Danny King was born in Slough, England in 1969 to Dot and Mick. The middle (and best) of three brothers, Danny went on to do many amazing things, like leave school with no qualifications, carry bricks up a ladder for really very little money, and get arrested a lot. In 1992 he came to London with the pie-in-the-sky idea of being a journalist, but ended up plying his trade in the murky world of sex, porn and model railways. So far, he has worked for *Club International*, *Mayfair*, *Escort*, *Club Confidential*, *Soho*, *Men Only* and *Model Railway Enthusiast*. He lives in Crystal Palace and invests most of his money in beer and kebabs. If you'd like to know more about this fascinating . . . sorry, nauseating, fellow, then please check out his website, dannykingbooks.com.

Also by Danny King and published by Serpent's Tail

The Burglar Diaries
The Bank Robber Diaries
The Hitman Diaries

The Pornographer Diaries

Danny King

Library of Congress Catalog Card Number: 2004103021

A complete catalogue record for this book can
be obtained from the British Library on request

The characters and events in this book are fictitious. Any similarity to real persons, dead or alive, is coincidental and not intended by the author.

First published in 2004 by Serpent's Tail,
4 Blackstock Mews, London N4 2BT
website: www.serpentstail.com

Printed by Mackays of Chatham, plc

10 9 8 7 6 5 4 3 2 1

This book is dedicated to Jim Hundleby, Andrew Emery, Nat Saunders, Barrie Smith, Chris Hayward, Ben Ashby and Pete Cashmore – friends, colleagues and pornographers one and all.

'Real orgies are never so exciting as pornographic books'

Aldous Huxley

Contents

All the names and situations in this book are purely fictitious. If you go into any corner shop in the country you'll see a million and a half-odd colourful grumble mags cluttering up the top shelf at any given moment, so there's bound to be a few similarities between those and the mags portrayed in this book, though these are purely coincidental. All the characters, publications, company titles and anecdotes in this book are purely fantasies of the writer's imagination – except for Matt Sanders, who not only exists, but still owes the writer either £17.50 or a look at his girlfriend in the shower. Which is it to be, Rat?

Acknowledgements

Once again, I'd like to thank my editor, John Williams, for helping me snip the many rubbish bits out of the first and second drafts. I think we got them all but there may still be one or two laboured jokes/paragraphs/chapters. Please just try and read around these. To Pete Ayrton and the whacky gang at Serpent's Tail for continuing to publish books that have been effectively written by a semi-literate hod carrier; to my agent Lucie Whitehouse at Darley Anderson for putting up with all my endless, pitiful belly-aching; to the Booker Prize Committee for overlooking me again last year, the bastards; to Ross Beasley, a fan from Grimsby, and more importantly, a talented drummer who's going places (hey, prison and the dole are places too); to my best mate Brian McCann for putting me up for two weeks when I found myself between flats and for laughing like a hyena when I spilled my king-sized doner all over his brand new sofa, just three minutes after him telling me not to eat it anywhere near his sofa because I was far too plastered (now that's friendship for you); to my younger brother Robin and my older brother Ralph for their sage advice and literary guidance (meddling fools); to Clive Andrews for reading through my manuscripts and for marrying Jo Hall this year – Congratulations & Best Wishes (that should save a wedding present); to Rob Swift, my old boss, for giving me my start on *Club International* and for all the laughs, beers and tears that stemmed from that lapse of judgement; and to Paul McCann, Pete Shirley, Joel Trilles, Adrian Smale, Sparky, bad Alan Johnson, Nicola Swift, Neil Aldis, Lisa Baker, Luke Palmer, Cem Ceylan, Rebecca Eden, Dave *'C'maaaannnn!!!'* Gibbs, Claire Bull, Matt Wheeler, Jack Southon, David Rider and Billy Chainsaw for the various roles they play in my life. And lastly, and most pointedly, I'd like to thank Jeannie Crockett for putting the smile back on this big old miserable face. I'd been wondering where that had got to. Thank you.

Moonlight Publishing Personnel

Position	Name (aka)
Publisher	Philip Goss
MD	Peter McMenamin (Dirty Mac)
Production	Jennifer Ball
Reception	Wendy Pickles
BLING	
Editor	Stuart Toldo
Sub	Godfrey Bishop (God')
Designer	Roger Noble
FROTH	
Editor	Roger Montgomery (Monty)
Sub	Matt Sanders
BANGERS!	
Editor	Susie Potts
Deputy	Hazel Smith
Designer	Don Atkins
ACE	
Editor	Ryan Breen (Paddy)
Sub	Paul Tompson (Fat Paul)
Designer	Hasseem Abdul
EDITORIAL ASSISTANTS	
Bling/Froth	Jackie Griffin
Bangers!/Ace	Mary Clarke

SOME OF THE GIRLS

Rebecca (chap. 2)	Jennifer (chap. 5)	Traci (chap. 5)
Gemma (chap. 5)	Zoe (chap. 6)	Claire (chap. 7)
Jerry (chap. 11)	Sophie (chap. 13)	Tanya (chap. 16)
Cindy (chap. 16)		

Prologue: The questions

Working for a porn mag, you're always asked the same questions over and over again when people find out what you do. They vary in style and phrasing a little but basically they boil down to the same five questions.

1. *Can you get me some mags?*
2. *Can you get me a job?*
3. *Are the letters real?*
4. *Do you get to go on photo shoots?*
5. *Do you get to shag the models?*

The quick answers to all of these questions is yes, no, yes, yes and sometimes, if you're lucky.

The long answers are, well, they're a little more involved . . .

1: Papier mâché porn

'Ow!' I yelped.

'What's up?' Barry asked from the track.

'I got a thorn stuck in me,' I told him, pulling my hand out of the brambles and sucking at the little black dot that had buried itself into my palm. The thorn showed enough of itself so that I could get my teeth on the end of it and yank it out, which brought a couple of tears to my eyes and made my lip wobble a bit. Luckily, I had my back to Barry so the rest of the school never got to hear about it. I wiped the blood onto my jeans and began crawling through the bush again.

'Haven't you got it yet?' he whined again.

'You ask me that one more time and I'll smack you in the fucking mouth!' I hissed back at him, meaning, 'You ask me that one more time and I'll chuck your bike in the river while you're in the shops and pretend it was Neil Barratt who came along and did it.'

I caught hold of a few more muddy and tattered pages that had been torn from the rest of the mag and gazed upon them in awe. The colours were dark from the damp and the dirt and some of them showed only fragments of pictures – but there was enough. Curvy, voluptuous ladies stared back at me wearing nothing but vacant expressions and an unidentifiable sludge you find under bushes in Berkshire – er, thorny bushes that is, not lady's bushes.

This was my first ever glimpse of a nudey mag, and I liked what I saw. Sure I was no stranger to the Great Universal catalogue underwear and shower curtain sections, and if you took mine and every other lad in my geography class's textbooks and hurled them across the playground, they'd all fall open on one particular page, but this was different.

This was a nudey mag.

Real, no joking naked ladies nudey mag. And it was amazing. Big round boobs and big hairy fannies that were so real I didn't need to use my imagination any more. Whole glossy pages of pink, bare flesh with just a hint of bird shit and mildew that was suddenly more fascinating and exhilarating than hunting Christmas presents or finding my big sister's diary.

See, just lately I'd been finding women's bodies fascinating – not girls, not the little girls in my class, I still didn't care about them, I'm talking about women – my friends' mums or even some of my mum's friends and I had a recurring fantasy about my form tutor Miss Jenkins keeping me behind after school to sit on my head, but I was still in the process of putting all the pieces together. Nudey mags seemed to hold some interesting clues.

I'd heard all about these magazines before, of course. Gary Allison had told us that he'd seen one of his dad's stashed away in the shed and it was stacked full of pictures of ladies that had to take all their clothes off and stand in front of the camera while people took pictures of them. Barry had asked if they were covering themselves up with their hands or standing sideways or something and Gary had reassured us all that they were 'standing facing the camera and you can see everything.' At this point someone might as well have told me that the universe went on forever for all the ability I had to comprehend this.

'Everything!' David Tinnings exclaimed and normally we would've told him to fuck off and go and play with his flute, but most of us were suddenly far too busy rearranging our trousers at this point.

'Bring it in,' Barry urged him.

'No, I can't, it's my dad's, he'd kill me,' Gary replied.

'Yeah, Jimmy Hill. Your pants are on fire,' Neil Barratt responded, then added, 'He's lying,' for those of us who didn't know what the fuck he was going on about.

'I'm not,' he insisted.

'Then bring it in,' the whole of the first year waded in. Suddenly you could see it in his eyes, Gary was wishing he'd never said anything about the mag because now he was backed into a corner and there was no way out without losing all face – and when you're only eleven years old, this simply isn't an option.

The next day Gary swiped his old man's mag and brought it to school. An enormous cluster around the tennis courts resembling Mecca at rush hour alerted Mr Escott-Neu that something was amiss. Gary tried to stuff the offending contraband back into his bag before our House Master clocked it but it was simply impossible in the feeding frenzy he'd created.

Gary was dragged off to the Headmaster and bloody lucky not to be caned. Then a letter was sent home to his dad and his luck ran out. Still, serves him right. Imagine nicking your old man's wank mag? He must've been mad.

Unfortunately, I arrived just too late to catch even a glimpse of the sacred article and tortured myself about it for weeks afterwards until Barry told me that he'd heard there was one in the bushes in the new field and did I want to come along and see if we could find it? Ten seconds later we were legging it up the road and across the old field and crossing the stream and . . . well, I guess this is where you came in.

'Come on, God', pass 'em back,' Barry was urging me.

'Hang on a sec,' I told him and savoured one last look at her. I didn't know how old she was – when you're eleven you can't judge age – but she looked about forty-five (see what I mean) and really quite scary. Her face was scowling and she had a wide gap between her teeth and heavy eye make-up and her hair was this enormous curly bush (up and down). She was leaning back on her hands and glaring at the camera with a look I took at the time to be contempt, though remembering back I'd say it was probably meant to be lust. Well, if you'd never seen lust before, I suppose it would be easy to confuse one for the other. Maybe this was why we all assumed they were being *made* to take their clothes off. Certainly, none of them looked happy about it. Also, I guess we just couldn't imagine a lady taking her clothes off and letting herself be photographed voluntarily. I mean, why would they? No, there had to be a room somewhere, somewhere where they kept ladies and made them take their clothes off and the ladies had no choice. All they could do was what they were told to do and scowl at the camera. Remember that song?

There's a place in France where the naked ladies dance,
There's a hole in the wall where the men see it all.

I just assumed there must be a place in England similar to the one in France, probably in London, where girls slouched in chairs in the nude and generally looked fucked off about not being allowed to go home. And this was the proof. I'm ashamed to admit it but far from feeling sorry for these ladies and wishing they could be reunited with their families and friends, I just wanted to be able to visit this room and watch the girls being made to take their clothes off. Well, a room like this was probably a good thing, wasn't it? A great thing even. This was just what I thought back then, you understand. Though . . . no, no, I'm not going to go there.

She was an amazing-looking lady though and despite the thousands upon thousands of women I've seen since – in mags, videos and occasionally in person – I can still remember her as clear as if it were yesterday. She has become my epitome of sex; naked, scowling, big bush and covered in mud and filth. That's my conditioning, it's what my brain has told me I'm into. Like the duck that hatches next to a teddy bear and thinks that's his old lady, that scowling naked lady has forever shaped my perception of sex. Bit of a shame really, not too many birds are willing to cover themselves in filth and crawl around underneath brambles with me. I sometimes wonder where that lady is and what she's doing now. I hope they've let her out of that room, it can't be much of a life now, can it.

I finally laid my fingertips on the stinking soggy mass that represented the bulk of the mag and dragged it towards myself, leaving several dozen beetles homeless and confused. The cover was almost black with filth, though I managed to peel a few pages apart to reveal bright pink flesh tones and backed out of the bush, mission accomplished.

'Gis a look, show us, show us,' Barry squealed, hopping from one leg to the other.

'Hold on, I bloody got it, be careful or you'll rip it.'

We laid it carefully on the ground and I wiped some of the gunk off of my hands and onto my jeans, then set about trying to carefully separate the pages. I'm not quite sure what was on the first dozen because they'd become one big organic wad of filth (in every sense of the word) but on page 14 there were pictures of a blonde lady sitting on a windowsill staring out through a net curtain. She reminded me of that woman in the Flake advert, only with this one you could see her knockers.

Barry exhaled heavily but neither of us spoke as we studied the pictures. Overleaf, she'd lost her knickers (and her head too as we only managed to turn half the page) and we stared at her wiry ginger bush as it caught the sunlight that poured in through the big window.

'Fucking hell, I've got a real stiffie,' Barry decided to share with me, indicating towards his cords. You know what, I know this is going to sound strange but I'd never realised everyone else got them when they looked at, or thought about, naked ladies too. It just hadn't occurred to me that this might be a universal problem. I'd always thought it was just me and that there was something wrong with me. Now that I knew the truth, I felt mighty relieved. That had been one doctor's visit I hadn't been looking forward to.

'Here, Dr Henderson, what d'you suppose this is?' standing there with a big hard-on. What can I say, I wasn't the brightest of lads.

'We should keep this at the camp,' Barry said. 'It can be like our camp treasure.'

'Yeah, though don't tell anyone else otherwise they'll nick it,' I said, then promptly nicked it after Barry went home for his tea.

The mag dried out nicely in my old man's shed during the summer but went missing at the end of August, along with that evening's dinnertime conversation, and I never saw it again. Nevertheless, I'd kept the picture of the woman with the big hair separate up in my room underneath my wardrobe (must've sounded like we had the removal men in upstairs every time I was 'doing my homework') though she too disappeared one gut-wrenchingly horrifying afternoon when I came home and found my bedroom had been rearranged. Again, nothing was said though I was subtly warned against concealing anything in my bedroom again by my old lady, who liked to comment every now and then that she must get round to giving my room a good 'sort-through', just to keep me on my toes. After that, I kept all my bits of mags in my younger brother's room (under his wardrobe).

Yep, that was a landmark year for me, that was. I spent most of that summer putting two and two together before finally coming up with five – fingers, that is. See, after a whole summer staring at that picture and my own bewildering stiffie, nature finally took its course and at the tender, impetuous and innocent age of just gone twelve I strummed my first one home.

And I haven't looked back since.

2: Can you get me a job?

So, I'm in reception and it's all very nice; polished wooden floors, pine or beech panelling on the walls, a large black leather sofa to wait on and a couple of really quite realistic plastic trees to lend the place a touch of class. They'd really done a nice job on the interior decoration, though there was one question I couldn't shake out of my head.

Where were all the tits?

This was supposed to be a porno company, wasn't it? What was with the New York City skylines on the walls? Why couldn't I see any arses?

Sure, they provided some magazines for visitors to browse; *The Spectator*, *The New Statesman*, *Private Eye*, *What Mortgage* and *Tatler* (in case, I suppose, you fancied banging one out while you waited). But there was no *Bling*, no *Ace*, no *Froth* and not even the slightest hint of *Bangers!* and yet these were the magazines that Moonlight Publications produced.

Disappointed.

I picked up *The Spectator* and tried flipping through it while I waited for my interview. The receptionist looked up at me for a moment through half an inch of bullet/nutter proof glass, then got back to her reading – Harry Potter.

Shouldn't she at least be poring over *Bling's* famous blowjob column and reading about naughty Natalie's latest gulletful? I would if I worked here, I thought to myself.

If I worked here. 'If' being the operative word.

I was here for my interview for the position of sub-editor on *Bling*. I was suitably qualified for the job (I wasn't just chancing it) having spent the last three years working as sub on a car magazine (alright, caravan magazine) but this was a job I really fancied. I'd seen several such vacancies advertised in the media pages of the national press over the years, and they were always worded the same:

> SUB-EDITOR
> Hard-working, talented, full-time professional required for market-leading title. Must have minimum eighteen months' publishing experience on consumer titles and be proficient in Word & QuarkXpress. Circa £17k. CV and cuttings to Stuart Toldo, Moonlight Publications Ltd etc., etc., etc.

They weren't fooling anyone – Moonlight Publications? Anyone who's been bashing off to porn since the seventies should know the name Moonlight Publications, so that would be most of the adult male population of Great Britain. Like I said, I'd seen a few of these adverts crop up in the past and I'd always applied for them, you know, just on the off-chance. The way I looked at it, even if I didn't get the job, just the interview in itself would be something I could tell my grandchildren about.

So here I was, third time lucky. They'd got in contact with me, liked my CV and asked me to write them a 500-word dirty story, a 500-word fictional porn star interview, half a dozen dirty soundbites and an 800-word humorous feature on *Baywatch* (I later found out that they'd strung the vacancy out for over two months before making up their minds because they had some three dozen hopeful applicants doing all their work for them). Six weeks after dropping my contributions to issues three and four in the postbox I got a call from a young girl who invited me along for an interview.

This would be the first and only time I've ever managed to talk to someone on the phone and stare at their tits at the same time.

The interview was for 10 a.m. sharp and it was now 10.25 a.m. I tried reading *The Spectator* and got quite engrossed in the first four words of an article by Gore Vidal before chucking it in and picking up *What Mortgage*. It was no use, I just couldn't concentrate, not knowing (or at least fantasising about) what was behind the glass doors and the Muggle on reception.

Would I see a naked girl? Would they just be walking around out back? What if the whole place was just wall to wall with pictures of tits and fannies and I couldn't look anywhere without seeing them? I hadn't looked at a porn mag in the company of someone else since I was fourteen years old and I wasn't sure a job interview was the right time to start again. What if we were looking through a couple of issues together and the editor turned around and told me he had a stiffie?

Jesus!

Normal job interviews were scary enough but this one had me unable to sit still for five seconds straight. My heart was thumping inside my chest, my armpits were sticky with sweat and my heavily gelled hair was itching like mad. I tried scratching it without messing the rest of it up too badly and took a few deep breaths. The receptionist hadn't given me so much as a glance in the last ten minutes, though I felt like I had a hundred eyes on me.

I bet she knows the score, I thought to myself as I stared at the receptionist. Working in a place like this she had to be a bit open-minded. I mean, sex was probably no big thing to her, second nature and all that. She certainly had nice tits. I wondered if she'd ever done any modelling herself. More than likely. Perhaps she'd even done hard-core, it wouldn't have surprised me. I was just starting to wonder if she had anything on underneath the desk when I managed to stop myself before I got to the point where I couldn't stand up if called upon to do so. My train of thought was further disturbed by a courier arriving with a large A3 envelope marked 'PROOFS'. The receptionist buzzed him through the security doors, signed for the envelope, then picked up the phone and dialled. The courier paid me no attention and I paid him even less, my attention was firmly fixed on the envelope and my mind was galloping off in half a dozen directions when all of a sudden some guy leaned out of the security doors and asked me if I wanted to come through.

The only thing I was about to come through was my pants.

'Sorry to keep you, one of those mornings. Stuart Toldo,' he said, introducing himself and offering me his hand. I took it, shook it and returned it to him, then followed him through the security doors.

Alice was stepping through the looking glass.

'Good luck,' the receptionist smiled, looking up from her book, and I almost managed to return her smile without looking at her tits. Almost.

'Well, we've got four magazines in the company, *Bling*, *Ace*, *Froth* and *Bangers!* I edit *Bling*, which is the one we're going to be testing you for today.'

Testing?

'You've read *Bling* before, I take it?' he asked.

If it had been anyone else in the world asking me that question I would've replied, 'No! But my mate's got a stack of copies, I've had a look through his . . . you know, just for laughs, that's all, nothing else.' What I actually said was, 'Yes, I've read a few copies . . . good mag . . . very . . . I liked it,' though again this wasn't strictly true. I hadn't actually 'read' them, as in the strict definition of the word, what I usually did was spread four or five issues about me and open them up onto my favourite pages, then lob my seed on stony ground. It sounds ridiculous, I know, but even up to this point I was half-expecting him to point at me and laugh, 'He admitted it, everyone, he admitted it, he buys porno mags,' then for everyone to pour out of the various offices either side of the corridor and laugh too while the women viewed me with contempt.

'Christ, we just produce them, we're professionals, but you actually *buy* them. What a creep!' the receptionist would shout after me, then scream, 'Rapist! Rapist! Rapist!' as she pulled her cardigan tightly across her big, fat, enormous, round, firm, bouncing . . .

'Yes, well, *Bling* is seen as the classiest of the titles we produce,' Stuart replied, bringing me back to reality. 'We get the best girls, at least we try, and generally work with the best photographers to produce a mag that's the fourth best-selling in the country.'

'What's your circulation?' I asked him, trying to show a professional interest.

'Around about 90,000,' he replied and I stopped dead in my tracks.

'A month?'

'Yes, give or take. It generally goes up if we've got a free video or some other gift on the front cover but it basically hovers around the 90,000 mark.'

This was staggering: 90,000 copies sold every month! I was expecting him to say 5,000 or even 10,000, but 90,000! Fuck me! And that was the fourth best-selling mag on the top shelf. What the fuck was the best-selling one doing? I thought for a moment about all the dozens of different mags up there in the newsagents and then about the numbers I'd just heard and put it together that Britain must shift something like 500,000 to a million dirty mags every month.

Every month!

Hang on a minute, let's just work this out. Say, for argument's sake, we took a good month and porn mags made a million sales (as it makes it easier to work out). There were 60 million people living in Great Britain, half of them were fellas. Now say the average life expectancy for blokes in the UK was three score and ten and let's just say that no-one under the age of 18 ever bought a mag, because they weren't able to. Alright, so 52 as a percentage of 70 was just over 74 per cent (I'm using a calculator now so don't get too impressed) and 74 per cent of 30 million was . . . hang on, I pressed the wrong key . . . was 22,200,000. That's just over 22 million blokes of nudey mag-buying age. Let's knock the pensioners off that total, because they probably weren't up to it anyway, and get it down to a manageable 20 million. That meant that on average, one in every twenty blokes in this country regularly went down the newsagents (or in my case the 24hr service station at midnight) and bought a dirty mag every month. One in twenty. With such a common phenomenon going on around us all the time, you'd think you'd see more blokes buying them, wouldn't you? I'd seen a badger once but to this day I've never seen anyone walk out of the newsagents with a dirty mag under his arm; mind you, I'd seen plenty of people walking out of the newsagents with a suspiciously thick issue of *Exchange and Mart* rolled up under their arm.

It suddenly felt good to know that it wasn't just me buying them.

'Yep, people are always surprised how many we sell,' Stuart said. 'We're like the Masons, in a way.'

'Yeah, you both have your secret handshakes, I suppose,' I replied, but didn't get the laugh I was looking for.

We carried on walking up the corridor, past offices on either side, then twenty yards later through a big pair of double doors and into a large open-plan editorial office. There were no pictures of the New York skyline in here, nor were there any copies of *The New Statesman* (that I could see), the place was wall to wall with pin-ups, posters and polaroids. Great piles of mags overflowed by the side of every desk and boxes of mags, videos and slides were heaped on top of a large bank of filing cabinets against the far wall. There was even a shelf close by with something like a dozen dildos laid out like a weapons rack.

It was an Aladdin's cave of porn.

'This is where we work,' Stuart told me while I gaped about. 'All four mags are done in this room and there's probably about –' he started quickly counting under his breath, 'about a dozen of us who work in here, though it's a bit early so no-one's in yet.'

I looked at my watch, it was 10.30 a.m. and there were three people sat about reading the newspapers and Harry Potter. 10.30 a.m. and a bit early? Fuck me, I wanted a job in this place, didn't I?

'Everyone's got phones, most of the iMacs have got email and pretty much everyone's on the net.'

'I bet this is about the only place in London you wouldn't

get sacked for looking at porn on the internet all day,' I thought out loud.

'It's probably the only place in London where nobody wants to,' he replied, making me feel stupid. I made a mental note to stop with the witty insights and shut my fucking gob. 'Alright, well, that's it really, just thought I'd show you the offices. Usual procedure from here on in now, we're going to do a quick interview in one of the rooms back there and then I'll give you a subbing test and then we'll see how you get on with it. Right, this way then.'

I followed Stuart back down the corridor and into a large but sparsely furnished office. There was a big table in the middle of the room with half a dozen chairs around it and a computer set up at one end. This was much more like the sort of interviews I'd come to know and hate.

'Take a seat,' he said, indicating to one side of the table, then slid in behind the other. He plucked several copies of *Bling* off the shelf behind himself and laid them on the table in front of me. One of them I already had at home, but the other two I didn't. I wondered if he'd let me take them with me.

'This is our mag, as you probably know. Lots of girls . . .' he said, flipping through it in front of me, making me blush inwardly, 'a few features, funny stuff, lads-type stuff. A few sporty things . . .' he was saying and I tried nodding along as if I'd even noticed one of his fucking lads/sporty features/things ever before, 'lots of readers' letters, true confessions, stuff like that . . . a shit load of adverts at the back you won't have to worry about and that's about that,' he finished and turned it over to me. 'Questions?'

'Are the true confessions really true?'

'I doubt it. They're all written by a regular contributor, and if you saw the state of her you'd wonder if she'd ever had it in her life. We just change her name every month. The readers' letters are all genuine, well, you know, we get real letters in, I can't remember if these are genuine or not,' he said, staring down at the page in front of me. 'They need subbing, which'll be your job,' he said in a way that made me think I'd already got it. 'That and you'll have to write the funnies and the reviews and the girl blurbs and, well, basically every word in here that isn't sent in by a contributor or in an advert. See what I mean, it's a lot of work.'

'What's girl blurb?' I asked.

'These bits, by each of the girl sets.' Stuart opened up to a page showing some tall slender blonde bird rolling around in a stable, butt-arse naked, and indicated a few paragraphs of text and a pull-out quote up in one corner of the picture.

'What, I'll have to interview the girls?' I said, hopefully.

'Be a bit fucking difficult,' he replied, flipping through the mag. 'She's Hungarian, she's a Czech, so's she, she's Estonian, this one's Russian and this one's from Wolverhampton, so none of them speak English. No, you just look at the pictures and get a feel for the set. Maybe look up a few back issues if they've been in before and then write a few words as to what you imagine they would be saying, if they were asked the right questions.'

'Imagine,' I mused, quickly reading the girl in the barn's fantasy about taking shelter out of a storm and getting done in both ends by a couple of wandering farm hands while the horses watched.

'Yeah, you know, make it up. We got you to do some before and send them in, stuff like that.'

'Oh, right,' I replied and tried to hide my disappointment. I'd always thought the girls had really said these things. Had I bashed off to something some geezer like me had written in the past?

'Right, so, why do you want to work for *Bling*?' Stuart asked, looking across the table at me.

'Well, I think it would be great working with naked birds all day and getting sucked off left, right and centre.' Obviously I didn't say this though if you've ever been for a job on a porn mag, this is your motivation, so don't even pretend it's not.

'Well,' I started, wondering how the fuck I was going to answer this. I'd known about my interview for a few days now and had been dreading this question and I still hadn't come up with anything convincing. 'I've always been interested in fashion.'

'What's that got to do with porn?' Stuart asked, making me back-pedal frantically.

'I don't know,' I admitted. 'Nothing at all. As for working here, I just thought it would be a bit of a laugh, that's all. I work in a very stuffy office at the moment and I just think that perhaps it would be nice to work somewhere fun for a change,' I said and half-expected him to tell me that this was a serious business, not Alton Towers, but luckily he didn't.

'Yes, it can be alright,' he admitted. It was about the best answer I could've given. If I'd told him I'd always been fanatical about porn and that it had been my lifelong ambition to work in the industry, I doubt I would have stood a chance. I mean, who wants to work with someone who's frothing at the bit about being surrounded by dirty mags all day long. Pretty unsettling, no? Same as Mr Kipling, how would he fancy some thirty-stone lardarse working in his cake factory?

'How much notice would you have to give at your current place of employment?' Stuart asked.

'Four weeks is the standard but I can negotiate if you need

me sooner,' meaning I'd drop them in the shit and jack in tomorrow if you give me this job.

'Money?' he asked.

'I can only afford to pay you a hundred a week,' I joked. We both laughed and Stuart made a mental note to knock two grand off the number he'd first thought about.

'Seriously, how much are you looking for?'

'Well, if possible it would be nice if you could match my current salary,' I told him, then chucked four grand on the top of my current salary.

'Okay, I'll see what I can do. Right, let's get you set up on this subbing test then. The page should already be up onscreen. It's a 500-word dirty story, I just want you to go through it and correct and rewrite where you think it needs it and fit it to the page. If you could bold out any changes you make, that'll save me reading the whole fucking thing again.'

I sat myself down in front of the computer and looked at the Quark page open up onscreen.

'Alright, if you start now you've got 15 minutes, that should give you plenty of time,' he assured me.

I quickly skim-read the story which seemed to be about a posh housewife, a broken sink, a plumber, his mate and a big smelly faceful of fat. It over-ran off the page by a couple of hundred words and there were a number of spelling, grammatical and physically impossible mistakes that all needed to be amended as well as a big pull-out quote which just read 'FILL ME FILL ME FILL ME FILL ME FILL ME FILL ME FILL ME'. I was half-tempted to leave it as it was, as it seemed like the sort of thing she'd say.

'Is blowjob hyphenated or two words?' I asked Stuart, who'd just phoned his secretary for coffee.

'Hyphenated,' he replied so I changed it to 'blow-job'. At

that moment there was a knock at the door and when I looked up I couldn't believe my eyes. It was like there was an explosion of realisation in my head and my heart leapt into my throat. Standing before me, asking me if I'd like tea or coffee, was a tall, slender blonde girl, say twenty-one or thereabouts, wearing nothing but high heels and a couple of hair clips. I couldn't believe my eyes, and I'm serious, I literally could not believe my eyes.

'Would you like a cup of tea?' she asked again, giving me a slight smile.

'Erm . . . please,' I replied, finally finding my voice.

'One lump or two?' she asked, barely three feet away. Her big round tits swung slightly as she leaned over to address me and her belly button stood at about my eye level, at least it would've been had I been looking at her. It seems daft, I know, there was a beautiful (and I do mean beautiful) naked girl standing not three feet away from me, talking to me politely, and the only place I could look was my shoes. I was burning up with embarrassment and my collar suddenly felt like a garrotte. I can't explain this, I guess at the end of the day, all fantasies aside, most normal people feel fairly uncomfortable confronting bedroom stuff outside the bedroom, particularly if you're trying to sit a test.

A test?

That's what it was. This was a test? The article didn't matter, that was a red herring, this girl in front of me was the test. Fuck, what was I meant to do?

First things first, I think she needed answering.

'No sugar for me, thank you.'

'Cream?'

Oh God!

'Just milk, thanks,' I replied and she gave me a little wink and left the room. Being the gentleman that I was, I waited until her back was turned and then stared at her as hard as I could to try and indelibly imprint her image on my brain.

I looked over at Stuart, who hadn't even looked up from his notes. I thought maybe he'd be smiling or laughing or trying to hide his boner like I was but he was completely unmoved. Was this a test? Perhaps not. Perhaps they really did have naked women who worked here full-time. What am I talking about, why would they? What would be the point? Sure it was a porno company but that didn't mean everyone who worked here had to wander around butt-arse naked all the time. Or did it?

No, it had to be a test. But again, what sort of test? What was expected of me? If Stuart had turned around to me and told me to oil her tits up or take pictures of her then at least I would've known what to do, but he hadn't. He hadn't said a word. The initiative was all with me.

Not my specialist chosen subject.

They weren't expecting me to get naked as well, were they?

No, they couldn't be. Or could they? Why else bring a naked girl into the room? Oh lord, she was back.

'There you go,' she said, putting a mug of tea down next to me.

'Rebecca, could you take a letter for me please?' Stuart said and Rebecca sat in the chair next to me, picked up a pen and pad and started scribbling down whatever it was Stuart started banging on about. I couldn't hear him. All I could hear was the blood coursing through my ears, my heart thumping in my chest and my zip starting to give.

I ploughed my way through the article, trying to take my mind off the naked woman beside me by reading about an altogether separate naked woman who had two cocks in her mouth.

Oh no, this wasn't the test, was it?

I didn't have to have sex with this girl in front of Stuart, did I? Oh Christ, I couldn't do that, no way. I had trouble taking my top off at the beach, but getting my old fella out in front of another man? Oh no, oh no no no!

Was that what I was expected to do? I mean, this was the porn industry after all. Presumably they were looking for a certain type of person who could work in the industry; a person who – like in the stories – enjoyed spit-roasting posh housewives in the afternoon while high-fiving their mates across her back. They didn't want prudes or namby-pamby shy boys working with them. And if I wanted this job, I was going to have to overcome my inhibitions and prove I could be like the nastiest of them too. That was the real test, wasn't it? To see if I was man enough to work in the industry. Me and Stuart were both going to have to do her and presumably high-five and say, 'Yeah, take it, bitch' at some point.

Oh God, what if my balls accidentally touched his? I knew they'd shrivel up and retreat to the size and hardness of small diamonds and never be seen again.

I couldn't do it, I just couldn't. I knew that was what they were both waiting for; for me to stand up and say, 'Come on then, let's party!' but fuck that! No way. If this was what it took to get a job in porn then I had to admit I just wasn't up to it and good luck to whoever was.

I cracked on with the article and subbed it back and proofed it one last time before announcing that I was finished and asking if that was all?

'Good, well, time's about up by now anyway. Did you bold all the bits you've done?'

I told him I had.

'Well, that's about it then, unless there's any final thing you'd like to ask?' Stuart said.

I thought about this for the briefest of moments, this was my last chance.

'Just one thing,' I said and looked at Rebecca. 'Which temp agency do you use?'

A joke. One feeble joke, that was all I could manage. What a feeble excuse for a man I was. Stuart and Rebecca smiled and Stuart said he'd show me out. As I got to my feet, slowly and carefully, Rebecca glanced at the front of my trousers and then up at me and smiled. I could've cried. What was I doing? I'd never had anyone this beautiful taking an interest in me in my life (and wasn't ever likely to) and I was turning tail and running like a coward. I caught her eye one last time and she gave me a wink.

Wasn't life cruel?

If only Stuart had left the room, just for five minutes, not even that. Thirty seconds would've been long enough, the state I was in.

So unfair.

Stuart shook my hand again, told me they'd be in touch and pointed me towards the door. I didn't believe him for a minute. What must he be thinking of me right now? I thought to myself. The receptionist asked me how it had gone as I passed by and I told her not too good.

'I'm sure you did fine,' she replied and added, 'Basically, with this company, if they like you, they'll hire you. I mean, how many people are likely to have the sort of experience we're after?' making me feel no better about myself. You know, it's funny, but I could see right down her cleavage as I said goodbye, but it didn't even register with me until I was out. I wondered if the receptionist had picked up on this too and came to the same conclusion as Stuart.

Probably gay.

'Jesus, he seemed more interested in me than in you,' I could hear Stuart telling Rebecca back in the interview room.

'I could've turned him,' she was arguing back, 'if you'd just left us alone for five minutes. I would've done anything for him.'

This conversation raged across my brain for the whole of the Tube ride home and culminated in Stuart giving Rebecca my home phone number and address so that she could come after me. She was probably on a Tube right now, I told myself, and due to start banging on my front door any minute. While I waited for her to get here, I slipped off my jacket, kicked my shoes across the room, drew the curtains and had the biggest and baddest wank of my life.

3: Welcome to the pleasure dome

'Unbelievable,' Barry said. 'Un-fucking-believable.'

'When d'you start?' Gary asked excitedly.

'Two weeks from Monday. I've given in a month's notice at *Caravaning* and I'm using my last two weeks' holiday to cut it short so I can start as soon as possible,' I told them, unable to wipe the broad grin from my face.

'But I thought you told us it went shit?' Gary said.

'I thought it did, just goes to show what I know,' I told them and downed the last of my pint. 'Can't wait, I can't fucking wait. Two more weeks and I'm out of there. I've done it. No more specky, no more sad wankers and no more Elenor. Thank Christ!' I exclaimed, a wave of relief washing over me.

'Never shag any bird you work with,' Gary pointed out like the wise, happily married, old sage he was. 'That'll learn you.'

'Fuck me, Gaz, don't tell him that, consider where he's going to be working. Fill your boots, my old son,' Barry quickly countered. 'You're going to be getting so much it'll be amazing,' he half-snarled, staring off into oblivion. 'And of course if there's any spare knocking about . . .'

'Don't worry, you can have my left-overs,' I agreed.

'Gratefully received,' he said.

'Geezer on *Caravaning*, you know, matey I told you about, bloke I sit next to, he reckons I won't pull another bird as long as I work there. He reckons no self-respecting girl will have anything to do with some, his words, "sleazy pornographer". Funny thing is, old Elenor, she reckons the opposite. She reckons birds'll be flattered by it. "This is a man who works with beautiful women all day long, if he's interested in me then I must have something pretty special,"' I said, putting on my well-worn Elenor voice and face. 'Trouble is, he's a middle-class PC Oxbridge ponce and she's just some old nightmare who's been playing with my head for the last year and a half.'

'You know, I think I must be looking forward to you getting another job almost as much as you are just so we can change the fucking record,' Gary said. 'Forget her, she's gone, or as good as.'

'I'll second that,' Barry agreed, waving at the barman, who simply waved back.

'Well, I'm very sorry if I've bored you over the last eighteen months with my pain, I wish you'd've said something sooner so I could've just shut up.'

'Hey, apology accepted,' Gary said with a regal wave of the hand. 'Just get us some free mags and don't mention her again and all is forgiven and gratefully forgotten.'

'Oh yeah, me too. Free mags every month, you reckon you can?' Barry said, hopping about on the spot.

'I'm sure I can, which ones you want?'

'I don't know, whatever. All the same, aren't they,' Gary shrugged.

'*Froth*, *Ace* and *Bangers!*' Barry said, putting in his order. 'Do you do *Asian Babes*, as well?'

'No, I think that's someone else. Don't you want *Bling*? That's the one I'm going to be working on.'

'Oh yeah, send us that one as well, but make sure you don't forget about *Froth*.'

'You like that one then, do you, Barry?' Gary smiled.

'No, I mean I don't get 'em or nothing, it's just a laugh. Bloke at work had some, just saw them, just thought it would be a laugh, that's all. I don't seriously want them, or nothing,' he protested.

'You want me to send them to you then or what?'

'Yes.'

'Here, don't send them to my house either or Karen'll open them, she opens all my mail, I can't send away for nothing. Here, I'll give you my work address, and remember to mark it PRIVATE AND CONFIDENTIAL otherwise my secretary might open it. Do they come in a plain envelope?'

'I don't know, I haven't even started there yet, have I? Give me a chance.'

'Man, you have just landed the best job in the world,' Barry breezed.

If I was nervous for my interview I was even more nervous for my first day. I'd come to the conclusion by now that they hadn't wanted me to bang Rebecca in front of Stuart and was fairly confident having sex in front of other members of staff wasn't going to be something in my contract, but I was still nervous.

First day nerves and all that.

I arrived five minutes early and was buzzed through the security doors by the receptionist with the tits.

'Congratulations,' she said, smiling at me. 'Welcome to your first day.'

'Godfrey Bishop,' I told her and shook her hand.

'I know, Wendy Pickles,' she replied.

'Really, thank God, we both have stupid names. Please call me God' or Bish.'

'Please call me Wendy or Wendy Pickles,' she replied, dropping the smile from her face.

'Er, shall I . . . er . . .'

'Go on through if you like, you know where the editorial offices are, don't you? At the end of the corridor. Just go and make yourself a cup of tea and find your desk.'

'How will I know which one's mine?' I asked.

'*Bling* hasn't had a sub for about three months now so your desk will be the one covered with everyone else's crap.'

'Oh, thanks, and sorry about the name thing.'

She flashed me her teeth and went back to her book, all in under half a second.

I walked up the corridor and through the doors and found the office in darkness. I groped around for some lights, flipped them all on and was immediately struck by one desk at the far end of the room which had all but disappeared under dozens of boxes and scores of mags. I shifted a few so that I could see my computer and saw that it was already on and that someone had set a hardcore still from a porn movie as the desktop picture. It featured two guys getting orally pleasured by one girl on her knees between them – or rather, they'd been pleasured by the girl between them. Urgh! I stared at it, transfixed for a good few moments before quickly looking away when the door swung open and a young girl walked in. She set her bag down at a desk across the room from me, took off her coat, turned her computer on and eyed me suspiciously before walking out again without saying a word. I picked up a few boxes off the floor and piled them back up on the desk in front of the computer.

The girl poked her head through the door again and looked at me like I was some kind of specimen before asking if I wanted a cup of tea.

'Please,' I replied, using my best Sunday school manners. 'No sugar, thanks.' She disappeared again, giving me two minutes to lose my coat and sneakily turn over a few pages of a copy of *Bling* that was lying on my desk before she returned.

'I'm Jackie,' she said, handing me my tea. 'I forgot how many sugars you said you wanted so I put in one and a half.'

'Thanks,' I replied and set my cup down. 'Godfrey,' I told her.

'Yes, I know, the new sub. I'm editorial assistant for *Bling* and *Froth*.'

We shook hands formally and I got a psychological blast of icy air up my pyjamas in the process. I've never met anyone so starched and joyless in all my life. This was a girl who worked for a porn mag yet she looked like a strong passage of Jane Austen would have her marching on Parliament with a megaphone blocking her view. She handed me the latest copy of *Bling* and asked me if I'd seen it yet. I hadn't, but even if I had, Jackie would've been the last person on Earth I would've told.

'It's looking quite good since the redesign, quite nice. Have a look,' she insisted, scrutinising me carefully.

I had a flip through and tried to make out that this was water off a duck's back to me as she hung over my shoulder. I'd never looked at a dirty mag in the company of a girl before, particularly that girl from the *Addams Family* after I'd only just met her five minutes earlier and while I was horribly sober. It's not something I'd recommend.

'Now this girl,' Jackie said, stopping me on a big double-page spread of a brunette lying across the page with her legs behind her ears, 'this is Tanya, she's our regular girl. We get loads of letters about her but I can't see it myself, I think she's ugly, well, not ugly, but just, you know, boring-looking,' she said in all seriousness.

Tanya didn't look boring from where I was standing, I could tell you that. 'GO AHEAD, PICK A HOLE,' she was saying, or rather my predecessor had typed in quote marks next to her face.

'Don't you think so? Boring? I can't see it myself, and she's got a horrible noony,' she said, shaking her head, and for one moment I thought she was going to get hers out and use it as some sort of control git. I suddenly realised that the people who worked here must have altogether different levels of squeamishness compared with the rest of the civilised world.

'God, yeah, awful,' I said, burning up with embarrassment. 'When does everyone else get in?'

'When they bloody well please,' she told me. 'I'm always here at ten on the dot but no-one else bothers to be on time. It's like they don't care or something. I hope you won't turn out to be like the rest of them.'

'No, no,' I assured her, not even convincing myself.

A third person arrived, to my relief, and dropped her coat and bag down on the desk next to Jackie's and wandered over.

'Alright?' she said.

'This is Mary, Mary's the editorial assistant on *Ace* and *Bangers!* This is Godfrey,' Jackie said, taking over proceedings.

'Alright,' Mary repeated and stared at me vacantly.

Mary looked like she was at the other end of the joy spectrum from Jackie completely. I know they were only my first impressions and everything but if Mary had ever turned down a fag, drink, pork pie or cock in her life I would've been seriously amazed.

'How was your weekend?' Jackie asked her.

'Alright,' Mary replied and continued to stare at me.

'Did you see Duncan?' Jackie asked.

'No,' Mary replied, stretching her vocabulary to its very limits. 'I went shopping with me mum.'

'Oh yeah, what did you buy?' I asked, trying to show an interest.

'Some pants and a pencil,' she replied expressionlessly.

'What d'you want a pencil for? We've got tons of them here you could've had,' Jackie asked.

'No, for my eyes,' she replied, pointing at her eyes. Mary then pointed them at the magazine I was holding and made a similar observation to Jackie's earlier noony comment. 'That Tanya? She's got a horrible cunt,' she said. 'It's all mangled and horrible.'

'Don't say that, Mary, that's awful,' Jackie objected.

'She has though, you're always saying it too an' all,' Mary insisted.

'I don't use the "c" word though. It's a horrible word.'

'What, "cunt"?'

'Mary, don't, it's vulgar.'

'Why? Everyone else always says it all the time.'

'That doesn't mean you should say it. You should rise above that sort of thing.'

'But I've got more right to say "cunt" than everybody else 'cos I've actually got one and they haven't,' she said, indicating between her tubby, fat legs.

This conversation went on for considerably longer than I like to remember, though thankfully it drifted away from my desk and finally I was left to my own devices. I spent the next half hour stacking the boxes in a neat pile on the floor and resetting the desktop picture on my computer to a neutral pattern.

I flicked through the issue of *Bling* again, feeling a little more comfortable about doing so this time, and tried to appreciate the redesign but tits and arses kept getting in the way. I put the mag away and spent an age shifting awkwardly in my chair, while I waited for the room to fill up with porn-hardened strangers.

A few materialised after 10.30 a.m., glared at me and got on with their own thing and it wasn't until 10.50 a.m. that someone finally came in and sat himself down at the designer's desk next to mine. He looked considerably older than everyone else I'd met so far, late forties I would've said, and he looked tired and confused, as if he'd just come round in a ditch.

'Who are you?' he said, furrowing his brow.

'Godfrey Bishop,' I told him and offered him my hand, but he was turning on his computer so he missed it.

'Are you new?'

'No, I've been here for years, you've just never seen me because I've been hiding under the desk.'

This must've been a company of starers because he was at it now.

'Oh,' he said all matter-of-fact. 'My name's Roger. I'm a designer. You're going to be working on *Bling*, aren't you?' I told him I was.

'Is that the one you work on?' I asked.

'One? One my fucking arse. I do *Bling* and *Froth*,' he murmured aggressively. 'It's a fucking joke, I'm the only bloke in here who has to do two mags every month, every other fucking designer in here just does the one but I get fucking two. Is that fair? You tell me. What other company would have their designers working on two mags, fucking wankers! I'm getting really fucked off with it, I can tell you that, fucking two mags? It's just a joke, that's all it is to them, a joke. They couldn't give a shit, not a shit. Every time they've got a poster to do or a supplement to design, who do they come to? They don't go to Don, yet he's only got one mag, and it's twenty-odd pages less than both of mine, no they come to me, fucking muggins. Well, I tell you what, much more of this and I'm fucking off, I don't give a shit, I've had enough. It's a fucking joke.' Roger turned his back on me, unpacked his sandwiches and went on for the next ten minutes, muttering to himself before silence once again descended over our little corner of the office.

Several faces looked my way from a cluster of lads laughing and smoking around one of the desks close by before a tall fella approached me.

'The new sub, yeah?' he said, in amiable contrast to Roger.

'Godfrey Bishop,' I said, stood and held out a hand.

The fella took it and said with a flick of the head, 'Come and meet the rest of them,' so I followed him over.

'I'm Paddy,' the tall fella said. 'I'm the editor on *Ace*, this is Hasseem and fat Paul, my designer and sub . . .'

'Hey!' fat Paul objected, though I don't know on what grounds.

'This is Don, designer on *Bangers!* and Matt, sub on *Froth*. All the other people in here are of no consequence,' he said with a dismissive wave of the hand, which I noticed took in the editorial assistants and Roger. There were still one or two other people dotted around the office but they were paying us no attention. 'This is Godfrey Bishop,' Paddy told the other, 'new sub on *Bling*.'

'That's your name? Godfrey Bishop?' Don said, shaking his head. 'Jesus.'

'So, you fancied a job on a porn mag, did you? Well, it can

be alright here at times, once you get all the sex bollocks out of the way,' Paddy said, making very little sense to me.

'What did you think of that bird in your interview?' Hasseem asked.

'Oh yeah, what was with that? I didn't get it.'

'It was just a laugh more than anything, see how you all reacted,' Paddy explained. 'Stuart got her in for the day for a couple of hundred quid to sit in in the interviews, to see who could manage to finish the subbing test with her rubbing her tits next to them. You, apparently, were one of the few who managed it.'

'Get this,' Matt grinned. 'One guy even got his cock out and started undressing there in front of them both and got kicked out.' Everyone broke up at that. Everyone, that is, except me, who felt icy hands squeeze my heart.

'So, she doesn't really work here?' I asked naively.

'Course not, you fucking donut, what would be the point of that?' Don said.

'Everyone thinks we've got naked birds stashed around the place,' Paddy sighed.

'The thing is with that model, right, what was her name, Rebecca, the thing is, Stuart was meant to take pictures of the different applicants doing their subbing tests next to Rebecca so he could make a feature out of it and cost off her fee but he forgot, so he's got to try and bury £250 somewhere in the books.'

'Where is Stuart?' I asked.

'It's Monday,' Paddy replied. 'He's probably still unconscious somewhere.'

'Hold on, I'll check,' Matt said and picked up the phone. 'Stuart called in today?' he asked and 'uhuh-ed' a bit, then hung up and told me that Stuart had phoned in sick and wouldn't be in today.

I scratched my head and wondered what I should do.

'Read my paper if you want,' fat Paul replied, reaching for the paper in his back pocket.

'Should kill a couple of hours till lunchtime,' Paddy said, 'then we can go over the pub and get a drink. You need one Mondays, don't you.'

The next two hours dragged by, and were made all the worse by having nothing other than *The Sun* crossword to occupy my time. No-one else seemed to be doing anything either. Roger was playing poker over the internet with his credit card behind me and losing quite badly by the sounds of it while Paddy, Don and the rest had dispersed around the office and were now chatting to other people, chatting on the phone or, in the case of fat Paul and Hasseem, playing baseball with two rubber tits that had been sellotaped together, and an enormous plastic dildo. Every now and then the ball would careen into Jackie's desk and knock papers or cups of tea flying and she'd have a mad fit and they'd stop playing for ten minutes, before the whole process would repeat itself. One time, the ball flew across the office and smacked Mary on the side of the face. Mary blinked a couple of times and then started laughing.

By Christ, Paddy was right, I needed a drink.

One o'clock finally came and I was lassoed and taken to The Abbot, three doors along from Moonlight Publishing.

'Guinness, Paddy; Don, Guinness; Export for Matt and a Fosters and a plate of chips for Paul,' the landlord said, reaching for glasses and tapping the till without waiting for confirmation. 'Where's Hasseem?'

'He's just talking to Peter but he'll be in, in a minute,' Paddy replied and the landlord went about pouring another pint of Guinness. 'What d'you want?' Paddy asked me so I said a pint of Stella. 'Cliff, this is Godfrey, he starts work today on *Bling*,' Paddy said, introducing me to the landlord (I'd never been introduced to a landlord before).

'Yeah, when did you lot start fucking working?' Cliff retorted. Ominous bells were tolling.

'You come in here a lot then, do you?' I asked Paddy.

'Every now and then, when the mood takes us,' he shrugged and we all went and sat down around a table by the fire. It was a traditional-looking pub, and by traditional, I mean it didn't look like it had had so much as a lick of paint since the sixties, though there was a television up in one of the corners showing the racing and a fag machine that now took decimal currency.

'How are you enjoying your first day in porn?' Paddy asked me.

'I haven't exactly done a lot.'

'No? Oh well, I wouldn't worry about it. You'll probably do something tomorrow,' he replied, savouring a few gulps. 'Ah, just what the doctor ordered . . . me to stay away from.'

Believe it or not – I didn't at first – but Paddy was an Oxford graduate with an MA in something brainy (I forget what) and an IQ you'd be chuffed to hit with three darts. He'd graduated some five years ago with a bright shining future in front of him and had come to London to make a go of his life, but had somehow got sidetracked along the way. In his first couple of weeks in The Smoke, he'd fired out dozens of letters to dozens of companies and received back dozens of job offers for his trouble. He had his pick of the cream of promising jobs, but then one particular letter stood out from all the rest. He'd only applied for the position as he'd applied for everything else in *The Guardian* that week, and what was one more letter, but now they'd invited him in for an interview and Paddy was suitably intrigued.

Five years on and Paddy could barely remember that

optimistic young grad. His wholesome, healthy and respectable upbringing had left a sleaze vacuum in his soul that only a drug and booze-fuelled lifetime of porn could sate, and now he was on the hook, there was no getting off. He'd drunk away more brains than I was ever likely to have and regretted none of it. He was still a clever bloke, but these days his cogs concerned themselves with more worldy matters than anything that could be solved by going into a library.

To call him my porn mentor wouldn't really be true; Paddy went places and did things I wouldn't have touched with yours, but he was a good guy to know and the person I would come to turn to whenever I needed advice. Or, more importantly, my conscience absolving.

4: Are the letters real?

'Charles . . . pulled his cock out . . . of . . . my . . . dripping . . . hole . . .' I muttered to myself as I typed, 'and . . . splashed . . . his . . . sticky . . .' no, 'hot . . . and . . . sticky . . . fat . . . in . . . my . . .'

My what?

I stared at the screen and chewed one of my nails as I considered the possibilities.

Face? Hmm, I'd done that one to death just lately. Mouth? No, that was how the last story I'd wrote ended. Tits? Maybe. I decided to have a think about it.

I twiddled my thumbs and looked around the room for inspiration. Jackie was glaring at Paddy, who was leaning right back in his reclining chair and seemed to be asleep; Mary was joining all her paper clips together in a big chain; fat Paul was looking around shiftily and unwrapping sweets in his drawer (I couldn't actually see this but he'd been doing it all week so I knew his look by now); Monty was behind me getting Roger to redesign the official *Froth* t-shirt again; Susie (editor on *Bangers!*) and Hazel (designer on *Bangers!*) were both burning up Moonlight Publishing's phone bill while Don hadn't finished brooding over the bollocking Susie had given him for lateness in front of everyone this morning. Nobody else was in.

No inspiration.

I stared at the space right after 'my' then typed 'pocket' and giggled to myself. I then went on to replace 'pocket' with 'handbag', 'hair', 'eyes', 'dinner', 'granny's purse', and finally 'homework', stopping to giggle at it each time before deleting the last word to leave the cliffhanger unresolved. 'Tits' finally got the nod simply because I couldn't be bothered to think of anything else.

God I was bored.

For two months now I'd been working on *Bling* and in all that time, all I'd done was either type in letters or write sex stories or girl blurbs. Now, you might think this sounds like a laugh, writing smut for a job, but it's not. Writing smut for an afternoon is a laugh, but doing it eight hours a day, five days a week (alright, four, we were all in the pub all day almost every Friday – and sometimes Thursdays too) was soul-sapping.

It wasn't that I found them difficult or anything, quite the opposite, it had become tedium beyond tears, but somebody had to do it and that was what I'd been taken on to do.

Out of all the questions I was asked while I worked in porn, 'are the letters real?' was by far and away the most common, so pardon me while I take a few moments here to elaborate.

Bling, and all the other mags, got sent in letters every day, probably half a dozen or so and they always fell into four main categories: *the enquiry*, where the reader wanted a model's address so that he could write to (stalk and murder) her; *the editorial comment*, where the reader wanted to compliment or complain about the state of the girls in the last issue and tell us how we should do our jobs; *the application*, where the reader asked if there were any vacancies (sex) going; and finally, *the sex confession*, where the reader pretended he'd recently had sex with one, two or three stunners and wanted to see it in print.

The first of these is fairly self-explanatory. Here's a quick example:

> Dear Tanya,
>
> I am aged late 30s and I have never been married. I have over the years bought a fair few magazines but honestly, yours are the sexiest pictures I've ever seen. I once had a pretty girlfriend who 'borrowed' money off me whilst shagging with someone else.
>
> I am quite good looking – not that bad.
>
> Perhaps you might feel sorry for me and ring me on xxxx xxx xxxx one evening.
>
> I am currently looking at your lovely tanned body with a sexy wet look. I look forward to hearing from you and I am sure I could love you.
>
> Love from ——, Doncaster

Obviously, I'm not going to give out the poor bloke's name or telephone number here, you'd all be ringing him up with marriage proposals. This letter was remarkable in only one way – he didn't make a single spelling or punctuation mistake. Quite astonishing. We should've got him in to read through my letters, because I was fucking useless. Anyway, the point is, how tempted do you suppose Tanya, an utter sex goddess, would be by this letter? This was the thing I never got and still don't to this day, how guys, who in all probability were not that successful with women for one reason or another, could believe that any of the knockout tens in our magazines would need to respond to their pleading letters in order to have sex. I don't know that much about women but I'd bet that most of the models in *Bling* and *Ace* couldn't go into a pub or a bar or a club anywhere in the world without having to take a big stick along to beat off all the blokes who tried it on with them; how would women like this, who have the pick of the cream of the blokes, even think twice about replying to desperate of Doncaster?

This was optimism on a scale I just couldn't get my head around.

The power of suggestion our magazines held over men was quite incredible though. Do you suppose for one moment if this same guy saw a stunner like Tanya in his local, he'd have the balls to go over and talk to her? I doubt it. Stick her in a mag with her pants down though and he assumes that her standards must include bearded men from local model railway societies.

I guess the only way I can explain this phenomenon is this; in the magazines we tried to portray all our girls as single. Nothing puts a crimp in your cock quite like some old bird banging on about the wonderfully cosy sex her and her boyfriend get up to all the time while you have to make do with a hundred stapled pages and an oiled boxing glove. So, what we did, to give the mag a bit more appeal, was have the models talk about how they were so hungry for cock that they pulled some complete stranger in the pub the other day and sucked him off out back by the bins. The reader reads this and, hey presto, he suddenly believes the country really is crawling with sex-starved girls who're not all that bothered about looks, money or body odour and are well up for a passing poke. Of course, this is just a passing fantasy, and the moment our reader blows his load and spoils the page, reality comes flooding back to him. But then, that's what fantasies are all about, the willing suspension of disbelief (as I think Blackadder once said). Women fantasise about film stars, blokes dream about easy good-looking girls who crave cock so badly that they're willing to drop their standards to our level. Blokes like sluts. Easy dirty sluts who are up for it and accessible. Fantasy girls like this press most guys' buttons, so this was how we portrayed ours.

The trouble was, some guys believed this for real. We'd put a quote next to a girl saying something like: 'I just love to suck cock. I could suck cocks all night and never get bored. And I always swallow' and suddenly get three dozen letters from guys saying: 'You like to suck cock? I like to have my cock sucked. We should get together. Give me a call on . . . etc'. It would never occur to them that a) she could probably have blokes flopping them out at her in Sainsbury's if she so wished so she wasn't likely to be going short, and b) that their letter was likely to be competing against three dozen other naïvoes who had also written in.

Oh, and c) their letter was destined for the bin before they'd even finished writing it. And not a bin anywhere near Tanya. Besides, if Tanya was up for it, didn't they think we'd have first dibs on her?

Just quickly, while we're on this type of letter, there was a sub-category here. In *Bling*, as in many other mags, we had a readers' wives section. Now, you would've thought that people would've understood what this meant, that readers sent in pictures of their wives for publication in our magazine. Not much area for confusion, but no.

> Dear readers wifes,
>
> I am writing this letter to tell you that I am very much interested to have a wife to come and live with me in my

flat. I like blonde ladies like Gemma and am very good at fucking. Please could you kindly get me a wife.

Thank you on your understanding and I look forward to hearing from you really soon

From ——

The second type of letter was the editorial comment. This was usually just a quick note saying something like: 'Loved the last issue. Jackie looked fabulous. I'd eat her arse out for breakfast. More of the same,' or 'I'd love to see Sophie Raworth (BBC newsreader) in your magazine, butt-naked with an assortment of fruit up her chuff.' I didn't pick Sophie at random by the way, for some reason she was far and away the most popular celebrity fantasy figure we received letters about. Hundreds and hundreds I saw on her, some with crudely drawn pictures of her wearing her ankles as ear-muffs and some featuring her doing a hell of a lot worse. Perhaps this is something Sophie might consider if she ever gets bored of reading the news. Whatever she decides, I always found it quite reassuring that so many blokes in this country took an interest in current affairs.

However, sometimes the requests were a bit more specific, if badly worded:

Dear editor,

This is where I have to flatter your mag to bits – and it is a true fact that *Bling* is the best mag . . . so other mags kneel to *Bling* – the master.

I have risen to enough courage to write this letter to you! When you come to read this letter I'll be twenty-one (and single!) and I thought . . . what can make my birthday special? I know . . . I'll write to *Bling* and propose a sexual challenge to all those gorgeous girls!

I like women with long hair (any colour). I feel it makes them more feminine and it brings out their beauty more (especially when their face retorts with pleasure – oooohhh!) Okay! The challenge is where these gorgeous girls get shagged by their racquet (tennis racquet) while shagging another woman with their racquets . . . If only I can draw!

They <u>must</u> own their own racquet . . . <u>tennis</u> <u>skirt</u> and the rest of the outfit . . . Not only are they going to get shagged by their own tennis racquet . . . by the others too. Not only that! One woman must be, say, the leader . . . who is the <u>only</u> <u>one</u> to touch me – unless she says otherwise!

To decide who'll be the leader . . .

1) Each woman will suck my knob – the more times they do it . . . The more chance they'll become the leader . . . OR . . .

2) I'll go round tasting each woman's pussy . . . The one I like the most will become the leader . . .

Okay! I think I got everything covered? Oh! How would you women – part of the challenge – be shagged by more than one racquet? (Or is it . . . tennis racket? – never mind!)

I hope everything is clear . . .

Write to me if anyone's interested . . . or for more info.

I'll leave it to you.

From ——

P.S. The women need to wear the tennis gear for the challenge – if they're interested!

Again, there's a level of optimism here not seen since England beat Germany 5–1 in Munich. However, I think he shot himself in the foot somewhat with his overcomplicated rules and regulations. He should've just asked if he could shag a couple of our models for his 21st. The answer would've still been no but at least he would've saved himself some ink.

We also got really moaning letters complaining that Abigail was wearing black knickers instead of white and that we hadn't had any white knickers for three issues now and stuff like that. Sometimes, they'd compile statistics and have charts showing a complete count of all the white knickers, full-frontal shots, bum shots, big boobs, shaven fannies, blonde girls and Chinese birds we'd had in the mag over the last five years (I kid you not) as proof that we were prejudiced against white knickers. The time and effort that must've gone into compiling all these stats is awesome. Again, these got to see how the rest of the world looked from the bin.

The insanest guy, however, was probably the bloke up in Liverpool who'd rip all his favourite pages out of the magazine every month, write on them 'I like this picture, more pictures like this,' then send them back to us. Sometimes he'd rip girls out of catalogues or newspapers and demand that we got the enclosed girl in our magazine. We could tell he liked them because he'd write 'lick lick' next to their privates. Occasionally he'd send back pictures from *Bling* that he didn't like with, 'She's not naked you stupid cunts!!! Get it right you fucking idiots!!!' if the girl still had stockings or a hat on or something. A genuinely scary fellow, but then nothing really surprises me about Scousers any more.

The third type of letter I mentioned was very common. Guys, and occasionally girls, would write in and ask if they could be in a photoshoot shagging the girls, or sometimes even just by themselves, oblivious to the fact that there were no blokes in *Bling*.

Dear *Bling*,
My name is ––. I'm nineteen and have a great ambition to be a part of a porno film/mag I believe my naked body is not disappointing and would be happy to send pictures of my nob or any other area you wish to see. My great ambition is to have people take photos of me naked: please could you help me with my ambition (info on what my next move is would be great)! if you need pictures or more info on this matter please please contact me on xxxx xxx xxxx.
(I will work for free)
P.s. this is no joke ring the mobile no. and speak to me to prove this.
please please please ring me if you can help me.

Or the slightly more simplistic:

Dear Editor,
Do you take Male Photo's Yes or No.
£10 Bum
£20 Front
Details in a Letter Please. Can come at Soho May 11th or 25th 2,00 Night Time because i will be Traveling on Bus to London Plus have to find Bed & Breadfest in a Hotel about £30 or £40.
Mr ––
Do you know any Guess House's it's more cheeperer'

Of course, there's a chance that the first of these letters was a joke simply because he kept claiming it wasn't and asking us to give him a call, probably one of his mates trying to set him up or something, but the second letter you feel is absolutely genuine. Some geezer wanted us to take pictures of his back and front and pay him £10 and £20 a pop for them like they were in demand or something.

As I said, we got a lot of this, and in fact, we got an even greater number of guys who'd actually send in pictures of their fronts. We had in so many that the editorial assistants started pinning them up on the wall over their desks as a sort of cock collage. It grew so much that within six months it measured five feet high by ten feet wide and started encroaching on the wall space over Matt's desk – which he was having none of.

I guess the guys used to send them in because posting them off was almost like a sexual act in itself, that thought of one of the models (because the whole place was staffed with models, right) would open their letter and see their cock and get off on it just as the reader had got off looking at their body. And if that happened there was a chance, just the slightest possibility, that she might decide to visit the cock and its fat, hairy, house-bound owner for a bit of ultimate fantasy.

This is just my interpretation and, again, I don't know a lot about how women's minds work but from what girls have told me, they don't get turned on in the same visual way that blokes do. Sure, they might froth and foam a bit if they see James Bond, the Chippendales or Blue Watch putting out a blaze at the thong factory, but pictures of cocks apparently didn't press the same buttons in women as pictures of women did for us blokes. Sure, there are always going to be exceptions and some women will moan how there's no decent porn for women and so on but by and large they're in the minority. There's no decent porn for women because there's no market for it.

That's not to say that women don't fantasise as much as us men because they do. What they seemed to love though, generally speaking, was the dirty stories. Women have better imaginations than men and it's this they seemed to need stimulating more than their eyes. What was it Marilyn Monroe replied when some reporter asked her what she thought was the sexiest part of her body? 'My mind,' I think she told him. Personally, I would've said it was her tits, but then, that just goes to prove what I'm talking about. Yeah, yeah, yeah, I know, blokes like to use their imaginations too, but where we're lying back wondering how many tennis bats we can fit up a bird's arse, they're fleshing out their fantasies and creating all sorts of sexy scenarios in their minds that result in a night of passion.

Which brings us neatly around to our last category: the sex confession. Now, I've probably set you all off in the wrong direction talking about women and what they like because that's not really my business. *Bling* and *Froth* and the like were aimed at blokes and hence catered for their tastes. Sometimes there was an overlap and sometimes there wasn't. A lot of women bought our dirty mags, surprisingly enough, but again it seemed more for the confessions than anything else. Blokes liked reading the confessions too but primarily they got off on the pictures.

'Yeah, but are they real or do you just make them all up?'

Bling genuinely got dozens of confessions through the post every week but before they got anywhere near the page they almost always needed to be heavily rewritten because they were usually a load of old unbelievable bollocks.

An example:

Dear Bling,

The train home from work is usually a dull affair for me, until the other week when I had to work late. On this occasion my carriage was empty apart from a stunning brunette in typical office gear. Not usually shy, I sat opposite her and we exchanged smiles. A few minutes later the woman leant over to me and said 'Want to make the journey more interesting?' whilst resting her hand on my knee. Looking down her loose blouse to see her bronzed cleavage I was quick to say yes. Instantly she thrust her hand onto my cock, rubbing it feverishly until it was hard. We snogged briefly before she grabbed my hand and a bag full of shopping and headed towards the toilet. 'What's that for?' I asked. 'You'll see,' she said, with a gleaming, yet dirty smile. As soon as I'd locked the door I pinned her to the wall, lifted her skirt and yanked down her tights and black knickers. My hand felt amongst her soaking black bush and caressed her pink lips. With the other I ripped open her blouse and lifted her bra, revealing pert tits with massive dark nipples. I sucked on these as she pulled my cock out of my trousers and wanked it mercilessly. 'Let's fuck,' I said, sweating in anticipation. 'My way,' she replied, reaching for her shopping. She pulled out a small cucumber and poured some shampoo onto my hand. 'You're going to be needing this,' she said and I knew she wanted it up the arse. I turned her to face the wall and began to lather her up with shampoo. I couldn't resist her plump bum-hole much longer, and threaded my meat all the way up inside her, which was met with a groan of contentment. As I began to stroke in and out of her arse, she inserted the cucumber up her cunt, stretching it as wide as I've ever seen a cunt open. As my excitement grew, I pummelled her faster and faster, gripping onto her curvy hips. Soon my motions matched the rhythm of the train rattling along the rails. At the same time the woman thrust the cucumber up her cunt quicker and quicker, and her slurping became as loud as the train. We both got closer and closer to cumming until, as she let out a squeal of orgasm, her arse clenched tight around my swollen cock, forcing me to shoot wads of cum up her arse and I groaned with delight. I quickly realised that my stop was approaching, so I pulled my cock out of the now rosy-cheeked girl, kissed her on the lips and dashed off, trying to make myself look presentable. I've not seen the girl since, but if I see her again I hope that she will have done her shopping.

Signed [etc etc]

This is a perfect example of the 'genuine' sex confessions we received. At least in the stories that appeared in the mag there was usually an element of 'Well, it could've happened' but with something like this we know for a fact – and that's *a fact* – that this never took place. How? Oh, come on, in the history of sex, do you really think any woman, never mind a stunning brunette, has ever turned around to a total stranger on a train and asked him to stick his cock and half a bottle of Head & Shoulders up her arse without so much as a 'nice day, isn't it'? Sure, strangers have sex all the time, but never bang, like that, out of the blue with no prompting and for no reason. Women just don't work this way. I wish to fuck they did, but they don't.

Okay, it's a story, and that's all it is, but knowing it's just a story, doesn't that lessen its appeal? Wouldn't it be sexier to read a confession that you could believe actually happened? Wouldn't it be nice to think that there really was a rampant brunette running around screwing guys at will? And this is why we ended up rewriting most of them. To make them just a little bit plausible and therefore more interesting.

Yeah, sure, nobody wants to have to plough through six chapters of 'How are you? I like your hat' before someone's getting pummelled into the wall but still, a few sentences just to set up the story, that's all it takes, and people are lazy. What's the common phrase? Oh yeah, 'To cut a long story short.'

> Dear Bling,
>
> I was walking in this pub with my mates when the tall, absolutely stunning blonde walks in with a couple of her friends. Anyway, to cut a long story short, we were soon getting undressed in the back of a cab on the way back to her place while her friend was down between my legs with my balls on her face . . . etc

You see what I'm getting at? Lazy. Set the scene a little and it makes it so much more interesting. Take our mate on the train, for example. Now the way I ended up rewriting that one was I made him a ticket inspector and her a fare dodger with a string of convictions behind her. One more time and it's the Big House for you. See? It gives it a little bit of edge and makes it a little bit more exciting already. At least, it did in my mind.

> There I was, standing over her with my notebook in my hand when suddenly she starts hitching up her skirt. 'Please,' she said, pleading with me. 'I'm really sorry. Don't put my name in the book. I'll do anything.' I looked down at her shopping. 'Anything? Is that a

bottle of Wash & Go?' I asked, and a thought suddenly occurred to me.

So, I ended up rewriting the ones I could and binning the ones I couldn't.

After a while, I started to realise that writing letters from scratch was actually a lot quicker and easier than typing in the genuine ones. Also, confessions sent in by women were at a bit of a premium so quite often I had to write these ones myself. And this was a bit of a shame really because these were the ones that most of us blokes wanted to read. Maybe it's the natural homophobia in men coming out but most blokes would rather listen to a bird talking dirty than another bloke. Think about it, really. It's like those 0898 sex-lines you get advertised in the back of our mags, you don't go phoning them up at £1.49 a minute to listen to some geezer banging on about how he pulled a nice bit of stuff on the train last night, do you? No, you want to listen to a good old dirty bird and hear about what she's been up to with the plumber while her old man's been at work. And then, after twenty-five minutes you can put down the phone, pull up your trousers, go downstairs and thank your Gran for letting you use the phone.

At the end of the day, the secret of a good sex confession, in my mind, was plausibility and a bit of a twist: the goody-goody-two-shoes girlie fresher who's so besotted with the senior lecturer that she lets him do her up the arse, only to find out that he's actually the janitor. The irate woman who discovers her boyfriend's been cheating on her so she makes a porno video with three squaddies plastering her from head to foot and leaves it behind after packing her bags and scarpering. The female journalist who's never swallowed a load in her life but has to write an article all about it for

Cosmopolitan in order to get her dream job there. Aren't these a bit more interesting than 'to cut a long story short'?

The overnight conference, the female boss, the recent divorce and the connecting doors . . .

. . . the missing stripper, the desperate club owner, the skint barmaid and the impatient stag party of rowdy firemen . . .

. . . the stranded female driver, the AA man, the lapsed breakdown cover and the roadside service . . .

. . . the dashing young cat-burglar, the female dormitory, the citizen's arrest and the on-the-spot penal punishment . . .

. . . the outrageous bet, the football team's showers, the manager's wife and the whole team pulled off at half-time . . .

. . . the Ann Summers party, the girl new to the neighbourhood, the suitcase full of products and the tube of lube . . .

. . . the odious boss, his naive secretary, her pay review and an unfortunate case for the tribunal . . .

. . . the middle-aged former beauty, the dried-out complexion, the bob-a-job Adventure Scouts and the interesting new moisturiser . . .

. . . the bored housewife, her insatiable lust for rough, the Parcel Force driver and the large packet leant up against her back door . . .

. . . the girls' night in, *Basic Instinct* on the telly, three bottles of wine too many and the itch neither friend can ignore . . .

. . . the unworldly shop girl, the teasing co-workers, the quest to find out what she's been missing and the rubber ring on the checkout seat the next day . . .

. . . the train home, the stunning brunette, the bag full of shopping and . . . oh, hang on a minute.

Well, anyway, I could bang on about this all night but I can't be bothered. I guess what I'm trying to say is yes, most of the letters were real, it's just what happened in them was a load of old bollocks.

But then, you probably all knew that already.

5: Talking dirty

Of course, it took me a good year and a couple of hundred letters before I worked this all out for myself. In those first few weeks I was more preoccupied with a more immediate question.

'Where the fuck is Stuart?' I asked Roger.

'I don't know,' he replied without turning around. 'Doesn't give a fuck, does he . . .' he started muttering to himself before his muttering became a mumbling and I was no longer able to make out what he was saying.

I phoned Wendy on reception and she told me she hadn't got anything written in the book and that Stuart hadn't phoned in. I replaced the receiver and wondered what I could do. *Bling* was late by about three weeks and we'd only got a couple of the features done: one about jetskiing and one about one 'crazy' night on the Ibiza clubbing scene. Both were extremely dull and wouldn't be read by anyone except the PR girl who'd taken Stuart jetskiing two months ago and Stuart's 'crazy' mate, Gerrard, who'd paid for half his holiday in Ibiza by writing about his 'mad antics' in Manumission. Not that they were that 'mad', all he'd done was drop a couple of tabs and get up on some stage with the in-crowd and dance around like a cunt in front of several thousand people all doing exactly the same thing. Gerrard had tried to convey the 'craziness' of it all though by tagging on the end of each sentence, 'it was mad' or 'it was wild' or 'it was unbelievable,' all of which were deleted from the feature in a charitable attempt to make him come across as less of a wanker.

Anyway, that was all by the by. I'd subbed the letters for this month and reviewed a couple of movies and was now stuck and bored. I twiddled my thumbs a bit more, picked up a copy of *Ace*, flicked through it for a few minutes but soon became bored again.

How bizarre! Only six weeks ago, before I'd started working here, I would've been poring over the pictures and fantasising about the girls until my trousers needed loosening. Only five weeks ago, I would've been sitting here surreptitiously stealing glances and shoving the magazines away the moment anyone looked over in my direction. But now, Hazel came up and asked me if I'd picked a loupe (a little magnifying eye-piece for looking at slides) up off her desk and I didn't even put the magazine down. She stood in front of me and complained about people nicking stuff off her desk all the time and how this was her third loupe to go missing this year and I just carried on flicking through the mag and looking at the naked girls bending over and spreading their arses without the slightest twinge of embarrassment. Well, why shouldn't I? They were only arses, after all. We all had them.

Paddy had been right. In my first week he'd told me that when he'd started he'd always known that the novelty of looking at naked girls would wear off. What had surprised him was just how fast it had worn off.

'Haven't you had her in your mag recently?' I asked

Hazel, showing her a picture of one girl resting her head against another girl's beaver.

'Gabrielle? She's our regular girl, she's in every month. I don't know what *Ace* are doing running her. Anyway, if you see my loupe let me know because I don't want to go ordering another one because it makes it look as if I'm stealing them.'

'You want to do what I'm going to do and scratch your name on it, that way everyone knows it's yours and no-one can nick it.'

'I bloody will next time,' she fumed and marched back to her desk.

'I'll let you know if I find it,' I assured her and scratched my name into Hazel's loupe. Well, it saved ordering one for myself, didn't it?

I was halfway through the afternoon and a bit sleepy after a couple of lunchtime pints when Stuart rang.

'Did you manage to speak to any of them?' he asked.

'Any of who?'

'The girls, did you phone them up?'

'Er . . .' I said, wondering if I'd nodded off during a briefing. 'What girls? Sorry, who do you mean?'

'Did Roger not give you those sets?' he asked, his voice now tinged with irritation.

'Er . . .' I said again, not wanting to get anyone into trouble.

'Let me talk to Roger, put Roger on.'

'Roger, it's for you. It's Stuart.'

Roger's shoulders sagged at the unfairness of it all and he took the phone off me without turning around.

'Yeah?' he grunted. There was a pause, then I listened to

one half of a sulky, petulant Q&A, then Roger handed me back the phone and turned back to friendsreunited.co.uk.

'I left some stuff for you with Roger, he'll explain what needs to be done. I'll speak to you in the morning.' And with that Stuart was gone again.

Roger didn't explain anything. In fact, he didn't even speak to me after I'd hung up, he just sat there clicking on the names of the class of '77 and muttering 'cunt' after reading each little biog. In the end I had to prise it out of him.

'Well, what's this stuff Stuart left for me?'

'Just some girl sets stuff,' he replied, clicking open another name.

'What girl set stuff? Where?'

'Doing the old bullshit that goes with 'em,' he muttered.

'Well, why didn't you give it to me earlier?' I demanded.

'Why should we have to work when he's not even here?' he replied.

'For fuck's sake, Roger, I've been bored out of my mind all morning when I could've been cracking on with this stuff.'

'Well, it's not my fault,' he replied without any trace of irony.

'Come on then, let's have it.'

'Oh . . . in a minute,' he whined and it took another five minutes before he handed over three sets of slides and a list of written instructions.

The three girls were all British and living in the UK so Stuart had decided that I should talk to them. I remembered him banging on about this a few weeks earlier, about how it would be better if all the little girl blurbs were true and that we should interview the girls and get them to talk dirty to us instead of just making them up, so here I was: three names, three sets of slides and three phone numbers. I was to call them up, introduce myself and get them to talk smut to me

– what they liked doing in bed, what they fantasised about, what was the best sex they'd ever had, that sort of thing.

How embarrassing.

This might sound like a giggle but try phoning someone out of the blue and getting her to say dirty things to you down the phone and see how dry your mouth suddenly becomes. Actually, I wouldn't if I was you, you'd probably get nicked if you did.

I looked at the first set of slides. She was tall, slim and blonde, and as bald as a baboon's arse downstairs. Her name was Jennifer.

I misdialled three times before the phone started ringing and when it was picked up I almost choked.

'Is that Jennifer?' I asked.

'Yes?' she replied. I'd never talked to a real live porn model before (well, not counting my interview) but here I was looking at pictures of Jennifer's horse's hoof through Hazel's loupe and speaking to her in person.

Suddenly, porn was no longer fantasy.

'This is Godfrey Bishop, I work for *Bling*,' I told her.

'Yes?'

'Hi. Er . . . well, how are you, okay? Right, erm . . .' I said and realised I should've thought out what I was going to say first.

'Yes?'

'Right, well, you had a set shot with our photographer Howard Parke recently and erm . . . we're just putting it in the magazine now.' She didn't reply. 'You know the set? You're wearing black fishnets and lying on a big round bed' – with precious little else on and your lunch in close focus in a good majority of the shots, I didn't add.

'Yes?' she repeated, parrot-like.

'Well, I just wanted to talk to you about them for a bit,' I told her.

'What about?' she replied, tripling her vocabulary.

'Well, you know in the magazine, we always have a little bit of text that goes with the pictures, a little bit about yourself. Stuart – that's Stuart the editor – asked me if I could interview you very briefly for it.'

'I don't know, my mum and dad don't know I do this and I'd rather not say anything,' she said, less than enthusiastic about the whole thing.

'What?' I replied, not understanding what she meant.

'I don't want you using my real name or details because I don't want my family to know what I do,' she explained, again making absolutely no sense to me. I got her to explain this to me again and she did. Jennifer didn't want her name or details used in the magazine because she thought no-one would realise it was her if she used a fake name. Seriously, like her mum could peruse through *Bling* and study all the pictures, but she wouldn't realise that she was looking at her daughter unless we included her in a fact box. Bizarre, huh, but I've talked to dozens of models since who all believed the same, that they could protect their anonymity not by wearing a bag over their heads or keeping their pants on, but by giving themselves a stupid name such as Tex, Jackson or I.Fux.Gr8.

'We're not doing an in-depth family portrait, I just wanted to ask you a couple of questions, that's all,' I reassured her and after a few moments of silence she responded.

'Er . . . go on then, what?'

'Ooh . . .' I started scribbling anything I could think of down on the pad in front of me. 'Well, er, for example, how do I phrase this? What's your favourite fantasy?'

She thought for a moment.

'To win the lottery.'

'No, I mean, your favourite sexual fantasy.' Several heads around the office turned in my direction, then went back to what they were doing.

'Why, you're not going to write that, are you?'

'What the fuck do you think I'm phoning you up for? And don't tell me your mum and dad will recognise you if I stick a caption on informing readers that you like sucking donkeys off.' Naturally, I didn't say any of this, but I was sorely tempted and screwed my face up as she became stupider and stupider in the slides before my very eyes. What I actually said was:

'Yes, of course I'm going to write it, that's the whole point. We've got to put a few little details next to your pictures for people to read. A sort of, I like it from behind or I've always fantasised about doing it this way and that. That kind of thing.'

'Well, I don't want any of that next to my pictures.'

'Er . . . but that's the style of the magazine. It's just a bit of fun.'

'But that's personal. That's none of anyone's business.'

Huh? Your fantasies are personal but you're happy to show everyone your arsehole across two pages?

'Well, what sort of stuff do you like?'

'Why?' she insisted.

'Because I have to write something,' I told her.

'I don't want you writing anything, what's wrong with just having the pictures?' she said, getting a little upset with me now.

'It's alright, there's nothing to it, everyone does it, all our models tell us their fantasies' – bullshit – 'you could tell me anything.'

'But I'm not like that. These things are personal to me, I don't want to share them with everyone.'

'But you're naked in the pictures?'

'But I don't want anyone to know anything about me.'

'You don't have to if you don't want to, you could just make it all up if you want to.'

'Well then, why don't you just make it all up?' she asked.

'Apparently, this is sexier,' I said and told her not to worry about it. 'Leave it with me and I'll write something myself.'

'What are you going to write?'

'I don't know, something silly.'

'You're not going to write anything rude, are you, because I don't want anything rude?'

'Well, of course I'm going to write something rude, we're a rude magazine!'

'But I don't want anything rude next to my pictures.'

'Sorry, but I've got to.'

'But why?'

'It's just something dirty for guys to read while they fantasise about you,' I said, amazed that I was having to explain this to a porno model.

'I'm phoning Howard,' she said and the line went dead.

Well, if that conversation didn't have the readers bashing their cocks to bits, I didn't know what would. Personally, I'd never felt softer or more reprehensible in my life.

The next girl I phoned, Tracy (modelling name Traci), wasn't much more forthcoming. She simply wanted to meet a nice man who could make her laugh and settle down with him by the sea and it took twenty minutes of badgering before she finally admitted, 'I quite like going on top' which was written up as 'I love to grind my hot cunt into my man's face and not let him up until I've cum all over him'. At least Tracy didn't seem traumatised by the whole idea that there might be some sexy stuff written next to her pictures, though she did say that she found it rather hard to speak because she was in the middle of Woolworths.

Paddy came over after I'd put the phone down and gave me a knowing smile.

'Let me guess, Stuart's quest for truth, yeah?'

'He's got me phoning up models.'

Paddy smirked and shook his head. 'Fuck me, when's he going to give that one up? Stuart goes through this at least once a year and it's always the same. "It's got to be true, it has to be real." This is such a load of old bollocks. This is porn, and porn has fuck all to do with reality,' he said as he offered me a fag and lit one up himself. 'You know what reality is? Reality is going down the newsagents to buy pictures of naked birds because you ain't getting it yourself. Or if you are, it's off your fat, and utterly broken-in, old lady who you can't bear to drill these days unless you've sunk half a bottle of scotch.'

'You know what I like about you, Paddy, is that you're refreshingly uncynical.'

'He's not fucking wrong though,' Roger said somewhere off behind me.

'Reality? Reality's girls who still live at home with their mum and dad, or girls who are engaged to be married, or girls who take evening classes in art. Girls who collect teddy bears, and girls who watch *EastEnders* and get upset when one of their favourite characters is written out.' Paddy paused to blow a couple of smoke rings. 'Reality is girls who get embarrassed the same as you and I do when someone finds out what they really get off on. Reality is, these girls are no different from the ones you've been encountering every day of your life, and how many of them have told you that they like taking two cocks up the arse? Not many, I'll bet,' he said with a wise old wag of the finger. 'Except your mum, of course.'

'Yeah, but they're porn models, they're expected to be different.'

'And I'm a porn editor, so presumably so am I. Still doesn't stop me from not getting a sniff in the last three months, does it? And I'm meant to be getting it left, right and centre, that's what all the lads down my local think and they refuse to believe me when I tell them I'm not. They think I'm just being modest or a bit circumspect but I'm not like that. I'm the first one to climb the holy tower and announce to the whole of Mecca that I've had a shag when I get one but I haven't because I live in the real world. I work in porn, but I live in reality. And it's the same for the girls. The readers might want to think that they're dirty, cock-hungry old slags who'll do or say anything to anyone because they've got low moral standards – well, they must have if they take their clothes off in front of cameras, mustn't they? But they're just people. And people don't talk like the old rubbish we write. Not even blokes. It's just fantasy, it's what guys want to imagine a woman is saying while they're bashing off because blokes find that sort of thing a turn-on. And yeah, you might get your girlfriend or some old tart you've just brought back from a night out to say "do my cunt" a few times when you're poking her – if you prompt her a bit – but you're not going to get these models to dictate these girl blurbs to you in the language and style that the reader wants to see them written in because they're models, not writers. This is why Moonlight employs people like you. And why, every time Stuart does this, he ends up with some boring tame issue full of girls all claiming that the most important thing to them is a nice cuddle and a bit of a chat after making love. And who the fuck wants to jack off to that?'

'I know what you mean.'

'Stuart's problem is that he's confusing real sex with reality. That's what the readers want, real sex, but they're fucked in the head if they think they're going to get it for £2.95.' And with that, he wandered off to leave me to make my last phone call.

Paddy was wrong, Gemma (real name) turned out to be a different sort altogether. Gemma seemed made up by the fact that I was phoning from *Bling* and giggled with devilment when she observed that this was like a dirty phone call.

'Are you looking at my pictures right now?' she asked and I told her I was. 'Do you like my pussy shaved? I did it especially for the shoot,' she said.

'Very nice,' I told her as I made notes with my right hand and adjusted my trousers with my left.

'I've never shaved it completely before, I used to just trim, but it feels so smooth and soft now that I think I'm going to keep it like this for a while.' I wanted to ask her if she was feeling it right now but I didn't know how to phrase it without Roger asking me who I was talking to.

'Smashing,' I settled for.

'Okay, ask me anything. Anything at all and I'll tell you,' she said all excitedly. I adjusted my trousers still more and wished I'd made this phone call in Stuart's office where no-one could hear me.

'What's the dirtiest sex you've ever had?' I asked, my voice low, my hand cupped over the phone.

Gemma pondered a bit then told me that she loved it up the bum, especially when she was stoned. I scribbled this down frantically and stared hard at her pictures through the loupe. There she was, in full glossy colour and talking to me on the phone. Suddenly her facial grimaces of mock sexual ecstasy didn't seem so mocked any more.

'And when was the last time you did that?' I asked, a bit nasally.

'Ooh, only last night. I was feeling really horny and I just had to have it so I lubed myself up and used my favourite dildo up there,' she said and I felt my cock pump air a couple of times.

'And have you ever done it with another girl?' I asked.

'Oh yeah, loads of times. I love eating pussy – but I only like it if there's a guy there to fuck me from behind while I'm doing it,' she growled down the phone to me.

'And lastly, what's your favourite fantasy?' I said, sitting impossibly forward in my seat.

'Imagining all the readers of – who is this again? *Bling*? – *Bling* wanking all over me and covering me from head to toe in spunk,' she said, emphasising every sensual word before breaking out in laughter. 'You've got the coolest job,' she said. 'Is this what you do all day, phone girls up in the middle of the afternoon and make them say rude things?'

'Sometimes,' I said, suddenly seeing an angle. 'Or sometimes I have to go round and interview them in person,' I lied.

Gemma laughed at this and purred delightfully. 'Well, next time I'm in London you can take me out for a drink and interview me properly,' she said, not taking the bait.

'No problem. Where do you live?' I said and looked at the code. 'Manchester, yeah?'

'Bit of a long way to come just for a five-minute interview, isn't it?'

'Yes, shame.'

'Never mind, you poor poppet. You just think of me next time you're doing some young girl from behind. Alright?' she said.

'I will do,' I assured her. Or the next time I was thrashing myself off . . . whichever came first.

Several of the slides from Gemma's set followed me home that night and wouldn't leave me alone until I'd knocked at least three good 'uns out to them while fantasising about awayday trips to Manchester.

I drifted in and out of sleep throughout the night, remembered our conversation each time I woke up and pictured all sorts of possibilities and scenarios through the early hours.

At work the following day I scoured the back issues and found four different sets of Gemma in four different magazines and these too made their way home with me that night. In one of the mags, *Ace*, Gemma was the centre-spread girl and I was half-tempted to pin her up on my wall until I remembered that my elderly landlady often let herself into my room while I was out to empty the coin-operated electric and gas meters. I doubted whether she would've approved. Instead, an unofficial Gemma shrine was set up in the linen drawer under my bed and rapidly grew as the week went by.

On Friday night, I had a couple of beers with the lads after work and bought two bottles of Bulgarian red on the way home, along with a small £10 bag of grass, 20 fags and a take-away chicken Madras. It had all the makings of a famous night in.

By 10 o'clock, Gemma was out of her drawer and laying about me in a crescent of best pages. I studied her pictures and fantasised that she was in the room with me right now, begging me to do her just the way she liked it. She really was the quintessential sex object for me at that moment and I wanted to fuck her so badly that it hurt. In fact, I had to. I simply had no choice. My life wouldn't ever be complete if I didn't. And I knew it.

I pondered this as I relit a joint and took a big drag.

'So why don't you?' said the little red demon sitting on my left shoulder.

'Why don't I what?' I asked him.

'Fuck her. Come on, you actually know her, it's not like you're just some fucking reader. You're in the business. Besides, you know what she's like, she told you herself. She fucking loves it. You'd have no bother there.'

'But she's all the way up there in Manchester,' I told him.

'So? Give her a ring, you've got her number in your wallet, we all saw you slip it in there. Give her a bell and tell her you want to go up and pay her a visit. Then just drill her. She'd be well up for it. Maybe not tonight but you could jump on a train first thing in the morning and be up there before lunchtime tomorrow. A fucking porn model man, and look at her. Imagine that.'

'She is something else, isn't she?' I said, staring at her centre spread and taking another big toke.

'And she's already as good as laid it on a plate for you, you'd have to be bent not to give her one. Go on, give her a ring. You know what they say, nothing ventured, nothing gained. You only live once and all that old bollocks.'

'That's all very true,' I told the demon. 'You've made some excellent points there. But hey, what do you think?' I said, turning to the angel on my other shoulder.

'Count me in, I'm with you lads.'

I dug my mobile out and tapped in Gemma's number. My pay-as-you-go credit was pretty low but I had enough for probably a couple of minutes. I pressed the green button and held the phone to my ear.

As horny and focused as I was, I was still a bit apprehensive about calling a porn model out of the blue and inviting myself up for a sex session. I mean, how the fuck was I going to phrase this one? I assured myself that Gemma would remember our call from earlier in the week and know what I was ringing about. I mean, she'd been chuffed to bits to hear from me last time I'd rung and she hadn't even known me then. Now that we'd shared a little telephone intimacy she was bound to be even more forthcoming. I took a couple of big swigs from my wine to steady my nerves and another big drag on my joint. My fingers were shaking as I held phone and drugs to my face and my heart pounded violently when the ringing tone started. This, however, was compared to nothing when the phone was finally answered.

'Hello?' I heard her shout.

'Hi, Gemma?'

'Yes?'

'Hi, it's Godfrey from *Bling*, we spoke the other day.'

'Huh? Oh, right, yeah, hi.' There was a bit of a pause as she passed this information on to someone with her, then asked me, 'What's up?'

'Oh, nothing, I just wanted to give you a quick ring, if that's alright?'

'Er . . . what about?' she shouted again.

'Well, just to say hello and all that, and follow up something we were talking about the other day.'

'I can't hear you, you'll have to speak up a bit,' she yelled. 'Hang on a minute, I'm going outside so I can hear you.'

There was a lull in the conversation as she made her way through a background of laughter and music and emerged out into the relative quiet of a street.

'That's better, I can hear you now. Okay, sorry, but what was you saying?'

'Oh, er, well, nothing important,' I told her and squirmed as I struggled to find the right words. 'Well, you know when you said the other day that it was a shame I wasn't up there in Manchester?' I said, trying to introduce the subject in a roundabout way. In my mind, when I'd planned this call, she'd remembered our conversation immediately and extended an instant invitation for me to come up and stay with her. This didn't happen quite like this in reality and I felt my heart sink a little when she replied:

'Er, no but go on.'

Not the recognition I was hoping for. I decided I'd better double check I was talking to the right person.

'This is Gemma, isn't it? The model, who I spoke to on Tuesday afternoon?'

'Yes. Sorry, who is this again?'

'Godfrey Bishop. I work on *Bling*, I spoke to you the other day.'

'Okay. Yeah?'

'Well, you said the other day that Manchester was a long way to go just to interview someone,' I said, not getting any closer to the point and finding it extremely hard to find the right words.

'Look, can this wait until Monday because I'm freezing my tits off here?' Gemma said and I pictured her little tits all goosepimply and pert. My phone started beeping to signal that my credit was disappearing fast so I realised I'd better get to the point and quick, but this wasn't easy. Why wasn't it easy? She'd seemed right up for it the other day.

'Well, when I spoke to you last you said that it was a shame I wasn't up there in Manchester and that I should think of you next time I . . . er . . . you know . . .' I tailed off as more beeps punctuated my train of thought. Get to the point! Get to the fucking point, I told myself, but my heart was going like the clappers and my voice was starting to croak. 'Anyway, er, tomorrow I was thinking of coming up to Manchester to see you in person, if that's alright, you know?'

'To see me? What for?'

'Well, it was what you were saying the other day, you know, when I spoke to you then? About me? Thinking of you?'

'Thinking of me what?' she said, failing to make any sort of connection at all. 'What are you talking about?'

'About . . .' I whined, then quickly concluded I'd misread the signals and was in the process of making a beauty of a mistake that would have me cringing for years. 'It doesn't matter,' I told her all urgently but she wouldn't let it go.

'What? Hello?'

'It doesn't matter. It doesn't matter.'

'Look, I'm with my boyfriend and his family at the moment and I don't work at the weekends anyway.'

'No, really, it's alright,' I tried to reassure her.

'What are you coming to Manchester for?' I heard her ask, but then there was a second voice in the background demanding to know what was going on.

'No, no, really, it's alright. Honestly, it's alright, don't worry . . .' I tried to tell her but it was too late, my phone suddenly died.

That hadn't gone as well as I'd hoped.

I looked at it for a moment, buried my head in my hands and didn't move for about two minutes. I stayed in this position, shaking my head and grimacing so hard that I'm surprised my cheeks didn't tear, before finally deciding the best way forward was a big drink.

What had I done?

A sudden, horrible realisation crept over me and threatened to devour my every last shred of self-worth as I tried to shake the words 'What are you coming to Manchester for?'

out of my brain but I couldn't. They were there now, and they were there to stay.

Whenever I'd think of Gemma from now on, I wouldn't think of her talking dirty to me or taking it up the arse or eating some other bird out while I looked on, I'd think of her standing in a cold pub carpark on a Friday night with her boyfriend at her elbow, asking me why I was coming to Manchester.

Jesus.

What an utter wanker.

6: Zoe bawl

What a wanker.

What a wanker.

What a wanker.

I spent the best part of the next few days cringing every time I remembered what I'd done, and remembering what I'd done about once every five minutes.

What a wanker.

Of course, in the cold light of day it was all very easy to see what had happened and why. Gemma, being an experienced pro, had simply given me what I'd asked first time I'd phoned up, whereas me, being a bit of a cock, had taken her at her word. Like all the dim readers I liked to mock, who are always sending marriage and sex proposals to the girls, I'd bought into what Gemma had said and believed it.

Jesus.

I was very sheepish at work on Monday morning and jumped every time the phone rang, expecting it to be Gemma or Howard Parke phoning up to complain. No-one said anything to me, though I walked about on egg shells like everyone knew and wished I could get away for a month or two until it had faded into memory.

Roger wasn't in, nor was Paddy or Matt, Monty, Fat Paul,

anyone from *Froth* or Stuart, so the office was mercifully quiet. Don came over and we chatted about the various football results over the weekend until Susie phoned him up (even though she was less than twenty feet away) and told him he had a shitload of work to be getting on with. Susie seemed like she was always doing this to Don. Why? For no other reason than because she could. Don was her worker, ergo her pet. Everyone else might get to talk, joke and laugh with each other but not Don. Don worked under Susie so he had to do what she said while he was at work and that was all there was to it. Why? Because she could, and because she was a cunt. Take your pick. It fucked Don off no end but Susie's other subordinate, Hazel, always got a real kick out of watching her colleague get humiliated and forced to return to his desk like a little kid. Why? Because she was a cunt too. It doesn't get much simpler than this. Whatever the ins and outs of it all, Don was gone and I was once again left alone with my thoughts.

I wrote a couple of girl blurbs that had been waiting since Friday but I really wasn't in the mood for this old nonsense this early on, so I borrowed one of Jackie's Harry Potter books and started reading about some four-eyed kid who could fly. Or something like that.

Just after twelve, Stuart arrived and called me into his office. I was dreading what was coming and wondered how best to bullshit my way out of the shame of it all, but Stuart didn't seem particularly angry or anything. He seemed hungover to fuck, but not angry.

'Right, sit down. Okay, I need you to do me a favour,' he started and I was fully expecting him to follow this up with, 'I want you to leave off harassing the girls. They're frightened and upset.' But he didn't. Instead, what he proposed really didn't sound like any sort of favour at all. 'I need you to go over to the studio and direct a shoot for me this afternoon. I've got to meet a bloke about . . . well, that's not important,' he said, with a dismissive wave of the hand and I caught a blast of Scotch in the face as he talked. 'It's over at Howard Parke's studio in Battersea. You'll be able to get a cab and claim it back and it's this girl here,' he said and handed me a polaroid of an incredibly cute young blonde.

'Zoe, her name is, though I'm sure it'll be fucking Bangers & Mash or something after today. She's a first-timer, never done any modelling before, sent her snaps in. I thought it would be a good learning curve for you because you're going to need to have to do this sort of thing more in the future, so what do you say?'

'Thank you,' was what I said.

'Er, yeah. That's not what I meant but, whatever. She's over there at the moment but she'll be in make-up for the next hour or so, so go and get your arse down there now and just get Howard to bang out a standard set. He knows what he's doing anyway, but make sure he shoots a few covers too, in case she turns out looking alright.'

Stuart scribbled down Howard's address on a piece of paper and shooed me off by opening the door next to me.

'Oh, and most importantly of all, make sure you get I.D. and a model release off her.'

'A what?' I asked, my mind already halfway to Battersea.

'I.D. We can't publish her pictures unless we've got photocopies of two forms of I.D. – driver's licence, passport, birth certificate, student card, that sort of thing – proving she's over eighteen, and a model release giving us permission to publish her pictures which has been signed by her and witnessed by, well, in this case it'll be by you.'

'Is that right?' I said.

'Of course, we can't just publish any old picture of

anyone we like otherwise we'd get taken to the cleaners. That's why it never works when some bitter divorcee sends in pictures of his ex-wife, claiming he's her and how she wants to be in the mag and the world to know that she loves it up the arse with a big stick. We can't publish these pics, no matter how saucy she is, without I.D. and written consent,' he said, then added, 'Unless the woman's dead. Then we can stick in whoever we want.'

'Yeah, but that's a bit sick, isn't it? I don't know if I could do it over those sorts of pictures.'

'Er, no, I mean pictures of her taken before she, erm . . .' Stuart trailed off with a look of horror etched across his face. 'You'd better get a move on, you don't want to keep them hanging about,' he told me, urging me away from him.

I grabbed my coat and left the building.

Zoe looked just unbelievable in real life. She was good-looking, sure, but she wasn't stunning. So what was it about her that I found so attractive?

Probably the fact that I knew I was going to be seeing her git, real soon.

She was sat in a big flannel dressing-gown in front of the make-up mirror while Howard's assistant (who was no pig herself) applied the finishing touches to her immaculate lip gloss. She shot a glance in my direction and gave a little nervous smile when I said hello, which was about all she could do while under the brush.

Howard was there too. He shook my hand and greeted me like a long lost brother and led me next door to a mocked-up bedroom studio set where we discussed clothing and possible cover shots.

'Stockings, suspenders, high heels, little frillies, that sort of thing,' I told him.

'And what about her?' he replied.

We laughed, good-naturedly, and he poured us a couple of vodkas, which we both made light work of.

'Who's the other geezer in there?' I asked as he refilled our glasses.

'Oh, him, the boyfriend, playing chaperone, for fuck's sake,' he said, shaking his head and drinking his drink. At that moment Howard's assistant, Pamela, Zoe and Zoe's boyfriend, Scott, all emerged from the dressing room and looked to us for approval.

'Doesn't she look beautiful?' Pamela said, and Zoe lit up with pride.

'Good enough to eat,' I agreed and noticed Scott's eyes dart in my direction.

'I'll be off then,' Pamela said and she and Howard swapped kisses.

'Alright, my love, thanks for everything,' Howard said, patting her arse.

'Are you going?' Scott asked.

'Yes, why, do you want a lift somewhere?' Pamela asked. The very notion of leaving his girlfriend alone with me and Howard seemed to horrify Scott, who denied he was going anywhere.

'Right then,' Howard said, clapping his hands. 'Shall we get started?'

Zoe took the frillies we'd picked out for her and disappeared back into the dressing room to put them on, which disappointed and confused me a little, then ten minutes later she emerged looking so gut-wrenchingly sexy that I would've happily killed everyone else in the room if she'd given me the nod.

Now that was a woman, I thought to myself, my tongue lolling out of my head. I tried not to make it too obvious and stare at her, but then suddenly remembered that I was a professional and, as such, was allowed to stare as much as I liked. So I did, and almost wore out my corneas in the process. I'd never really been a lingerie fan or anything like that before, but seeing Zoe three feet away decked out in that lacy black finery, I was immediately converted. I still don't think it suits me, but Zoe looked fantastic in it.

'My God,' I kept muttering under my breath. 'My God.'

What must've been going on in boyfriend Scott's head I can only imagine. Here was his girlfriend, probably looking more stunning than he'd ever seen her before, and he was sharing the moment with two other geezers. What sort of inner conflict must that stir up?

'Shall we get you on the bed then, darling?' Howard said, popping my intense concentration. 'Alright, come round here,' he said, guiding her into position and moving her this way and that with his great sticky paws. Zoe didn't seem to mind and co-operated like a shop dummy but Scott's face was a picture, especially when Howard took a light reading off her tits.

'So, er, so have you done many of these?' a voice asked behind me. It was Scott, he'd wandered over to make conversation but he was still watching Zoe and Howard like a hawk. As was I.

'Oh yeah, they're nothing, just work to me these days,' I lied, shifting the tube of extra strong mints I'd just found in my pocket.

'Do they take long? I mean, what's going to happen? I mean . . .'

'Oh, it's nothing, just the usual old routine,' I reassured him. 'Striptease and sex toys, that sort of thing.'

'No-one said anything to me about sex toys,' he protested, which was a coincidence because no-one had said anything to me about sex toys either. I'd just decided to throw that in for a laugh to see the look on his face. It was great.

'Well, we'll see,' I told him and moved closer to the set for a better view. Scott followed me step for step, unwilling to leave my side.

'Okay, and big smile,' Howard told her, looking through the viewfinder. 'Come on now, say "cheese" . . .' – which she did and SNAP. 'Now say "big cock please" . . .' which again she did and SNAP. 'Now "hot jizz please" . . .' – again SNAP. 'Now "spank me please" . . .' SNAP, etc. Howard carried on this way for several minutes while he snapped off a roll of cover shots of Zoe in various poses, pulling various faces. He could've just got her to say 'cheese' or 'please' or just asked her to smile, I suppose, but it was funny the way he kept coming up with something new each time and soon we were all laughing and a little more at ease with each other, which I guess was the point of the exercise.

Actually, to say we were all laughing isn't exactly true. One of us looked fit to bust and you ain't going to win a bun for guessing who.

'So, what did you do before you worked on this?' Scott asked, distracting me from his girlfriend, who was just about to start losing her clothes.

'Oh, you know, not a lot . . .' I said, trailing off as one of the straps fell down around her shoulders.

'So how did you get into doing this then? Did you go to college?' Scott tried again, but I wasn't biting.

'Yeah, something like that,' I replied.

'And so, I mean, if I wanted a job on your magazine, how would I go about it?'

'I don't know,' I told him, as all of a sudden one of Zoe's nipples hoved into view.

I can't tell you what a feeling of exhilaration I felt as that first little bud broke from ground. It was like . . . like . . . like . . . well, the only way I can describe it is like this; you know that bit in *Jaws*, when Roy Scheider's on the beach and he sees that little kid eaten on the lilo and the camera rushes into his face? That sudden surging realisation. Well, it was like that. A kind of 'Oh my God, this is really happening. She's going to get it all out with me standing right here and nobody in the world can do anything about it.'

Fantastic.

And it's a different sort of rush from when you take a bird home and she gets her kit off for the first time because there was no connection between me and Zoe, no relationship. She was just doing it, I was just watching. This was all purely voyeuristic, which I guess, in a nutshell, is what pornography is all about. It's seeing something you have no right to see. It's, like, seeing up some girl's skirt on the bus or accidentally wandering into the women's changing rooms at your local swimming baths. It's a taboo pleasure. It's like, say for example, if you've got a neighbour that you really fancy and one night she invites you in for a coffee and you end up in bed together. Well, that's all great and good, but doesn't it feel naughtier, more taboo, when you're standing on her garage roof in the middle of the night watching her through binoculars?

Well, that's what I think anyway.

So there it was, first one, then the other, separated only by the sounds of Howard's shutter snapping open and shut, and my swallowing.

Zoe gradually peeled the lacy basque away to reveal her bangers in all their glory (and a fine pair she had too) before going to work losing her stockings.

'So, I mean, how long have you been doing this?' Scott tried again, his voice now a little wobbly.

'Look, sorry, mate, I don't mean to be short with you or anything but I am trying to work here,' I said and went back to my silent vigil.

Scott looked around the studio, searching for what, I don't know, but he seemed to look absolutely everywhere except at his slowly undressing girlfriend.

'That's it, now peel each stocking off and make out as if you're going to flick them off the end of your toes,' Howard was saying. 'That's it, that's beautiful. You're a natural. Isn't this fun?' Zoe giggled in agreement and I emitted a guttural grunt, but Scott didn't seem to have anything to say on the matter and had disappeared off behind me somewhere, to my eternal relief.

'That's wonderful, hold that. Yep, now legs apart, really thrust forward. Oh, I say, that's superb . . .' SNAP SNAP SNAP. Howard stopped for a moment and looked up from behind the camera. 'Darling. Honey, all your hair's hanging down in your eyes. No, dear, just leave it. Godfrey will get it.' Then he turned to me. 'God', give her a hand, tidy her hair behind her ears, will you?'

Oh man, this was just getting better and better.

I moved forward while Zoe lay in position, now only her knickers in place, and gently brushed her hair from her face and tucked it behind her ears. As I did so she looked up and gave me a smile that almost had my eye out. At that moment she was the most sexually charged woman on the planet and had we been alone I would've given her the best five seconds of her life.

'Thank you, Godfrey,' Zoe grinned and I mumbled something along the lines of, 'Not at all, my pleasure.'

'Okay then, sweetheart, a couple more in that last pose,

then I want you to start pulling your pants down . . .' Howard started to say but this was about all Scott could take. He burst forward out of nowhere, held his hand up in front of the camera and seized Zoe by the arm.

'No! No! No!' he blubbed, imploring her. 'No more. Don't! Don't! Come on, let's go home. I don't want you to do this. I'm sorry, Zoe, please, let's just go.'

'Hey, get off me,' she protested, shocked, annoyed and clearly embarrassed. 'Let me go!'

'Zoe, no, you don't have to do this. Please, you don't have to do this.'

'Don't have to do this? This was your idea, remember?' she yelled as the pair of them played tug-of-war with each other across the bed. 'Get off!'

'I've changed my mind, I'm sorry, please, let's just go,' he was crying. *He was crying?* Yeah, he was, he was crying. Tears were streaming down his face and his eyes were all puffy and red.

Gawd dear, you're going to wake up in the middle of the night and remember this day for a few years to come, mate, I thought to myself with an inner smile.

'Please . . .' he was imploring her, crying more and more.

'No, I'm doing it and that's the end of . . . get off!'

'I love you, I love you, please don't. Zoe, no . . . boo-hoo-hoo,' etc.

Me and Howard had stood back without saying a word so far but now it looked like it was time to step in. Howard gave me the nod and we both went and wrestled him away from her and the bed and bundled him towards the door. Scott struggled and screamed in protest and we only let him go when Zoe blocked our path and told us to leave off.

'Let him go, it's alright.'

Scott broke forward to hug her but she pushed him back and spelt it out plain and clear.

'Now I'm doing this whether you like it or not, and I'm not doing this for you, I'm doing this for me. You don't have a say in it, have you got that clear? And if you disturb us one more time I'll be packing my bags tonight when we get home, do you understand?' she said, finally getting his attention. 'Now you've got a choice, either you can stay and sit quietly or you can go and I'll meet you at home. What's it to be?'

Go Go Go Go, I was chanting frantically inwardly but Scott was fucked if he was going to leave Zoe here alone with us and told her he wanted to stay.

'No, I can't have this, he's got to go. I'm trying to run a business here,' Howard objected but Zoe told him if Scott was forced to leave, she'd go too. I think Scott saw a glimmer of salvation in this but couldn't work out how to exploit it so, in the end, we all resumed our positions and got back to work.

Not much to tell after that. Zoe stripped down nicely and we posed, positioned and photographed her from every conceivable angle, though the fun atmosphere from before was now somewhat spoilt by Scott's gentle sobbing off in the corner. This didn't do anyone any favours, least of all Zoe, whose smiles now looked papered on.

To pay Scott back for spoiling my first porn shoot, I got Zoe to do a load of pink shots (pulling herself open) and insertion stuff. We'd never use them in a million years but I just wanted to put Scott through the wringer a bit more.

When the last shot was taken, Zoe got dressed and filled out all the relevant paperwork in exchange for a cheque. As she did this, Scott approached me and Howard and apologised to us for losing it in the way that he did and Howard gave him a brief lecture by way of response.

'This is a professional industry, Scott. We're not taking pictures of Zoe for titillation and thrills, this is how I make my living and this is precisely the reason I discourage boyfriends, husbands or any other chaperone from coming along. Not because I've got something to hide or because we want to force your girlfriend into doing something she doesn't want to do, but because people who don't work in the industry get all emotional and protective and get in the way of professionals at work,' he said, indicating the pair of us.

Scott apologised again and Howard told him no harm done and shook his hand just before he left. Zoe said goodbye and told us that she had enjoyed it but she didn't know whether or not she was ready to make a career out of it just yet. She gave Howard and me a kiss on the cheek and her and Scott linked arms and left.

And as we watched them walk up the road and loop their arms around each other in reconciliation, Howard lit a fag and said, 'Besides, if you hadn't have been here, mate, we could've probably both nailed your bird.'

7: Three's a crowd

Now, I took what Howard said about us both probably being able to nail Zoe with a pinch of salt but it turned out that he wasn't exaggerating. Like I've said before, people were always asking me if I got to shag the models and the general answer was no because, by and large, I didn't get to meet them. Most of my days were spent sat in front of a computer in the office, writing about how much I loved being taken hard up the arse by two truck drivers, while sucking off their mate on video (though I didn't spend all day writing my biography). It was the photographers who worked with the girls and, therefore, got the perks.

Take one photographer I knew; every new girl who came along to test shoot for him, he would ask them the same questions. Would they be prepared to do girl/girl? Most would say yes, that would be fine. Then he'd ask them if they'd be prepared to do boy/girl? Again, most would say yes. So then he'd pick up his camera, get his cock out and tell them, 'Off you go then.'

If the girl hesitated he'd explain that he wasn't 'going to fork out a load of money booking a make-up girl and a male model and reserving the studio for a day's shooting on an untried girl who, for all I know, will probably run off at the first sight of a hard-on, am I?' Then add, 'Come on, girlie, this is a professional business so get your chops around it,' and, hey presto, he'd get a blow-job off every girl who shot for him.

What a great scam!

And he wasn't alone in this. A lot of photographers I worked with liked to make the most of their positions and who could blame them? Women have always used sex to get what they want and blokes have always used whatever they had to get sex. This is the natural order of things. It's been going on since men lived in caves and will probably continue to do so right up until the hermaphrodites take over. The PC lobby won't have this though and reckon we're all equal in wants and desires, but when was the last time one of them got a shag? Well, the birds get it alright, partly as a way of getting their blokes to go along with whatever old rubbish they're trotting out with this week, and the PC geezers, they just play along to get inside their bird's knickers.

And that's a fact, by the way.

Me? I was just pissed off because I never had anything anyone wanted.

However, all that aside, there have still been a couple of times when models laid it on a plate for me – only for me to turn it down.

What? Are you joking? This sounds like bullshit. Nope, I'm serious and I'll explain why and you tell me if you would've done any different in my trousers.

See, the couple of times it's been offered to me were very much under conditions and along the lines of those few words with which Howard bade Zoe and Scott a fond farewell.

I.e., 'both of us.'

I was at a shoot only a few weeks later, around Howard's

again, when Claire made me a definite 'it's on a plate if you want it' pass at me. Claire was one of Howard's regular models and a sweeter, lovelier girl you couldn't wish to watch undress. Now, I'd been getting a few signals off her almost as soon as we started, with a bit of lingering eye contact here and a few suggestive remarks there, but I put all this down to the fact that we were just having a laugh, the wine was flowing and that Claire was very much at home with Howard. As the shoot went on though, Claire's come-ons became less and less easy to dismiss.

'Get it out, Godfrey, let's have a look at it then. Come on, let's see your cock.'

I'd stopped reading between the lines about five minutes earlier.

Claire was on a bed and she was playing with a selection of dildos for our Christmas issue (she had a Santa hat on) and she'd been getting a bit carried away with each of them, and me and Howard had to keep telling her to withdraw them from herself so that we could take the shots we needed – *Bling* not being able to show penetration, you see. Well, Claire was quite full of high spirits and, in between Howard changing films, she would demonstrate them for real, right in front of me, purring away like a cat and holding my gaze until I turned away (which wasn't happening too often).

'Oohh, this one's a good one. I like the feel of this. Tell me, Godfrey, are you about this size or will you have to do me up the bum before I feel it?'

Say what you mean, why don't you?

'Er, well, I, er . . . don't really know about that. I, er . . . ha ha ha. Do you want another glass of wine?'

'Mmm, yeah, my mouth's getting a little dry. Unless you've got something better for me to drink,' she said, slipping a dildo into her mouth and slurping up and down on it suggestively (can you slurp up and down on a dildo any other way?).

This went on pretty much non-stop for about two hours as we were doing the shoot and Howard eventually leant over to me and pointed out, 'She likes you.'

'Have you got a girlfriend, Godfrey?' Claire asked.

'No, I'm between girlfriends at the moment,' I told her.

'What, like Yosser Hughes is between jobs?' Howard asked. We had to spend ten minutes explaining to Claire who Yosser Hughes was before the conversation could move on, but when it did, she said to me:

'That's a shame, isn't it, no girlfriend? What do you do about sex then? Do you tug yourself off all day, do you?'

'Not all the time, sometimes I have to go to work,' I told her.

'Have you ever tugged off over pictures of me?'

'No, I'm afraid I haven't,' I apologised, but decided that I bloody well would from now on.

'Oh, I'm hurt. You've hurt my feelings,' she simpered, so I promised her that I'd crack one out over her as soon as I got home, and this seemed to cheer her up.

'Why wait?' she asked and set about herself with gusto with one of the sex toys by way of demonstration.

This was killing me.

It might sound like a right good sexy giggle, but at the time it felt more like Hell in hot grots. Can you imagine having an amazingly beautiful and breathtakingly dirty 22-year-old doing everything she can think of to entice you into doing her and you can't do a thing about it? That's right, not a thing. I was a professional doing a job. Stuart had sent me along with a brief and I had to make sure that we got the shots that we needed for the issue. I couldn't just go steaming in there with my big cock hanging out and ask

Howard if he wouldn't mind stepping outside for half an hour while I had a bit of a ding-dong with the girl he'd paid £250 to get in for the afternoon now, could I?

Of course not. That sort of behaviour would find its way back to the office before I could, and where would me and my smug, self-satisfied grin be then? Out on my ear, that's where. I knew that much for a fact and had heard too many stories of luckless predecessors who hadn't exercised the same control I was struggling to maintain in the face of such temptation and had found their P45 waiting for them when they got back to their desks. People might like to imagine that working for a porn mag is a bit like clocking on at a Roman orgy but the only thing it's got in common with those ancient times are the sirens that lure you into the rocky shallows (even though I think those ladies were actually Greek, but still, my parallels are all over the place so what does it matter?). The powers that were at Moonlight Publishing left us in no doubt; you're employed to do a job so keep your pants on during working hours and don't expose yourself or the company to any possible legal unpleasantness. 'You want to shag models?' MD Peter McMenamin once said in a now famous Christmas speech. 'Do it in your own time.' Cue much incongruous laughter.

Of course, this all only applied if they found out, but seeing as Howard was about as discreet as those cats that went at it outside my bedsit window every night, I decided not to risk it.

And yet again, after another half an hour of putting Claire into various poses with various dildos we found we'd shot five rolls, more than enough for what we wanted, so I decided to call time. I looked at my watch. It was gone five. No point going back into town just to sit at my desk for ten minutes, so I also decided to give myself the rest of the afternoon off.

'What are you doing? D'you fancy a few drinks?' Howard asked. 'The fun's only just beginning,' he assured me, pointing towards Claire with his eyebrows all over the place, not very subtly.

'Yeah, don't go,' she said, 'we can have a little party, the three of us.' I watched Howard packing away his camera and lighting and I suddenly saw that Claire was expecting both of us to supply the custard.

Er . . . hello! thinks I. Things are taking a turn for the decidedly unpleasant.

'Actually, I'm not sure I can stay,' I said, taking a big step towards the door. 'I'm meeting a mate tonight and I've gotta shoot.'

'What!' Claire exclaimed, jumping to her feet. 'No, don't be silly, stay a while.'

'Yeah, hang about, we'll have a laugh,' Howard urged, waving his eyebrows about even more, as if I didn't understand what he was getting at.

'No, no, seriously, I have to. I'm really sorry, but I can't get out of it. I'd love to, but I can't. It's my mate, see, he's getting married next week and I'm the best man and we've got to go over the running order for the day. It's a real bummer, if only I'd known because then I could've rearranged it but he's coming all the way over from Cardiff. Sorry about that.' I shrugged, slipping into my coat and aiming myself at the door.

'You get back here right this instant, Mr Godfrey Bishop. I'll tell you when you can go,' Claire stomped, all school mistress-like, but I was way too freaked out at the thought of me and Howard rolling around in the buff together to give in to any strong-arm tactics.

I don't suppose Claire got too many rejections because my behaviour seemed to baffle and irritate her something rotten. Howard, on the other hand, tried a couple more times but eventually chucked in the towel when he realised that it was no use, I was off no matter how much he Roger Moored me. He did look pretty narked though at having to stay and give Claire a good seeing-to on his own and I felt a bit bad about that, until I remembered that I hadn't been alone with a girl in months.

I apologised to the pair of them for my shoddy manners once again, just as Claire was telling me that, if I went, I wouldn't get my present, and I slipped out of the door to last-ditch cries of 'Wait, wait, wait. Just wait a second, I want to show you something really important.' It was no use though. I had a good idea what that thing was and it was the very thing I was running from.

Out on the street the reassuring hustle and bustle of traffic restored some sort of normality to my senses and I shook my head in disbelief.

What was I doing?

I was running away from a definite shag with a porn model who was absolutely gagging for it, that's what I was doing. Jesus, I felt like George Formby in one of those old movies where the evil Nazi slapper's trying to shove her hands down his trousers and he's fighting tooth and nail to stop her and the audience is sitting there, scratching their heads and wondering why he doesn't just let her have it all over the knuckles.

So just why did I do a runner then?

Well, at the end of the day, I suppose it all came down to a bad case of Cockclashophobia – i.e. the fear of my cock accidentally coming into contact with another man's. I don't know if this is a genuine phobia but if it is, I'm an extreme sufferer.

See, no matter how hot, horny and willing Claire was, I just didn't want to get my cock out in front of Howard. And it's not because I'm ashamed of my body or that I was frightened that I wouldn't be able to perform or anything like that, I just didn't want to be aroused and having sex when there was another bloke in the same room. Equally, I really didn't want to be on hand when some other bloke was thrusting away like a horny dog with a bone. I make no apologies for this. I can't. It's just the way I am. You can pile in as many birds as you like but the moment another bloke hoves into view I'm off. Consequently, the thought of me and Howard standing around in our socks, thrusting, laughing and high-fiving each other across Claire's back was quite enough to send shivers down my spine. I can't tell you why, it's probably because I'm British (or more specifically, English). I was born and raised in these frigid isles and we Englishmen generally don't like to drop our guard and expose our vulnerables unless we're watching the football. It's just not the done thing. Not the done thing at all. Can you imagine David Niven *tally-hoing* his way up Margaret Lockwood's arse while Cecil Parker *hot-danged* it all over her knockers?

No, sex in Britain is a rather shameful little act performed by intoxicated adults in dark rooms under the covers. That was what I was brought up to believe and, thinking about it, probably the reason I spent most of my late teens driving into the next town in a hat, dark glasses and a big coat to buy a staggering number of porno mags.

Of course, this is just me. There are plenty of blokes who have no such hang-ups, though these are generally ex-public school types, rugby players or squaddies; blokes who like to rough and tumble, grab each other's nuts for fun and devise initiation ceremonies for newcomers which usually involve sucking everyone else off. I mean, come on, these sorts of bloke are so used to staring at each other's cocks across digestive biscuits that of course they're not going to have any qualms about having it off in front of each other.

Me though, I just couldn't do it. Does that make me less of a man? I don't know. Maybe. But then if in order to be regarded as a man I've got to drink some scrum-half's piss through a sock or kiss cocks with the rest of the battalion then you can call me whatever you like. Though this is slightly getting off the point.

Like I said, I'm not shy in front of other blokes. Whenever I play five-a-side I have no worries about getting stripped off and jumping into the showers with the lads because this is just getting clean after the match. It's no more sexual than washing your hands after working on your car or combing your hair. If, however, all of a sudden, one of the lads turned around and had a big hard-on, that would change everything. Me, and I'm sure everyone else, would feel distinctly uncomfortable and want to get out of there and get dressed as quickly as possible (unless it was Michael Owen and he'd just won us the World Cup, then who knows what might happen). But this is just my natural homophobia at work and that's the truth. I'm not against gays or lesbians or anyone else who wants to swim against the tide, I just don't want to myself. I'm happy for the homosexual community if they want to do what they like to do and enjoy the same sorts of freedoms and liberties as the rest of us, but it's just not my flavour of crisps, that's all, so I'd rather stay well out of it.

Same as I'm not into stamp collecting or *Robot Wars*; you can crack on if you like but personally I find you all a bit creepy and would rather be in the next pub.

I used to work with this gay bloke a few years ago when I was on the caravan magazine and always got on alright with him, except when he would absolutely insist that I was actually a bender myself but hadn't come to terms with it yet. This, he would say, was why I was afraid to try shagging another bloke, because I was bent and frightened that I'd end up liking it. I mean, what sort of sense does this make? I'm gay and the proof's in that I won't let some geezer in a tight t-shirt give it to me hard up the arse? Am I a murderer too? My response was usually, 'You don't have to smack your hand with a hammer to know it's going to hurt,' followed by, 'and even if I was going to try it, it wouldn't be with you, you fat ugly cunt.'

No, I don't know. I'm pretty sure I'm not a shirt-lifter (though you can never tell with these things) because my overwhelming desire is to be with women, who I am totally and intoxicatingly attracted to. Sometimes I wish I was a bender because I bet it's a fucking hell of a lot easier getting a shag than it is being straight.

And so, somewhere among these disjointed thoughts is probably the reason I fled from Howard's that day.

I've been in a few similar situations with models since and I've always reacted like Mr Grimsdale's assistant with the microfilm down his pants. I did a runner. I wish I didn't, but I did. What can I do? We all have to accept our own limitations.

It particularly confuses and pisses off the models when you do this though because there they are, stark-bollock naked with not an inhibition in the world and there you are unwilling to join in. It hurts their feelings and makes them feel a bit cheap, like you're saying to them, 'Oh no, I couldn't possibly do that. Your sort does that, I'm above all that sort of thing.' This isn't true, of course. I have only the highest admiration for women who get their clothes off for me. I'm just far too fucked up to do it myself.

And that's the answer to that question – do you get to shag the models? Well, if you don't mind getting your cock out in front of the lads and bumping balls with your mates then yes, you do occasionally get to shag the models.

If, however, you don't go in for that sort of thing, well, then no, you just have to be content with going home and whacking off over pictures of girls who've chased you around the studio and out the door, begging you for sex.

8: Hitting bottom

I guess my subconscious homophobia must've still been bubbling away just below the surface a few days later because I turned to Don and asked him, just hypothetically like, what he'd rather have; some big black bloke shag him up the arse or his mum beaten up by muggers?

Don thought about this for a moment or two, then said, 'I don't know. Can't I have both?'

'Why is it always a black bloke who's got to shag you up the arse?' Matt asked from across the room.

'Yeah, who is he and what does he want?' Paddy joined in.

'No, seriously, seriously. Whenever anyone's got a hypothetical gun at their heads in this room it's always the same big black bloke that gets wheeled out to shag us all up the arse or make us suck him off,' Matt said. 'Would it be alright then if he was white or something? I mean, the whole point of these questions, as far as I can make out, is to test whether we're benders or not, ain't it? I don't think we necessarily have to chuck in the race issue too.'

Hasseem looked up. 'Don't look at me, I'm staying out of this one.'

'No, no, hang on a minute, let's put it like this then;

Godfrey, who would you rather get bummed in the arse by, me or Hasseem?' Matt asked. All eyes turned to me as I considered this question.

'Have I got a gun to my head?'

'Yeah, yeah, don't worry about that, you've got to do it, you ain't got no choice. Now come on, which one of us would you rather get done by?'

'I don't know. Who'd be the nicest to me afterwards?' I asked.

'You know, this is getting a little weird, lads,' Paddy said.

'Come on, come on, answer the question,' Matt insisted. 'Me or Hasseem.'

'Fine, if you're going to be like that, I'll go with Hasseem then and you can fuck right off,' I told Matt in no uncertain terms.

'Cheers, God', very sweet of you,' Hasseem said, blowing me over a kiss, which I pretended to catch and stick in my top pocket.

'Oh yeah, like fuck you would. I'd put any money on it that in real life you'd really rather get shagged up the arse by me,' Matt said, sounding a little bitter.

'I wouldn't. I fucking wouldn't,' I insisted.

'Yeah, Jimmy Hill.'

'Tell us then, Matt, why should God' go with you rather than Hasseem?' Paddy asked.

'Why? Because I'm white, and that's not meant to be an insult on you, Hasseem, or nothing. It's just an observation based on what you lot are always coming out with, that this big black bloke's going around shagging you lot up the arse, so that says to me that you're all inherently racist. Not in an evil way, I don't mean that. But just in that us in this country, no matter how fucking integrated and politically correct we all are, are still deep down scared of old darkie.

It's been this way for fucking centuries and it's going to take more than a generation or two of living side by side before institutionalised racism vanishes from our collective consciousness.'

'Bollocks,' said Fat Paul.

'You don't even listen to yourselves when you talk, do you?' Matt said.

'Alright then, Nelson Mandela, if we're all so fucking racist, how comes God' chose Hasseem over you?' Don asked.

'Oh, he didn't, he's lying, because he just wants to disprove my point.'

'That's not true,' I told him.

'It is, it so fucking is.'

'You know, you're just a bad loser,' Hasseem said.

'I'm not,' Matt protested. 'I couldn't give a shit.'

'You are,' everyone told him.

'I'm so fucking not . . . alright then, let me ask you this, God'; why Hasseem over me? Come on, the truth. What swung your decision?'

'Well, I don't know. He's a nice bloke, I suppose; we get on well together, got quite a nice body . . .'

'Okay, that's it! I'm out of here,' Paddy said, heading for the door.

'You know, you blokes talk about this so much I swear you're all really gagging for it with each other,' Susie piped in.

Susie hated our daily theoretical discussions, and not just because we shouted our thoughts from all corners of the room, right across her desk, rather than get out of our chairs (well, who could be arsed?), but also because she had a typically girlie pragmatic mind. See, in my experience, career women almost always make for the biggest fucking moaners at work. They're forever watching you and moaning when they see you skiving. They're forever taking themselves and their jobs way too seriously and they're always competing with everyone around them to see who can be the most conscientious at work. And it winds them up no end when they look about and see all the competition's fucked off down the pub or are standing around in front of the mirror drawing Mexican bandit moustaches on themselves with big black marker pens. They hate the Devil-may-care-but-I-really-couldn't-give-a-fuck weariness that envelops most blokes after ten years in the workplace and don't get our lackadaisical attitude towards time-keeping and petty theft because they haven't been working as long as us. It's a simple fact. See, when a bloke's born, he's told from day one that he's going to work, and that's it, mate, end of discussion. Whether you leave school at sixteen, eighteen, twenty-one or twenty-eight (put it off as long as you like, egghead, but you're still going), eventually you have to get a job and go to some soul- and spirit-sapping office/factory/field and put in eight hours a day until you're an old man. And then, and only then, are you allowed to stay at home and talk about what a fantastic life you had polishing car bumpers for the last fifty years, and please can you cut up my blancmanche for me because my hands are a bit fucked?

Women, though, women have only just started colonising 'meaningful' full-time employment so they've yet to discover just how shit a life-time in the workplace really is. Also, whether you like it or not, they've got the ultimate 'get out of work free' card, although I'm sure you've all marked me down as a right chauvinist for bringing this up. Well, bollocks to you, it's true and that's all there is to it. When the thrill of sending me sixteen memos a day wears off for Jennifer in Production, all she's got to do is have a shag and it's 'so long, work' and 'hello, coffee mornings and walks in the park'. And 'Darling, could you buy an extension lead on your way home from work so I can stick the telly in the garden?' This is a fact. Women can and do have babies. Men can't. If men could, then I really would be bent over the desk having Hasseem throw all he could up me – gun or no gun.

Which brings me rather neatly back to my original point and Susie's snipe.

Like I was saying, she hated our little think-tank and thought it was a pointless waste of everyone's time. No big black bloke was ever going to come in here with a gun and demand sexual favours from us, so why did we insist on discussing tactics for such an inevitability five days a week?

It drove her barmy.

This was a good thing, we all agreed, particularly Don, who was waging his own incredibly petty revolt against the woman who'd made his last few years a misery. Why had she made his life a misery for the past few years? Like I said before, she was a cunt. And this is what cunts do. We all know them. It probably wasn't even anything to do with Don himself, it was just that he was a bloke and that she was a miserable old cunt. I don't know for sure but all the smart money was on her having been fucked over a couple of dozen times before in the past so Don got to bear the brunt of her retaliation. Not a particularly nice or fair thing on Susie's part but then she wasn't a particularly nice or fair person. She was a cunt. Get the picture?

'One of these days we're going to walk in here and there you'll all be on the floor rolling around together,' she added, completing her all-encompassing put-down.

'People who live in glass houses shouldn't throw stones,'

Fat Paul warned her, then added, 'especially lesbians like you who've actually done it with other birds.'

'Oh yes, and here it comes. I'm very comfortable with my sexuality, thank you very much. I'm about the only one in here who is. The rest of you are a load of repressed fags.'

'Fuck me, make up your mind, either we're a load of racists or we're a load of poofs. I don't think we can be both,' Don said.

'Have you finished those pages yet?' Susie snapped, flexing her authority over Don and making plain her disapproval concerning his continued participation in this discussion.

Don didn't reply. He merely held her gaze for a moment, gritted his teeth, then went back to work. It didn't matter that he hadn't answered, Susie hadn't asked it to get an answer, she'd asked it to bring him to heel. We all saw this and cringed for Don.

Paddy, back from the bog and the only one of us with equal status to Susie, asked her why she was always giving Don stick but went pretty easy on Hazel.

'Are you two muffers at it or something? Because you want to try and make it a bit less obvious if you are.'

Hazel, who up until this point had stayed more or less out of it, burst into a string of denials.

'Don't be so fucking ridiculous, of course not, you stupid prat. Why are you lot always having a go at me? I haven't said anything to you, it's just all the time, fucking childish wankers, the lot of you . . .'

She went on for a bit longer than that and I couldn't help notice the hurt look on Susie's face, as if she was taking Hazel's vehement reaction to such an idea as a personal knock, which I guess was Paddy's plan.

'. . . you lot might want to fuck each other but count me out . . .' she was saying as if her life depended on it.

Hello, I thought to myself, something's gone on there then. I made a mental note to try and wheedle it out of Hazel with booze the next time she came over the pub.

'Hey, there's nothing wrong with it,' Paddy said. 'I don't care, live and let live as far as I'm concerned. If I was a bird I'd probably be a lesbian too.'

'I'm not a lesbian,' Hazel insisted.

'Neither am I,' Susie echoed.

'Alright then, bi-sexual, whatever you want to call it, it's still gay, isn't it?'

'No it's not. There's no gay or straight as far as I'm concerned, I just have sex with people. I don't exclude half of the population from my bed,' Susie said.

'So I've heard,' Matt chipped in.

'You know, you are all truly pathetic. How anybody as closed-minded as you lot ever got into porn I'll never know. You're no better than those idiots out there on building sites or in factories, you're a lot of reactionary Neanderthals,' Susie told us. 'Let me ask you this then, and there's no gun involved or million pounds or anything, what would be so bad about sleeping with another man?'

'Fuck off,' Paddy smiled, lighting a fag.

'Why? Why fuck off? Have you even ever wondered what it would be like? Seriously, have you? Aren't you even a little bit curious?'

'Not in the slightest,' Matt said, followed by a unanimous round of 'no ways' by the rest of us.

'Then how do you know you don't like it until you've tried it?' Susie asked.

'It's alright for you lezzas, sorry, bi-planes, because you're all just munching down on each other but for us, if we wanted to go that way, we've got to get a big cock up the arse,' Paddy explained.

'Yeah, and a big black one at that,' I shouted over.

'So what? That's where your G-spot is, that's the male pleasure point. Get shagged up there and you'd love it.'

'And this is something you'd know all about then, is it?' Paddy asked her.

'Doesn't work like that. The female G-spot is some other place.'

'Oh, how convenient,' Matt said. 'So while we're all off buying tubes of Analsooth and wiping the tears from our eyes, you're in a field somewhere having your elbow patted.'

'It doesn't hurt that much,' Mary looked up and said.

'Mary, you don't?' Jackie said, shocked at such an admission.

'Yeah, I love it. Why, haven't you ever done it?'

'No I haven't and never will. It's horrible, it's not for that purpose.'

'Well, neither's your mouth but I love that too.'

'Hey, Mary's a party in one body!' Fat Paul pointed out, reminding me of Howard and Claire's offer the other day. 'Come on everybody, dive in.'

'I'm up for it,' Mary giggled.

'See, look at the double standards,' Susie was still banging on. 'It's alright if Mary takes it up the arse but none of you are willing to try.'

'Ah no, just hold your horses,' Hasseem said. 'I had a bird do this to me once while I was shagging her. She kept trying to stick her finger up my arse, telling me that I'd love it, so in the end I just let her.'

'Yeah, what was it like?' Paddy asked.

'It was like someone had their finger up my arse,' Hasseem replied.

'Oh yeah,' Paddy nodded thoughtfully.

'A finger's nothing,' Susie objected. 'That's not the same thing at all.'

'She was wearing cricket gloves at the time,' Don said, causing Susie to scowl at him.

'Do you mind? We are trying to have a serious conversation here.'

'Correction,' Paddy pointed out. 'You're trying to have a serious conversation, the rest of us are trying to fuck about.'

'Yeah, yeah,' Susie nodded, her patience ebbing fast. 'You know what, I don't know why I even bother, you lot are a waste of time. I don't think you're even capable of having a serious conversation, that's why you'll never do anything with your lives. You're going to end up sad, lonely old men that no-one will ever want to talk to because you can't be serious.'

This was girl logic if ever I'd heard it, and I had, come to think of it, several times before from several different girls. The argument, from what I understood of it, went something like this: Because we're always fucking around, cracking jokes and generally having a laugh, no-one would want to pay us the time of day because they'd know that serious and important issues such as feelings, relationships and hopes for the future would be brushed aside in favour of jokes about masturbation. No-one would ever learn anything from us because we'd refuse to face up to cold hard truths in a stern and sober manner, therefore talking to us would just be a waste of time as they searched for truth and answers.

Now, I can see this and would even agree with it if it weren't for one thing; namely, that there are fucking hundreds of thousands of blokes like us up and down the country who live to talk bollocks, so surely we'll have them to talk to, won't we? We won't have to sit around the kitchen table discussing the problems of parenting with sour-faced killjoy mooses because we'll all be over the pub taking the piss out of each other or talking about football till the day we drop. And that suits me just fine.

'What's so great about serious conversations?' Paddy asked. 'We're not curing cancer here, we're publishing wank mags for crying out loud. Why have you got to be so miserable all the time? It'll get you nowhere. Lighten up, enjoy life while you can because we'll have enough real problems to worry about in just a few short years, you can count on that.'

'Really? What are they then, Pad?' Matt asked.

'You know, old age, illness, World War III, they're all on the way so we don't have to go looking for things to worry about, they'll find us.'

'This is precisely the reason these things happen, because nobody is willing to discuss them. Everybody's so busy making jokes that the real issues get lost!' Susie exclaimed, like this was so obvious that she couldn't believe we'd all missed it.

'How does Godfrey taking a cock up the arse from Hasseem start World War III?' Don asked, not unreasonably in my opinion.

'HAVE YOU DONE THOSE PAGES YET?' Susie screamed back at him.

There was a second or two's silence as this latest humiliation sunk in then Don suddenly exploded.

'BOLLOCKS TO THIS! BOLLOCKS TO IT! I'm not taking this shit any more. Fuck it! Fuck it!' he shouted, jumping up from his seat. I thought at one point he was going to launch himself across his desk at her but instead he just looked her straight in the eye and squeezed as much bitterness into the following statement as he could muster. 'You . . . are . . . a *fuckingggg* . . . *WANKEEERRRR!*' he told her, practically spitting out each word. He then looked down at a startled Hazel and told her, as if the thought had only just occurred to him, 'And so are you.' He grabbed his bag and started stuffing his personal belongings into it, all the while raging about how there was only so much shit a man could take and how working with 'you two lesbians' was enough to put anyone off women for good, and how their only redeeming quality was that they were both mortal and one day they'd die, but why didn't they do the world a favour and go and chuck themselves in the Thames because that's all they were good for etc etc etc.

'I'm not a lesbian,' Hazel objected.

'Well, you fucking should be. And what the fuck you two ironing boards are doing working on *Bangers!* I'll never know.'

'Right, that's enough,' Susie said, finally finding her voice. 'Sit back down and get on with your work otherwise you'll find yourself with a written warning.'

Don almost laughed.

'I quit. Write me up all you like but you'll have to post it to me at home because I'm out of here.'

'That's where you're wrong, you can't just quit, you have to give a month's notice.'

'Watch me,' he said, pulling on his coat.

'Don, wait. Let's just calm down and talk about this.'

'You're a cunt. You're a cunt. You're a cunt. That's all I've got to say. You're a cunt and a lesbian and a fucking ugly cunt and I'm not taking it any more.'

'You can push me only so far,' Susie told him.

'Push me? You want to watch yourself because if you were a bloke I'd fucking lump you one right in the gob and still might. Ah, bollocks to it, you're not even worth that. You're nothing. You're just a cunt and that's all you'll ever be. And you,' he shouted across to Roger sitting next to me, 'you're a boring miserable wanker.' Roger looked up, a little surprised to be singled out seeing as he hadn't said a word all day. 'And if Monty or Toldo were here I'd tell them what a couple of wankers they were too, but they're not. Hold on, I'll leave them a note each. Hazel, give me your Post-its.' Hazel complied and Don wrote a quick goodbye to both Monty and Stuart and stuck them on their screens.

'Right, as for the rest of you, you're all invited to my leaving drink which'll be kicking off in The Abbot in about 30 seconds' time. Bring your wallets because you're going to be needing them.'

Susie made one last desperate attempt to try and stop Don from leaving. Under normal circumstances she would've loved to see him hand in his notice and disappear from her life without a fuss (which I think was what she'd always hoped for) but upping and leaving like this was going to reflect really badly on her. And she knew it.

'Wait, just wait a minute. Think about what you're doing. Your blood's up, you're angry, things were said but that doesn't matter. I don't care about that. Let's just sit down and talk about this and we can work this out. If not for me, then do it for the mag.'

Don stared at her, absolutely incredulous. She'd threatened him with the sack so many times that he'd once told me that he felt like he was working on death row. And now, here he was, finally strapping himself into the electric chair and she was trying to give him a last minute reprieve. For what? So that three weeks down the line when he wasn't expecting it she could throw the switch herself? Don knew her too well for that. He wouldn't give her the satisfaction. It was his call and his fate and if he could fuck her up at the same time then that was just one more reason to go.

And as if to prove that conversations turn full circle if you talk for long enough, he had for her just seven last words.

'Go stick it up your fucking arse.'

9: The morning after

'Urghhh . . . what time is it?' Paddy groaned, rubbing his face.

'Morning,' I coughed, shredding my throat to ribbons. This caused me to cough even more until all I could do was grimace with pain, and right myself into the airline passenger emergency position until my throat simmered down enough for me to take a sip of whatever was in the glass on the coffee table in front of me.

'Fuck me, you're starting early,' Paddy said as he dragged himself up off the sofa opposite and scratched his nose and arse, in no particular order.

'Gin and tonic, oohhhh,' I said, but took some more.

Don's living room was dark with the curtains drawn but the bustle and traffic outside told us that the world was up and on its way to work.

Matt told us to pipe down as he was trying to sleep, so Paddy told him it was gone ten and we were late. 'I don't give a fuck!' he shouted angrily and neither of us could argue with that.

Don had turned in a few hours earlier and gone to bed to leave the three of us to fight over two sofas. Me and Paddy had won, albeit through a battle of attrition with Matt, who'd collapsed behind the sofa about an hour before us.

My neck was really stiff and I felt fucked. I tried to stand but had to sit back down again after a bit of light-headedness and nausea. I rubbed the sleep from my eyes (all three hours of it) and took a few deep breaths but that just kicked off my coughing fit again.

So, so tired.

'Bollocks to it, I can't be arsed,' Paddy announced and curled back up on the sofa. 'Fuck it.'

Neither he nor Matt showed any further sign of life other than a persistent sniff sniff sniffing and an occasional moan/sob.

It was different for me though, I couldn't blow out work. I had to go through all the proofs with Roger and return them to our repro-house. Actually, I was meant to have done that yesterday but after Don jacked, we all got a bit side-tracked in the pub. The stuff was late. It had to be done today otherwise I'd be in for a right bollocking come Monday. I had to go in, no matter how I felt, it was as simple as that.

What a nightmare.

Fucking Roger. He could do the stuff without me no problem, but he wouldn't if I wasn't there, in order to demonstrate he was in a strop over the fact that I'd stayed in the pub all afternoon. Roger never went to the pub. He didn't like going to the pub, but he was one of these petty killjoy bastards who hated to see other people enjoying themselves. He was a wanker, a fucking wanker, and at that moment in time I hated him, because it was him who was making me have to get up and go to work.

I felt really tired, really rough and really fucked off, all in one.

I was also quite unbelievably thirsty.

I went to the kitchen, filled up a cup and drank and refilled it three times before turning off the tap.

Man, I was fucking hungry too. It was then that it occurred to me that I hadn't eaten anything since Wednesday. It was always the same with coke. All thoughts of survival and safety would go straight out the window after a few lines as I threw myself and all my efforts into drinking myself stupid and getting my cock sucked.

Oh no . . . hang on, I suddenly thought to myself as a memory flashed across my mind. Shit, what did I do? I concentrated my mind and tried to remember. 'Cock sucked?' When I finally remembered I suddenly wished I could forget again.

Fuck, I'd followed Mary around the pub all last night in a drunken stupor, practically begging her to give me a blow-job. Oh no, I was wrong, there was some actual begging going on as well. Oh shit.

Did anyone see me doing it?

Yes, nearly everyone.

Would they remember?

Oh fuck!

My face burned with embarrassment as more and more details came flooding back to me.

I'd kept touching her leg, trying to feel her up, grabbing her tits and guiding her hand onto my hard-on – in the pub.

Oh no, why did I do all that? Why? Because I was coked off my tits and hornier than an Alsatian with a beach ball, that's why. I tried thinking some more. Did she take it all as a joke or did she seem to mind?

She seemed to mind.

I think she told me to fuck off at one point and Wendy had tried to steer me away from her.

Oh no, I'd tried it on with Wendy too.

Shit. Fuck. Shit.

The memory of me banging on at Wendy at great length about the pros and cons of her sucking me off (there hadn't been many cons) actually hurt when I recalled it to the point where I tried to shut it out and pretend it hadn't happened. She had been really angry at me and had kept telling me to go home, and I told her I would only go home if she came with me.

'Go on, you might as well,' I think was the phrase I'd used over and over again. 'Go on. It won't mean anything,' I'd reassured her, then . . . oh no, gone into graphic detail about what I wanted to do to her – as if this would somehow convince her into giving herself to me. I can even remember the logic behind my thinking and what I was trying to get at, but it was pissed-up, mad logic based purely on a kind of animal instinct that was telling me if I wanted something hard enough, I'd get it. Wendy had told me to fuck off and go home for the umpteenth time before Paddy had come over and taken me aside, and the memory faded once again into fog.

I was mortified.

How could I have done such a thing? What would people think of me now? I couldn't ever face Wendy again, that was for sure. I'd have to do a Don. I couldn't ever go back there.

Oh shit, what if she or Mary put in a complaint to the police about what I'd done? You could get locked up for that sort of shit these days. What was it, sexual harassment or something? Sexual assault even. Just imagine that, being interviewed by the police for something like this? Jesus, what would I tell them? Would I just hold up my hands and take everything that was coming to me or should I try and wriggle out of it, take the 'it was nothing, just mucking about, everyone does it' stance as I sat in front of two stony-faced policewomen from the rape squad.

'Would you call repeatedly pulling someone's hand onto your erection after you'd been warned not to do it "just mucking about"?' they'd ask me. 'Would you call grabbing a girl's breasts or trying to put your hand up her skirt when she wasn't looking "just mucking about"?'

'Well, would you?'

'How would you like it if we did it to you?'

'How would you like it if we kept grabbing your cock?'

'How would you like it if we flashed you our panties and made you get down on your knees in front of us and undid your trousers and . . .'

Jesus, I really needed a wank too, something else I hadn't taken care of since Wednesday. I'd have to have one later, I had other things on my plate at the moment.

I turned my thoughts back to Mary and Wendy, and this immediately poured cold water onto my little impromptu police fantasy. What was I going to do? Should I apologise to them? It would seem like the proper thing to do but in order to do that I'd have to confront and admit what I'd done and I really just wanted it all to go away and be quietly forgotten. Fat fucking chance of that.

Maybe they'd been so drunk that they wouldn't remember it. Maybe everyone else had played up too and my actions would be lost in a night of drunken debauchery and outrageous behaviour. And maybe if I grabbed a big enough handful of straw I could stop myself from falling out of a hay loft.

Would they go to the Old Bill? Probably not, but they might go to Stuart or even Peter or someone and put in a complaint about me to them. But what could they do? It wasn't in work time or the work place so what business is it of theirs if I want to sexually assault my co-workers?

Fuck me, was I for the sack, or what?

Maybe Moonlight wouldn't have a watertight legal case but what was I going to do, take them to a tribunal and stand up in front of a panel of arbitrators and argue that rubbing my boner up against Mary's arse while she was trying to play pool in no way affected my ability to perform my job to a satisfactory standard?

Christ on a bike, it weren't long ago that they'd brought in laws just to stop people like me from moving near schools.

No, when they sacked me I'd go quietly and know that I'd fully deserved it. Probably best if I saved them the bother and never went back. At least I'd never have to face them again. It might be the coward's way out but it would spare everyone any further unnecessary embarrassment.

Do that and it might even allay legal action. Maybe Mary and Wendy might think getting the sack was punishment enough and just let me be. Maybe they might even end up feeling sorry for me and realise that they'd over-reacted to what was really just a drunken misunderstanding. But it was more than that, wasn't it? It wasn't just a bit of horseplay, no matter how much I tried to convince myself, I was burning up with the horn, unable to think rationally and being a real pest.

'Oh, you twat, you twat, you twat,' I muttered to myself over and over again.

Why did I do this thing? What's the matter with me?

Drink, that was it. Drink and coke. Everyone else seems to be able to have a couple of pints and the odd line and have a good time. Not me though. Oh no. Me? Me? I turn into a fucking nightmare. A rambling, drunken, desperate, old wanker who, when he's not trying to get in the sack with anything in tits, is boring them off everyone else with his theories on why everyone is either his best mate or an utter cunt.

I crept back into the living room and saw that both Matt and Paddy were out for the count again. I was half-tempted to wake them up and ask them if what I'd done was really that bad but I was too embarrassed and too afraid of what else they might tell me.

See, there were great swathes of the evening that I couldn't remember. I know people who don't want to admit what they drunkenly did the night before always claim amnesia but I was serious, there were some worryingly large gaps.

We'd gone somewhere else after The Abbot, I remembered that. Some little drinking club in Soho, and we'd stayed there for about four hours, but for the life of me I couldn't remember more than five minutes of it.

I racked my brains and tried to remember who was there. Paddy, Don and Matt, obviously. Hasseem had come along too, as well as Fat Paul and even Monty, whatever the fuck he was doing there, but I couldn't remember seeing Wendy or Mary there. I racked my brains even harder and desperately tried to picture them either sitting around the tables, dancing away on the little dance floor or beating me off with their handbags, but the pieces weren't fitting. They obviously must've bailed earlier in the evening to get away from me and who can blame them? Thank fuck for that, I thought to myself, at least there'd been a limit to my idiocy (which was a bit of a first), but then somebody else started coming into sharp focus. There had been a girl there. I'd been talking to her at great length. Shit, who was it? What had I said?

Hazel.

Hazel?

I slowly remembered. She had come along and found us after The Abbot because she didn't want to say goodbye to Don on bad terms. To be fair, Don was all conciliatory and explained that his blood had been up and that he was sorry for what he'd said and that he really liked her, really (he was well drunk and coked up at this point too) and they'd had a hug and a few drinks and a line of this and that . . . and then I'd sidled up.

Bollocks.

The dam burst and our conversation came flooding back to me. I'd been probing her about Susie. Earlier on in the day, when Don and Susie were having their little shouting match and Don had kept on accusing the pair of them about being lesbians, Hazel had really gone to town vigorously denying any and all pot-holing. This had alarm bells ringing all over my bullshit radar station so I thought I'd subtly try and wheedle the truth out of her the next time I saw her – and after seven hours of solid drinking, I was feeling spy-masterly subtle.

'So, what's this that's gone on with you and old whats'er-face then?'

'What do you mean?'

'You know what I mean, you and old 'er . . . fucking 'er . . . Susie, you know?'

'I don't know what you're talking about.'

'Look, it's alright, you can tell me, I ain't going to tell no-one else. Have you shagged her then?'

'No, I haven't.'

'That's not what she said,' I told her tactfully.

'I don't care what she said, I haven't shagged anyone at work.'

'Alright then, not shagged, what do you lot call it? Licked her out then?'

'Listen, I don't know where you lot get this from but nothing went on with me and Susie.'

'So something did happen then? Go on, tell us about it, don't be a cunt.'

'What business is it of yours to go asking me questions like this? You're just as bad as all the rest.'

'Look, do you want a line of coke?'

'I'm not telling you anything.'

'I don't want you to, I'm just being hospitable and offering you a line of coke, that's all. Don't be so paranoid.' (This ought to loosen her tongue.)

We nipped into the women's when no-one was looking and darted into an empty cubicle, locking the door behind us. I dropped down to my knees and polished the top of the seat with toilet paper so as to save snorting up a load of piss while I was at it, then scraped two decent-looking lines out of my rapidly dwindling gram. Behind me Hazel rolled up a £20 note and dropped down beside me and snorted the first line, then handed me the note. I did the same and snorted the other, then with a quick sleight of hand, pocketed her twenty and gave her back the tenner I'd already rolled. Well, this stuff did cost money, you know. We dabbed the rest on our gums, waited until the coast was clear, then rejoined the pub.

Only then did it occur to me that I'd been alone in a bog cubicle with a woman and some drugs and hadn't tried it on at all. Where was my head? I decided to save a couple of lines for later and give it another go then.

Me and Hazel chatted quite amiably for the next half hour, each of us telling the other more and more irrelevant stories about our childhoods as the minutes went by, until the conversation turned around to Susie again and I decided to try another tack.

'You know, I don't know why people get so protective of

their sexuality. I agreed with old whats'erarse when she said that, you know, just being straight is discounting half of the population.' (See where I'm going with this?)

'Really? So have you ever been with another bloke?'

'Me? No, fuck off! I mean, no, I haven't, but it's, well, it's complicated.'

'What do you mean?'

'Oh yeah, like I'm going to tell you.'

'Why not? Go on, tell us. I can keep a secret.'

'What, and I can't, I suppose, is that it? Birds can keep secrets but blokes can't.'

'Hey? I don't get you.'

'Your Susie secret. You want me to tell you all about my big secret but you're not willing to tell me about yours. That's hardly fair, is it?'

'There is no secret.'

'Yeah, well, whatever.'

Hazel spent some time mulling this over then leaned in and lowered her voice so that I could just about hear her.

'Oh, look, it's nothing really, but you can't ever tell anyone about it, ever, alright?'

'Yeah, no, definitely, tell us,' I urged her.

'No, you first, tell me your supposed big secret first.'

'No, that's not how it works. What if I tell you mine and then you don't tell me yours?'

'As if I'd do that. Come on, I will, but I'm not saying anything until you tell me yours.'

'It's not that simple,' I faffed.

'What do you mean?'

'I'll tell you afterwards.'

'Bollocks. Look, you brought this up, you have to go first otherwise I'm not doing it at all.'

'We go at the same time,' I suggested.

'How can we go at the same time? We won't be able to hear each other speak.'

'Alright then, we'll write them down. Agreed?'

Hazel agreed and pulled some paper and a pen from her bag. She handed it to me and I had a think about what I could write. Obviously I hadn't done anything and I was just trying to use it as bait to get her to spill the beans but I had to write something. What could I write that would sound like a deep and dark secret? I wasn't about to put down that I sucked off geezers every Sunday afternoon no matter how many times she'd sat on Susie's face, as there was a limit to these things, but it had to be something suitably fruity.

In the end I wrote down that I liked getting shagged up the arse by girls wearing a strap-on, as that seemed to be the sort of thing people wouldn't admit to in public that didn't involve geezers.

By the way, I don't.

When I was done I handed Hazel the pen and she spent a few minutes writing her confession down before announcing that she was ready to exchange. We swapped papers and I eagerly unfolded hers to find that she'd written only one word: 'Sucker.'

I looked over at her as she shrieked with laughter at my bullshit confession and desperately tried to snatch it back out of her hand, but it was like trying to get a small child off a Rottweiler.

'Oh my God,' she was laughing as I was wrestling with her over the seats.

'Give it to me. Give it to me,' I was yelling, making her crack up even more for some reason. 'I was only joking – that's just bullshit, I wasn't serious, I just wanted to hear about you and fucking whats'ercunt,' I yelled as she elbowed me in the guts and kicked me onto the floor.

'Right, then I'm definitely not telling you anything then.'

I slumped down on the seat, humiliated and fucked off with her and wishing that I'd written something like that too.

'You're just a cunt,' I told her. 'I thought we had a deal.'

'Look, don't worry, I'm not going to show anyone else. I'm only teasing you. Go and get me a drink and we'll be friends again.'

I told her to go and spin on it but she said she'd show everyone at work what I'd written if I didn't buy her a drink.

'You're blackmailing me?'

'Yes. Get me a drink, ding ding ding. Go on, I'll give you this back if you do.'

I went to the bar and bought her a vodka Red Bull and was about to hand it to her when I had a thought and demanded to see what was written on the paper. Predictably, it had 'Sucker' written on it again so I withheld her drink until she handed over the real one.

I didn't get to shag her in the bog later either because her boyfriend showed up and scuppered my last remaining chance of drunken sex.

All in all, the evening had been a bit of a shitter.

I stood in Don's living room and remembered all of this and wondered what Hazel would do or say about it today . . . or Monday . . . or the day after that. I hadn't heard the last of this, that was for sure, but what could I do short of going around and telling everyone in advance that I was trying to bullshit some scandal out of her in the first place and that I'd just made it all up? No-one would ever believe for a second that I actually didn't take it up the arse.

They wouldn't want to believe it.

Shit, you know, this sort of thing has a tendency to follow people around for life. I mean, look at Richard Gere. Who hadn't heard all those rumours? He was probably just doing the same as me and trying to get Kim Basinger to admit she'd done it with donkeys or something and look where it got him?

Bollocks.

I picked up my coat and pulled on my shoes, but even as I did, more memories were triggered. It was here, here in this room around this coffee table that me, Paddy, Matt and Don ended up talking and drinking and doing the last of our gear till the very early hours of the morning. Hang on, I'd told Paddy all about my little Hazel episode already and they'd all been cool about it. In fact, oh yeah, fuck, Paddy had even told us the real dirt on Hazel and Susie (he'd gone for Susie a few months earlier with similar suspicions and she'd proved a bit easier to tap up). Apparently, 'and you can't tell anyone this' I think was the obligatory non-disclaimer phrase that was tagged on the front of this story, Susie had tried it on with Hazel when they'd both gone over to LA to visit a couple of their photographers. By all accounts (or at least Paddy's anyway), they'd both got a bit drunk and a bit coked up after a shoot and carried on drinking back at the hotel when Susie began to kiss and fondle Hazel all over the bed. What had started out as a playful wrestling match ended up in a bit of a snog (as it always does in these lesbian stories) only for Hazel to suddenly freak out just as things started to get a bit interesting and run back to her room. Susie had spent half the night and pretty much every siege tactic in the book trying to get in there with Hazel, but Hazel was having none of it and a rather uncomfortable working relationship was born.

Hee hee hee.

Susie, being Susie, couldn't understand why Hazel had flipped out so badly over something that was water off a dyke's back to her, and had confided in Paddy as much to assure herself that she'd done nothing wrong more than anything else. Naturally, Hazel was less keen for the story to break.

Well, I'd show her who couldn't keep a secret.

I was just starting to feel a tad better about myself when one last image flashed across my brain. Again, it was here, we were all sitting around the table doing the last few lines and Paddy was telling us his story when I was struck down with a severe case of honesty and I'd told them about . . .

Oh bollocks . . .

. . . about phoning Gemma in Manchester. No no no, I thought, screwing my face up as I cringed at the image of myself going into every tiny embarrassing detail as I unburdened myself. Even after ten minutes of banging on about it, when they were starting to get bored with the whole confession, the coke told me to keep their attention with ever more humiliating revelations. Fuck.

Why couldn't I keep my mouth shut?

What was wrong with me?

Well, that was it, I was giving up the booze. I'd been kidding myself that I was going to cut down for years but this put the lid on it. No more. I just couldn't go on the way I was going. Jesus, I was just becoming known as a real cock when really that wasn't me. I was a serious-minded, sensitive, even shy sort of guy who had things to say and wisdom to pass on; not someone who'd walk around with the fat end of a pool cue sticking out of his flies for half an hour in the hope that someone might notice and laugh. I was sick of making a cunt of myself and it just wasn't me. Booze (and especially coke) was doing mad things to me, stupid things and I'd come to hate it. I loved a pint, I won't deny that, but in recent years I'd really started to hate getting plastered. I didn't want to do it any more, I didn't want to be seen as king of the wankers any more and last night was exactly what I was talking about.

Christ, no wonder nobody took me seriously. What an arsehole!

Well, that was it, that was my final session. If no other good came out of last night then at least it finally put me on the wagon. From this moment on I would be a quiet, easy-going and unassuming sort of bloke. A happy-go-lucky fella who spent his time reading or having dinner parties or going down the gym or something, and I'd be happier for it.

I didn't need to drink and I didn't want it any more. I was finished with it. Some blokes might piss away their lives on the sauce but I wouldn't be one of them. I'd seen the light and I swore that from this moment on I was a changed man. From now on, people would come to regard me as an intelligent and level-headed fella, someone they could rely on, someone they could trust. Someone who could be turned to for advice, someone to look up to, admire even. Above all, I would become someone to respect.

This was my future and I was looking forward to becoming this person.

In the meantime, I'd just lie and tell everyone that I couldn't remember anything about last night.

10: The Dirty Dozen

Naturally, I was in the pub and fucking steaming less than seventy-four hours later. I'd successfully managed to swerve the beer and lead a totally monastic existence for one weekend but all that went for a toss with the arrival of Monday lunchtime and Paddy's birthday. I tried to make my apologies and duck out of it but my will was crushed with a chorus of 'don't be a cunt' from the lads. A three-drink minimum was rigorously enforced by Paddy to stop people from gaying off and by pint number five I couldn't remember why I'd tried to give it up in the first place.

Male peer pressure? And we wonder why we die first.

It got my old lady's back up no end. I'd told her Saturday morning in a phone call that I was finished with the drink and she couldn't have been happier if I'd told her that I was quitting porn for a nice respectable accountancy job and settling down at the end of her road with some brainless baby-making blob. A few days later she phoned again to find out how things were going and I told her that the wagon hadn't so much gone over a bump as fallen off a cliff. She was very disappointed. I tried to explain that it was Paddy's birthday and that I had to go for a drink and then Tuesday there was a big Champions League game on and that that was only being shown in the pub and then Wednesday we always went for a midweek drink after work to kind of break up the monotony of it all and so on to Thursday which was so close to Friday that it practically was Friday and who doesn't have a drink on Friday? She didn't understand.

Well, it's a bloke thing to be fair.

As much as I was disappointed with myself for drinking again, it was a relief to be back in the bosom of my brethren. Not much was said about my behaviour from the previous Thursday by Paddy, Hasseem, Paul, Matt or any of the other boys because, by and large, they accepted it. I was off my nuts and that's what people do when they're off their nuts. It was very reassuring.

The same, however, couldn't be said of the girls. Neither Mary nor Jackie (nor Susie, for reasons of solidarity and because I'd supported Don's walkout) would talk to me. This uncomfortable silence lasted several weeks and had me walking around on eggshells, though even when they did come around and eventually spoke to me again, they did it with such ill-disguised contempt that I wished they'd go back to ignoring me.

And then there was Hazel. Hazel smiled at me from across the room, passed notes and spent weeks cracking arse jokes in front of everyone that were aimed solely at me. Paddy and a couple of the others knew what she was getting at but everyone else was left scratching their heads in bewilderment until one day, when she wasn't there, I told them that she'd confessed to me that she loved it up the arse and that she was just making jokes at her own expense. Most people believed this and from that day onwards got a little embarrassed for her each time she shouted some crude and graphic anal comment across the room.

All in all though, I didn't feel too good about myself around the office during this time and tried to spend as much of my working week in the pub as I could. And this was happily possible, thanks to Stuart being permanently 'away on a shoot' – 'away on a shoot' being Editor-speak for going on the lash or playing golf or learning Spanish in the garden or something. In fact, 'away on a shoot' had come to mean just about anything except being 'away on a shoot'. I didn't know this for a fact but Stuart went on so many shoots that *Bling* should've had a bigger cast than *Ben Hur*. And it was during one of Stuart's absences that I got the chance to go 'away on a shoot' myself with Paddy, though this time, 'away on a shoot' actually meant 'away on a shoot'.

And what a shoot it was too. What a shoot.

'Okay, can you all squeeze together and bend over for me. That's it, that's it, right, now smile,' Howard joked as twelve ladies' arseholes stared back at us.

'It's like a bike rack,' Fat Paul said, his jaw at knee level.

This was *Ace*'s shoot. *Ace* was celebrating its twelfth birthday so Paddy decided to commission a twelve-girl shoot and run it across a dozen pages; 'The Dirty Dozen' being the obvious cover line. Paul had come along to see the spectacle, Hasseem was meant to be here too but hadn't shown up (must've had something better to do), while Matt desperately wanted to come but had just started seeing a girl he was all dizzy about and she'd put a block on any and all future studio work. Matt could've simply lied to her and told her he'd never come but Matt had a serious case of the 'considerations' and insisted he'd always be honest in his dealings with Penny. The silly cunt would be dumped within a month and never live to see twelve naked women in the same room again. It would be a regret Matt would still be torturing himself with forty years later when he was old, grey and as impotent as a glass of water. In Matt's place, Paddy had invited me.

'We're doing this twelve-girl shoot round Howard's tomorrow. They'll be all the old faces there – Rebecca, Claire, Andrea, Traci and so on. Howard's laying on a load of booze and there should be a little of the old nose powder too. Do you fancy coming down, at all?'

I mean seriously, what did he think I was going to say? This was something I'd miss the birth of my son for.

Howard reeled off half a film from different angles and took a few close-ups too, then rearranged them into a different pose, stacking them up on top of each other and shooting them from between their legs. To me, they looked like one of those big legs of chicken doner you get turning against the heat in a kebab shop. I don't know if you can picture that but that's what they looked like to me.

I was rocked solid and starving hungry all at the same time.

'Fucking hell, hey!' Paul said and I couldn't agree more. Paddy said nothing, he merely sat silently watching, smoking a fag and sipping straight vodka, like an old master appreciating a painting.

'Give me some of that,' Rebecca said, pouring herself a vodka during a lull in the shooting. Half a dozen other girls all scrambled over to the drinks table and helped themselves too, while Traci and Claire did a couple of lines of Charlie off to the side. A girl called Natalie dropped herself into my lap and announced to everyone that I had a hard-on, then proceeded to grind her arse into it while holding my hands to her tits. This would've cost me a fortune if I'd been in a club up West but as it was I was the one getting paid. Claire suddenly bounded over and joined us on my lap, then started snogging Natalie – presumably for my benefit. Natalie snogged back, tongues and all, and I started to pant and gasp for breath as I looked on, partly through excitement but mainly because they were squashing my rib cage with their fucking elbows all over the shop. I turfed them both onto the floor and rubbed my battered and bruised chest.

'Oh, poor Godfrey. Did we squash you?' Rebecca cooed, then made a play for my trousers before I was able to stumble back, away from her grasping fingers. Claire then leapt on me from behind and rode me around the studio for a few seconds as I tried to shake her off and the others started dashing towards me when Howard told them all to line up for the next shot.

'We'll get you yet,' Claire giggled as she skipped away.

There'd been a lot of this horseplay from the girls during the course of the shoot and it seemed to be getting worse and worse as the vodka went down and the coke went up. They were all in ridiculously high spirits and bringing out the worst in each other like a bunch of overgrown schoolgirls. There were definitely a couple of ring-leaders though, Andrea for one and that Traci, riling up the others as they tried to out-outrage each other.

I'd been getting off pretty lightly up till now. Not like Howard's assistant, little Jon. Jon couldn't have been any more than nineteen and had been brought in for the day to help with the lighting as it was such a big shoot and the girls went for him in a big way. He looked young, helpless and shy, like a lamb amongst a pack of jackals, and pretty soon the girls could smell blood. At first it had all been verbal abuse:

'Are you a virgin, Jon?'

'Are you getting a stiffy, Jon?'

'Show us your stiffy, Jon.'

'Do you want me to suck it for you, Jon?'

'Who would you rather suck it, Jon, me or Traci, Jon?' Etc.

But soon enough things took a turn for the physical. They'd grab him, kiss him, pinch his arse, trip him up, push him over whenever he had to lean over and even hit him in the cock when he wasn't looking. Traci landed a really good one, doubling him over for a couple of minutes, then offered to kiss it better, making the rest of the girls laugh and offer to do the same.

'Fucking slags,' Jon wheezed as he pigeon-stepped past me.

I had to feel for him, I really did. It might sound like lots of laughs being the centre of attention for a dozen naked girls, but they were really giving him a rough ride. And, like I say, at nineteen years old, you haven't got the confidence to stand up for yourself and fight back. At least, I never did when I was nineteen, and Jon certainly didn't.

Howard let this all go on without a word because he was enjoying seeing Jon tortured almost as much as the girls were. He kept getting Jon to take light readings from here, there and everywhere, just to place him in harm's way, then rattled off a couple of shots as Jon struggled to break free. It was all a big laugh, though the object of the laugh wasn't having one himself.

Me, Paul and Paddy, however, had no idea just how out of hand things were about to get.

The girls were lined up for the next shot. Traci was lying on her back with her legs open while the others leaned in and licked her all over. Howard told Jon to get a light reading from Traci's tits and the girls sniggered with mischief as Jon reluctantly approached. He made it to the centre and clicked the meter, flashing the studio lighting, when suddenly Traci grabbed him and pulled him over.

'Come on, let's get his clothes off,' she shouted and all eleven collapsed in on him.

'No!' he screamed, but he was lost under a tidal wave of flesh.

The girls pinned him down by the arms and legs as Traci straddled his chest. He tried in vain to fight them off but he didn't stand a chance – well, he might've if me, Paddy, Paul and Howard had weighed in on his behalf, but fuck that. We just sat back and watched as they ripped, first the shirt off his back, then pulled his trousers and pants down, leaving him in just his socks. The moment his cock was out they were fighting over it like a flock of pigeons fighting over a hot dog bun. They grabbed it, pulled it, tried to push it back in (for some reason) and did all manner of painful things to it, short of cutting it off and flushing it down the bog. Traci had an idea though.

'Come on, let's get him hard,' she announced to the delight of the other girls. Andrea responded by lowering herself down onto Jon's face while Traci sucked, kissed and pampered him to unwilling arousal.

'No, help, get off!' Jon cried from under there somewhere as twenty-four hands caressed every inch of his skinny naked body.

Howard snap snap snapped away, chuckling with devilment, and before long Jon's body betrayed him and handed the girls a wood to play with. The shoot rapidly descended into hardcore as girl after girl took turns having their picture taken sucking on Jon's cock while the rest of them kept him pinned to the ground.

'I know, I'll have some of this,' Traci announced, manoeuvred herself into position and took him inside herself.

'Oh, he's pretty good, you know,' she announced to the rest of the girls as she steadily fucked him.

Me and Paddy looked at each other uncomfortably but neither of us knew what to do. Things had got this far incredibly quickly and really we should've intervened earlier but now we were stupefied into inaction. Jon never gave up struggling to break free or calling for help but we did nothing.

Traci clambered off of his cock and Rebecca took her place, though all the girls were suddenly taking numbers. Claire looked back when it was her turn and announced that I was next and all the girls grinned at me in agreement. Now, you might think that I wasn't entering into the spirit of things but I wondered how any of those same girls would've felt if they were grabbed by a dozen guys, stripped naked, sexually assaulted, then repeatedly raped while a photographer documented their ordeal for kicks. Moreover, I wondered how the courts would've viewed it. Seriously, if they were guys and Jon was a girl they'd all get ten years to life and be called monsters in the papers. Okay, some might argue that it wasn't actually rape, and that Jon clearly enjoyed himself and had given his consent by getting an erection, but this couldn't be further from the truth. Blokes aren't like girls, we're much more mechanical beasts and physical stimulation is often all that's required to induce an unwarranted rush of blood to the little head. I mean, fucking hell, I got one in the car going over speed bumps on my way to my Nan's funeral but don't remember feeling particularly sexy at the time (I drove back that way though). What the girls did to Jon was wrong, any which way you look at it, but the thing I couldn't believe, when I think back on it, was that this didn't occur to a single one of them. They were like a pack of dogs (in every sense of the word) toying with a soon-to-be-eaten rabbit and so excited with Jon's degradation that the studio was filled with sadistic giggles and shrieking.

'Make him cum! Make him cum!' Andrea was yelling.

'I'm trying. I'm trying,' Claire grunted back as she rode his cock into the ground.

'Stick your finger up his arse, that'll make him pop,' someone suggested, but Rebecca had a better idea.

'No, let's use this,' she said, holding a huge dildo up to twelve screams of delight and one of horror. It was at this moment that I knew I couldn't just sit back and do nothing any more. I jumped out of my seat and waded to Jon's rescue, pulling and pushing half a dozen of them off long enough for Jon to scramble to his knees and flee.

'Come on, a joke's a joke but this has gone far enough,' I was shouting angrily but the girls started sticking to me like pollen.

'Godfrey wants some. Let's give it to Godfrey now,' Claire was screaming, the weight of half a dozen girls suddenly pulling me to the ground. I tried to stay on my feet as long as possible but as more and more piled on top of me the sheer weight of numbers pulled me over.

'Paddy, help!' I desperately screamed, but Paddy and Jon just sat back and laughed. 'Get off me, you fucking slags!' I yelled as they took over control of my legs and I felt my belt suddenly loosen.

'Ooh, just for that, you're going to get it good,' Rebecca told me. Andrea and Natalie piled in with Claire and subdued my arms, kneeling down my wrists painfully.

'Let me in, let me in,' Traci shouted, stepping through the throng. Me and the girls saw the strap-on plastic cock she was lubing up at the same time and the volume went up as my trousers went down.

'Fuck, no, help. Seriously. No! No!! No!!!' I screamed but to no avail. My pants were suddenly down and cock and balls gripped by a dozen vices, but Traci was yelling at them to turn me over. 'No, help, Paddy, you cunt, help me!' but Paddy was enjoying the spectacle far too much to come to my assistance.

'Don't know what you're laughing at, you're next,' Rebecca told him.

'Try that shit with me and none of you gets paid,' he replied casually, reminding them all who was in charge here.

'Me too, let me go or you'll get nothing,' I threatened, but they weren't buying it.

'Don't listen to him, he doesn't write the cheques. He doesn't even work for *Ace*,' Claire told them, as they manhandled me onto my front.

Just when all seemed lost, Andrea adjusted her position, allowing me to pull my arm free. Before they were able to subdue it again I tried to push Claire off of me but I ended up accidentally catching Natalie a cracker right across the face with my flailing arm. Natalie shrieked and went over onto her back, freeing up my other hand, and I was just about to start pushing the rest of the girls off when there was suddenly no need. My lynch mob, to a girl, jumped off and rushed to Natalie's aid. When they got her sat back up, she was sobbing and trying to hold her nose on her face as blood gushed out all over her hand.

'You fucking idiot!' Rebecca screamed at me. 'What the fuck did you do that for?'

'It was an accident. You wouldn't get off me,' I replied.

'We were only having a laugh, you didn't need to do that, you stupid bastard!' she spat.

'Ooohh, by dose, ah finks ee's browkened it,' Natalie sobbed.

'She's right, it definitely looks broken,' Claire agreed, pulling Natalie's hand away.

'You bastard!' someone else shouted at me, but this time I didn't see who as all eleven turned on me, yelling and screaming and generally looking like they wanted to tear me several new arseholes.

'You better get out of here,' Paddy said, pushing me towards the door.

'You fucking cunt!' someone else screamed. 'My boyfriend's going to kill you,' she told me and I wondered if she'd tell him the full story or just that I punched one of her mates in the face. I turned to ask her this and a bottle of vodka exploded on the wall next to me, showering me and Paddy with broken glass and booze. Several other girls thought this was a good idea and grabbed missiles of their own, but Howard intervened, snatching dildos, cans and light meters back out of their hands while yelling at Paddy to 'Get him out of here'.

The door was yanked open, I was pushed through it, then it slammed shut and suddenly I felt really bad. Why should I have felt like this? What should I have done? Let them sodomise me? Let them assault and rape and humiliate me the same as they'd done to Jon? It infuriated me the way none of them could see that they were in the wrong and I was half-tempted to go to the police and report the fucking lot of them, but what would be the point? It would be like that old joke where a bloke staggers in to a cop shop and reports that he's just been raped on the beach by two Swedish nymphomaniacs and thirty-eight officers went to investigate. Ha-de-ha-ha. But it's true, and not just the police. What jury was ever going to sympathise with me? Every bloke I've ever told this story to always looks at me in disbelief and tells me I've got the best job in the world. I try and explain it to them again but all they hear is, 'No, you don't understand, twelve naked stunners pinned me to the ground and tried to have sex with me against my will. It was awful.' Even I think I'm a cunt when I put it like that. And then there's the women. They always – and I do mean always – tell me it's not possible to rape a man because of the old 'if he didn't enjoy it he wouldn't get hard' chestnut, but I've already explained this one.

So, nobody believed me. Or if they did, they couldn't understand what my problem was. I sometimes wonder if this is how prostitutes feel when they get raped.

Actually that's not true, one person believed and sympathised with me. The studio door was yanked open a second time and Jon came stumbling out. He was limping a little and looked in pain as we set off for the train station together.

He thanked me for helping him out and I apologised for not doing so sooner. He said it was okay, but I felt like a cunt anyway. When we got to the station and said our goodbyes, Jon pointed out that I had blood on my knuckles, but it wasn't mine. We looked at the blood and the little scuffs where I must've caught Natalie's teeth and Jon finally spoke.

'Fucking nice one, mate.'

11: Nutters

Actually, you know what the most common response I get when I tell blokes that last story is? 'You must be fucking mad.' Yes, mustn't I? Personally, I think working in the porn industry has opened my eyes to madness more than a degree in psychology ever could. And I don't mean in the 'you don't have to be mad to work here but it helps' jokey signs that painfully dull people put above their desks at work. I'm talking about being able to recognise madness and misunderstanding in others that I was blind to before. People in Social Services may think that they've got their finger on the mental illness pulse of this country but, believe me, it's only when you work in porn that you realise just how many loopy bastards there actually are out there.

I've already mentioned the letters we used to get. They were scary enough, but they were scary in a funny 'here, read this' kind of way. A letter's not going to hurt you (letter bombs, anthrax and those big boxing gloves on springs aside) because letters come from miles away and you can just chuck them in the bin if you can't be bothered to deal with them. No, it was the phone calls and the blokes hanging about outside and the visitors to reception and the crazy-looking headcases who would suddenly appear next to you in the office when Wendy forgot to close the security doors etc. that really freaked us out.

We had one such guy a few months back. He started showing up in reception looking for Jerry, one of our girls. He claimed to be her boyfriend and said that 'they' wanted to do a shoot together, so if we could just arrange it please that would be very good of us. Wendy, in an attempt to humour and get rid of him, told him that we couldn't use untried models and that, if he wanted to take a few amateur snaps of himself and Jerry 'together', then he should just do that and send us the Polaroids and we would have a think about it.

Unfortunately, this guy was always, always, ALWAYS going to get the wrong end of the stick on this one and sure enough, a few days later, he came back clutching a Kodak envelope.

'Godfrey, get you arse up here to reception, I've got some nutter coming in,' Wendy told me over the phone.

'So what? Why are you calling me? Get someone else to deal with him, I did the last one,' I told her as I ate my packet sandwich and read *Harry Potter and the Goblet of Fire*.

'There is no-one else, everyone's at lunch or out on a shoot. Now just get up here and help me deal with him or I'll just buzz him through and give him directions to your desk.'

'You fucking . . .' is all I had time to get out before she cut me off. I got up out of my chair and reluctantly made my way out to reception, where I was met by the sight of some smiling maniac waiting for me behind the glass security doors.

'Don't let him through, see him out there,' Wendy told me unnecessarily and pushed the doors closed behind me.

'Hello, can I help you?' I asked. Fuckwit went on to explain about his 'girlfriend' and how the 'nice lady sat behind me' had told him to go away and get his pictures done so that we could then arrange a porno shoot with him and Jerry, so here they were.

'I'll go through them with you because I also took some of the cat, and I'd rather you didn't publish those ones,' he said. I nodded to show him that I understood and tried to mix in a little shrug of disappointment. 'There's the first one,' he said, handing me a blurry, over-exposed shot of him standing around in his socks and pants in what looked like Reginald Christie's front room. 'I didn't bother with any start-off dressed shots, I thought I'd get straight into it. That's okay, isn't it?'

'Er, yes, fine,' I replied and he handed me over the next one, this time *sans* socks.

'It's difficult using a self-timer, isn't it? Can never quite get yourself squarely in the picture, can you?' he said as he handed me one where he was no longer wearing his socks, pants or head.

'Look, if you just want to drop them off, I can have a good look through them later,' I told him.

'No, no, it's okay, I want to go through them with you because there's a few things about the lighting and stuff I need to explain.'

'Oh, that's not necessary, I know all about lighting. I can just take them off you and have a look at them in the office.' I knew exactly which bin they were going in.

'Oh well, I'll come with you then.'

'I'm afraid you can't, office policy. Sorry. It's to do with insurance.'

'Insurance?' he asked in confusion.

'Yes, see, if you have an accident in our offices you can sue us for thousands.'

'Oh, don't worry about that, I'll be okay.'

'Oh, but if you weren't, we'd be liable.'

'Well, I'll be very careful then.'

'I'm afraid we can't take the risk. I'm sorry.'

'Well, is there something I can sign, where I promise I won't sue? Here, get me a pen and I'll write something down for you,' he was saying and I saw there was no easy way out of this one.

'Well, alright then,' I said and his eyes lit up, before I continued, 'let's quickly go through them here then.'

'Oh! Er, okay then,' he replied, a little deflated after thinking he was going out back to where all the miracles happened. 'Right, yeah, here's the next one of me,' he said, handing me a picture of his scrawny little carcass now sporting a swollen, lop-sided erection. 'Ooops, there's one of the cat, I better just take that one out. You don't want to see that now, do you?'

'I don't want to see any of them, mate,' I almost said, but it doesn't pay to go upsetting these doo-lally cunts.

'Ah now, here's one of me crawling along the floor. Yeah, I quite like that one. What do you think?'

I looked over at Wendy, who was making faces at me from the safety of the front desk. Fuckwit looked around too but missed the faces.

'Do you think she'd like to see these too?' he asked excitedly.

As tempting as it was to drag Wendy into this mess I decided to keep things nice and simple and just try and get him out of the door without any part of me getting bitten.

'Probably best just to go through them with me,' I told

him, but he held up a couple for her to see and she smiled and nodded at him.

'Very nice,' she told him, then answered the phone even though it hadn't actually rung.

Matey seemed taken with her approval and held up several close-ups of his cock and balls, but Wendy was suddenly far too busy giving our address and fax machine numbers to the dialling tone to notice.

'Never mind,' he said, returning his full attention to me. 'Look, another one of my cat there.' Jesus, this was doing my head in. It's always a slog going through someone else's photos with them but when they're of that person masturbating . . . urgh, over pictures of Jerry . . . maintaining polite interest is near impossible.

'Well, I really must be getting . . .' I started but he grabbed me by the arm.

'Oh no, there's only a couple left. Here, I didn't actually manage to catch it in full flight because I was using my timer, but it proves I can do it,' he said, handing me the pop shot.

'Well . . . err . . . good stuff. I'll be sure to pass these on to . . . the person who deals with this. Thanks for dropping by.'

'When do I get to do it with Jerry? I can do it any time this week if you like,' he reassured me.

'Oh, I don't really know, I'm afraid she's very busy at the moment, not that I have to tell you that. We'll give you a call,' I told him, anything just to get rid of him for now, then I'd leave it to someone else to deal with him when he came back in next . . . tomorrow probably.

'Do you want my number then?'

'Sure, why not?' I said and he wrote out his name (Colin Daish), address and telephone number.

'And you'll definitely give me a call?' he asked.

'Yeah, sure. It might be a little while though, I hope you understand.'

'Yeah yeah, of course, but you'll definitely call?'

'Well, it won't be me, it'll probably be the photographer, I'll just be passing on your details,' I said, edging towards the security doors.

'Okay, brilliant. Sorry, what's your name?'

'My name? Er . . . Don, Don Atkins, just phone up and ask for me before you come in next, save you wasting your time coming in if I'm not here.'

'Brilliant. Thanks very much then, Don, and I'll see you soon,' he said as Wendy buzzed me through the security doors. 'Ooh, actually, just one last thing. Can I just have a quick word with Jerry while I'm here? There's something I wanted to ask her,' he said, looking past me towards the offices out back.

'I'm afraid she's not here, she's out on a shoot.'

'On a shoot,' he said, looking a little choked up. Well, it's not easy hearing that your bird's away getting her kit off with someone else, is it? 'What time will she be back?'

'Well, she won't come back here, Colin, she'll just go straight home. I expect you'll see her tonight.'

'Where?' he asked.

'At your place,' I said. 'Well, goodbye.'

'No, she's not coming to my place tonight,' he told me. 'I'm going to hers, but the trouble is, I've lost her address. Could you give it to me please?'

Boy, he did that so cunningly I almost fell for it.

'Oh, I don't think we can do that, Colin, it's company policy not to give out our girls' addresses to anybody we don't know,' I said, getting both feet behind the security doors.

'But you know me.'

'Ah, yes, I do, but it's just company policy, a bit like the insurance, our hands are tied.' I wish yours were, mate. 'My advice to you is, give her a call.'

'Yeah, yeah, that's a good idea. What's the number?'

'You haven't got her number either?'

'I lost that too.'

'Oh dear, that's awkward. I'm very sorry, but we can't give out numbers either. It's the rules.'

'Can't you just bend them this once, for me?' he implored.

'I'm very sorry, I could get the sack if I did.'

'I wouldn't tell anyone.'

I leaned forward and whispered to him very quietly, 'No, you might not, but she would,' flicking towards Wendy with my thumb. 'Sorry.'

'But I am her boyfriend!'

'Yes, yes, yes, we know you are, but if we gave out numbers to everyone who asked, any old nutcase off the street might get hold of them,' I said and waved goodbye to him through the suddenly shut glass.

Of course, this all made for a very amusing story when Paddy and Matt and everyone else got back that afternoon, and Paddy told me one in turn.

A couple of weeks previously Mary had got a phone call from some matey who was near to tears with apologies. He explained that he'd gone down his local the night before (in Leicester somewhere), taken his usual seat and got the paper out, but had the strangest feeling something was amiss. When he looked around, everyone in the pub was staring at him and smiling, and he recognised them all from somewhere but he couldn't think where. Anyway, he shifted a little uncomfortably in his seat, quickly downed his pint and went home, puzzled and a little upset as to what he'd seen down the pub. It was only when he got home that he realised what had happened.

Ace had thrown him a surprise party down his local and he hadn't noticed.

'I'm so, so sorry,' he told Mary. 'I wondered why people were looking at me, waiting for me to speak and I just sat there without saying a word. Please, please, believe me, I'm sorry. You must hate me now. You went to all that trouble and I just left,' he went on, actually breaking down at one point.

Mary told him to hang on and asked Paddy if he'd thrown one of the readers a surprise party last night.

'What the fuck are you talking about?'

Out of curiosity, Paddy took over from Mary and asked matey what the problem was. Matey explained it all again so Paddy tried to set his mind to rest that *Ace* hadn't thrown him a party. Matey was having none of it.

'You did, you did. You're just saying that.'

'We're not, mate, honestly. We wouldn't. I promise you, we didn't thrown you a party last night.'

'Then why was the pub full of *Ace* girls and why were they all looking at me?'

'Mate, I don't know. All I can tell you is that you're probably mistaken, I doubt very much they were *Ace* girls because . . . er, all our girls are in America at the moment shooting our calendar.'

'They're not, you're lying. They were in The Badger's Arms last night waiting for me to acknowledge them. I didn't realise, you see, I didn't realise. That's why I just went home. I'm so sorry, please, if you throw me another one I'll realise next time.'

'Look, mate, we didn't throw you a party. I mean, why would we?'

'I don't know, that's what I couldn't work out either. It's probably why I didn't say anything because I wasn't expecting it. I'm so sorry.'

Paddy went on to tell me that matey had even offered to refund some of the expenses and for a few seconds Paddy was half-tempted to take him to the cleaners. I mean, who'd believe him if he complained afterwards? He didn't in the end, he just reassured him that his apology was accepted and that was the end of the story, as far as *Ace* was concerned.

'Okay, thanks. Again, I'm sorry, and please, keep writing about me.'

'He was a Premier League mentalist,' Paddy told us.

'I had one like that not so long ago,' Matt said. 'A bird, surprisingly. She wanted to know why we kept superimposing her face onto all the models in our mag. She said it was ruining her relationship and her reputation in Stockport, if that's possible.'

'Well, that's alright for you lads, Leicester and Stockport are miles away. I've got this fucking psycho just round the corner and now he knows my face. You think he'll come back?'

'What, are you kidding?' Paddy smirked. 'Of course he'll come back. You ain't seen the last of him by a long way.'

The only surprising thing about Colin Daish's return was that it took ten days to happen. He must've sat at home all that time, masturbating his cock to pâté waiting for the phone call that was never going to come, before deciding to get up off of his ass to come and see what was taking us so long.

'Your mate's here in reception,' Wendy told me when I picked up the phone.

That was it, 'your mate'; no notice, no warning, just 'your mate', so of course I strolled down to reception expecting to see one of my 'mates', only to find myself instead coming face to face with the last man on the planet I wanted to see.

'You cunt!' I whispered to Wendy as I went past her. 'Why didn't you tell me it was him?'

'What, and me get stuck with him? Not likely, he's your mate.'

I walked through the security doors and Colin held out his hand for me to shake.

'I thought I'd just pop in because I haven't heard anything yet. I was thinking maybe you called while I was out and that I missed it,' he said, anxiously.

'No, I'm sorry, I haven't called you yet.'

I suddenly realised that there was no easy way of getting rid of this one, he was here for the long haul and it wouldn't matter how many times I fobbed him off, he'd keep coming back until we fixed him up with Jerry, something that was never going to happen. I was going to have to nip this one in the bud before it got too silly, not something I would've normally volunteered for. Colin didn't look like a man who took bad news well, though ironically, he looked like a man who'd had lots of practice.

Fucking Wendy!

There was nothing else for it; I had to stand before him, look him in the eye and give it to him straight.

'Has no-one else spoken to you yet?' I asked.

'No, I haven't heard anything.'

'Oh, this is very awkward because it's not really down to me, the photographer should've given you a ring.'

'What about? Does he want me to go to the studio?'

'Er, I'm afraid not. You see, and I'm really sorry about this and it's not my fault at all, I promise, honestly, but the photographer, he told me to tell you that he doesn't think he can shoot you.'

'What? Why not?' he said, with jaw-dropping disbelief.

'Well, I'm really sorry, I'm on your side, but he thinks that, well . . . he said, rather that,' then a stroke of brilliance occurred to me, 'that we don't shoot men. I mean, actually we don't. Look,' I said, darting through reception and grabbing a spare copy of *Bling* from behind Wendy's desk. 'Look, it's all women, there aren't any blokes in it, none at all, are there? We only shoot women.'

'But the lady said that if I took some pictures of myself I could be in it with Jerry,' he said.

'I don't think she said that exactly.'

'She did! She did! She said if I brought in pictures I could be photographed with Jerry.'

'No, I think what she actually said was that if you wanted to take pictures of yourself with Jerry, then we'd take a look at them.'

'No! No, that's not what she said. She said I could have pictures taken with Jerry if I brought in some pictures of myself. That's what she said,' he insisted.

'Look, it doesn't matter what she said or what you thought she said because she's just a receptionist. Here's what I'm telling you, and I'm very sorry but I'm afraid this is the way it is. We do not take pictures of men, we only take pictures of women.'

'But why? That's not fair.'

'Why? Because that's what the readers want to see. You buy the mag, don't you? Would you buy it if it was full of geezers?'

'But what about the lady readers? They might want to see something too.'

How I didn't ask him if he'd taken a look in the mirror lately ('you scrawny little fucking runt') is beyond me but I somehow managed to remain diplomatic.

'We don't have many lady readers, our readers are mostly men.'

'Mostly?'

'Yes, men and lesbians,' I told him, though this wasn't actually true. According to market research a great many women who regarded themselves as 'straight' read our magazines too, though just how 'straight' was 'straight' was anyone's guess. Put it this way though; if you caught me sat at home reading *Sexy Cocks Monthly*, just how 'straight' would you say I was? Still, there was no point in confusing the issue with this poor baffled bastard any more than I had to.

'Well, maybe if you had men in it, women would buy it too,' he said, hopefully.

'I'm very sorry, that's not down to me. I'm really just the messenger.'

'Oh,' he said, looking utterly crumpled. 'Well, can I just quickly have a quick word with Jerry then? I just want to ask her something.'

'I'm afraid she's not here.'

'But you said that last time.'

'Yeah, and she wasn't here then either.'

'Well, where is she?'

'I don't know, at home or down the shops or somewhere, I suppose.'

'What shops?'

'I don't know, Colin, I don't know her. I've never met her.'

'Well, I want to speak to her.'

'Can't you speak to her next time you see her?'

'But I don't know when that will be.'

'I thought you said you were her boyfriend?'

'I am and I love her.'

'Well, good, then that's all sorted then.'

'I know what you're trying to do,' he said menacingly.

'I ain't trying to do anything,' I told him.

'Yes you are, you're deliberately trying to keep her away from me. I just want to fucking talk to her!' he demanded loudly, freaking the shit out of me.

'Alright. Alright, you win,' I conceded, holding up my hands and motioning for him to calm down. I knocked on the security doors for Wendy to buzz me through and spelled it out for him. 'Okay! Here's what we're going to do,' I told him, stepping through the doors and closing them between us. 'I'm going to go in here and you're going to go away and never come back again, alright? Otherwise, we'll phone the police.'

Colin stared at me through the doors in angry disbelief for a moment longer, then exploded into a rage.

'You fucking bastard! You fucking piece of shit! I'll kill you, you fucking cunt. I'll smash your face in. You're a fucking wanker,' etc etc etc. Then he started looking past me and yelling at the top of his voice, 'Jerry! Jerry! JERRY!'

I don't think I helped matters by making mental faces at him through the glass but sometimes you just have to do what feels right.

Peter, June, Stuart, Paddy and pretty much everyone else in earshot piled out of their offices to see what the commotion was, so I quickly stopped with the Joeys and told them that he just went crazy for no reason. Wendy, for once in her miserable life, backed me up. Peter told her to phone the police.

'Doing it now,' she said, and I just managed to pull one last quick spazmo face at Colin, without Peter seeing, prompting Colin to go wild and start pounding on the doors to get at me.

'I don't think he likes you,' Peter pointed out. 'What set him off?'

'Who knows with these people?' I told him.

12: Look who's stalking

Colin didn't take the hint.

He phoned up the company a dozen different times and put on a dozen different voices, but as he asked to speak to Jerry every time, we all knew who it was.

'Jerry isn't here. She doesn't work from here,' he would be told time and time again but there would be no getting through to him. Sometimes he'd erupt into a temper and sometimes he'd plead, but most of the time he'd just try and con us that he was an agent or a photographer and that he wanted to hire her for a million pounds or something. Actually, I hope that was him.

Anyway, we gave his number and address to the Old Bill and they went around and frightened him with arrest, but like all good nutters he just denied everything and continued his fruitless attempts to get in touch with Jerry from phone boxes around London.

I told Paddy that we should get one of the girls to ring him up and pretend she was Jerry just to wind him up but Paddy thought that would probably aggravate the situation rather than help it.

It was another few weeks or so before he started showing up at the office again. He didn't come into reception this time but chose instead to hang around outside waiting for . . . well, presumably Jerry to emerge. That wasn't very likely seeing as Jerry lived in Budapest and had never even visited our offices. This too had been explained to Colin during one of his calls but he wasn't having any of it. As far as he was concerned Jerry was from Guildford; he knew this because she'd said it in one of the bullshit interviews I'd made up about her in *Bling*. He didn't quite phrase it like this but you know what I mean. Besides, when he'd made his first enquiries we'd maybe humoured him a bit too much, not realising what a persistent bastard he was going to be, and so that was that as far as he was concerned. Jerry was alive and well and waiting for him to find her, and we were the enemy keeping them apart.

'I still think we should get Hazel to ring him up,' I said.

'And say what? "Fuck off, you nutcase"?'

'No, get her to say something like, "Oh, Colin, I hear you've been trying to get a hold of me. They won't let me talk to you, but I've had it with them. I want to get out of here and be with you. If only I was sure you truly were the man for me. Prove your love to me, go and stick your leg on a railway track."'

'Yeah, or "knock over Barclays for us or something, will ya, you loopy cunt,"' Fat Paul chipped in.

'You don't think Colin would smell a rat then?' Paddy asked.

'Well, I don't know, I'm not his psychiatrist, am I?'

'I'm not telling him to do anything like that,' Hazel objected.

'Well, look, we can at least tell him to fuck off, can't we? Get him off our backs. You phone him up, pretend you're Jerry, tell him you're not interested or that you're getting married or something, and tell him if he don't like it he can go and chuck himself in the river. It's got to be worth a go, ain't it? Even if it's just for a laugh.'

'No, I'm not doing it.'

'Alright, sod you then. Jackie, d'you want to do me a favour?' but she wasn't having any of it either. Nor was Mary or Susie or Wendy. I thought Mary or definitely Wendy would've done it, but birds are like that, aren't they? As soon as one of them puts the kibosh on something none of them want to know. It was the same at school; you'd have one perfectly normal, decent bloke in class and some girl would take a dislike to him and put it about that he smelled or was covered in fleas or something, and that would be it. No other bird in school would ever talk to, or sit next to, the poor bastard again, no matter how much they sympathised with his plight, because he was Smelly Dirty Flea Bag and to show him anything other than vicious, joyful contempt would see them labelled Mrs Smelly Dirty Flea Bag. And no girl wants that.

Incidentally, answers on a postcard if you can guess what my nickname was at school.

We didn't phone Colin in the end but he kept us on our toes for a few weeks. In the absence of Jerry, it was me and Wendy he was after. We were the only people he'd dealt with in the office and the only people he seemed to remember. Matt, Hasseem, Fat Paul and Hazel all reported passing him in the street without him taking any notice of them so this seemed to confirm things for us.

We tried the Old Bill again and Peter set to getting a restraining order drafted, but Colin was still spotted here and there.

I was dreading running into him outside and so was Wendy, probably more so than me. People started seeing him so much that it got to the point where the pair of us would stay behind after everyone else left work so that they could give us a buzz and warn us if they saw him hanging about on their way to the Tube. A couple of times me and Wendy had to leave by the side entrance to avoid Colin, who'd been spotted lurking around up the street.

In a funny sort of way, it brought me and Wendy closer together. There'd been an unexplained frosty antagonism between us ever since day one, but our shared plight melted away much of the ill-feeling and we actually started getting on together. We'd sit and chat around the office while we waited for the all-clear, then walk each other to the Tube Station and see that the other got there alright. Occasionally we'd even smile and wish each other a 'good morning' when appropriate. What was it that Humphrey Bogart said? It was the start of a beautiful friendship.

I immediately wondered if I could bone her.

At the end of the day I decided not to bother. Nothing seemed to piss girls off more than me having a crack at them, particularly the ones I got along with (not a long list). I think they saw it as evidence that I was only actually interested in them for one thing all along, which is so fundamentally untrue. It's a good job blokes don't think like this otherwise you'd never be able to ask one of your mates if he fancied a game of golf for fear of him getting all upset with you and accusing you of just pretending to like him so that you could have someone to play golf with. Jesus! Anyway, like I said, I didn't try it on with Wendy but settled for pencilling her down as a possible Christmas Party target. It would keep, particularly if I kept on making an effort to play the non-threatening mate.

It was a Wednesday and no-one had phoned. Me and Wendy were sitting around the office waiting to get the all-clear from Fat Paul but we hadn't heard a dickie-bird in twenty-five minutes. The Tube Station was only ten minutes away too and he knew we were hanging on for his call. This was typical of recent behaviour from the lads. This would be the fourth time no-one had phoned us back and it was starting to piss us off.

'Oh, I forgot.'

'My battery ran out.'

'I thought Paddy was phoning you.'

'I thought you said don't ring.' Etc.

In fairness to them, they always rang in when they did see Colin so I guess I could understand it slipping their minds when they didn't – especially as half the week they were usually plastered.

'What do you want to do, give it another ten minutes or shall we just fuck off now?'

'Let's fuck off now,' I said.

We had a peep around the front door and up the street and the coast looked clear – well, it was full of prostitutes, crack addicts and angry piss-smelling drunks, but there was no sign of Colin, so we headed for the Tube.

'We should go for a drink one of these nights,' Wendy suggested.

'Yeah, that would be nice,' I agreed. 'Where d'you fancy, just go to The Abbot or something?'

'Hmm, maybe not. Not if that bloody idiot's going to keep hanging around, I wouldn't want to bump into him on the way home afterwards. There's a few nice pubs up my way though, if you didn't mind travelling up to North London,' she said, giving me a look that had me rearranging the lie of my pants without using my hands.

'Yeah, that's not a bad idea,' I told her. I lived way down south and she knew it. There was no way I'd be expected to face an hour-long Tube journey come half-eleven when we would both be hammered, what with her place being just around the corner. 'We could make it tonight if you want?' I said, keen as Colman's.

'No, I'm afraid I can't, Liverpool are playing at home tonight,' she replied.

'Oh,' I said, suddenly understanding. 'Urgh!'

'What? No, no, not like that. I mean Liverpool really are playing at home tonight – in the Champions League. It's on the telly and I'm off round my brother's to watch it.'

'Oh, right, yeah, I forgot, I'm meant to be watching that myself. Maybe tomorrow then?'

'Yeah, sounds good,' she said and smiled. This was great. I was going to get to shag Wendy and that was a definite cert. She had quite a cute body too. Fairly short, nice big knockers, blonde hair. As we walked along together I tried to conjure up a mental image of what she looked like in the buff and immediately realised that I was going to have to give myself the old one-two as soon as I got home this evening. In the movies, blokes take cold showers when they have thoughts like these. In real life, they smash themselves off into a sock.

Maybe it was because I had all this going on in my mind that I didn't hear someone shouting after me from up the street. That and the fact that they weren't actually using my name to get my attention. They were using Don's.

'Don! Don! Slow down. Hang on a second, I want to speak to you! Don!'

It took a good few seconds of hearing this phrase shouted over and over again, combined with the slap slap slap of rapidly approaching steps, before I was jerked back to reality. I almost broke my back spinning around to see Colin charging up the street towards me and Wendy. My heart screamed in my chest and the chewing gum dropped from my mouth as I saw the reds of his eyes closing fast.

'SHIT! Fucking leg it!' I yelled at Wendy and sped off down the road, leaving her for dead (in every sense of the word).

Wendy screamed in panic and sprinted off as fast as her high heels could carry her. Not very far, as it turned out. She managed about half a dozen paces before her stilettos got the better of her and she went tumbling tits-first into a discarded kebab. Not that Colin seemed to notice, he went straight on past her and after me like a man on a mission.

'Don, wait up, you bastard! Wait there! Don, stop or I'll fucking have you! Don!' Not the sort of encouragement that was likely to see me slowing down.

Now they say that madmen have the strength of five men when their blood's up, well, I have the speed of ten cheetahs when one's after my claret, and I tore away from Colin like a dragster with no brakes. Unfortunately, cheetahs and dragsters have the legs over a furlong or two but that's pretty much their bolt. I nipped and tucked around a few corners but Colin wasn't for shaking. I even considered darting up a couple of the alleyways, but I really didn't fancy getting caught and clobbered up one of those in case it was days before I was found. In the end I reasoned that my best bet was to stick to the main roads and rely on help and intervention from my fellow Londoners, if it came down to it.

I sprinted in the road to bypass the crowds on the pavements and Colin did the same. I'd put probably 30ft between us (that's around 9,000mm in case you're reading this in Europe and confused by our wacky system of measurements) but my lifestyle and Colin were both catching up with me fast and I started tensing up, readying myself to get hit.

'Fuck off, you nutbag!' I half-screamed, half-pleaded with him. 'Leave me alone.'

'Don! Fucking stop, you cunt! Donnnnn!'

'Bollocks to you,' I croaked and carried on running, clutching the stitch that had begun tearing away at my side.

I didn't know how much longer I could go on but I knew one thing – I really didn't want to stop. I really couldn't see any good coming of that.

My long powering strides had shrunk over the course of half a mile so that they now resembled stumbling quick-steps. I had no energy left, just the will not to be knifed. 'Come on,' I gasped, urging myself on. 'Come on!'

My legs burned with every step and my side ripped with pain; the sweat poured down my face, stinging my eyes and burning my cheeks; my heart thumped in my chest and I could hardly catch a breath as I plodded along the street, but nothing was going to stop me, short of my fags falling out of my pocket. I turned around and saw Colin closer, but no longer closing. He'd sunk into step with me about 20ft back and was mercifully looking about as fucked as I was. This was suddenly a war of attrition. The winner would be the guy who wanted their objective the most. For Colin, it was to smack me in the mouth. For me, it was to not be smacked in the mouth by Colin. That was basically what it boiled down to.

I soldiered on, out of Wardour Street and left along Oxford Street. The crowds swelled significantly and I wondered if I could nip into one of the shops up ahead and lose him. I wasn't sure, but figured if I could just find a big round display table or something, I might be able to put it between Colin and myself, and stay out of reach long enough for security to come to my rescue.

JJ Sports fitted the bill perfectly so I shoulder-barged my way through the throng and down the stairs into the sports equipment basement. Colin never missed a step and careered in after me as I desperately sought out a safe refuge.

A big square basket of assorted mini-footballs offered a decent obstacle so I skidded to a halt behind it, grabbing hold of the side to stop my legs from buckling beneath me. Colin reached me before I'd had a chance to draw two breaths and immediately started chasing me around the basket. When he realised that I wasn't going to let him get anywhere near me and that we were just going in circles, he suddenly stopped and tried going the other way. I was too sharp for him though and stayed a frustrating 180° out of reach.

'Come here, you bastard, I just want to have a word with you!'

'Not fucking likely, mate, you're a fucking headcase.'

'For fuck's sake, stop!'

'Stick it up your arse.'

'I'll kill you, I mean it.'

'Fucking help me, help me!' I started yelling, causing half the shop to look our way.

'Just wait there a minute!' Colin was saying, his voice full of frustration.

He skidded to a stop the other side of the basket and feigned to go anti-clockwise, before darting clockwise again, then stopped and started feigning this way and that, to try and catch me out. Unfortunately for Colin, I was synchronised to his every movement and he didn't gain so much as an inch (1/39,000th of a kilometre) on me as we danced about the basket together.

'Wait, just wait,' I urged him. 'Let's just calm down and wait a moment. Can we? Can we?' Colin agreed and simmered down just long enough for me to chuck one of the mini-footballs straight in his face, flattening his nose and blacking both his eyes.

Colin fell back howling in pain and I took the opportunity to put some distance between us. I wanted to leg it from the store and start running again but I got disorientated in my panic and I lost the exit. Colin was after me again and looking like he was ready to rip my head off with his bare hands.

'I'm going to kill you, you fucking bastard. You dirty piece of shit! Arhhhhhhhhhh!' he came screaming, prompting me to bawl with fear as I charged headlong straight into a rack of trainers.

I pulled myself up but he dived at me and caught hold of one of my ankles. I tried to shake him off but he clung on doggedly as I dragged him along the wooden tiles, screaming for help.

'You bastard!' he was still shouting as I dragged him along the floor on his face.

'Get off me, you cunt!' I screamed at him, kicking him whenever possible.

Finally, security guards from all corners of the store were converging on our position and shoppers scattered. Two of them fell on top of Colin and tried prising him off my ankle, but Colin wasn't having any of it. He clung on like a rabid dog, threatening to eat me and all sorts and only let go when I started whacking his hands with a pair of golf spikes.

'Ahhh!' he hollered in pain again, and I managed to land one last beauty right on his fingers as they lay flat against the floor, but that was about it, as I was suddenly bundled over by the rest of Group 4 and held in a headlock with this fat bastard on top of me.

'Tell him to call the police,' he shouted at his mate, who was jabbering into his walkie-talkie. Colin was still fighting for all he was worth to get at me but that was my lot. I was done in and more than happy to sit it out until the Old Bill arrived and carted Colin off to the nick. I was in no doubt that they would too. Colin had been warned to stay away from the company a number of times and here he was attacking a member of staff. The fact that Colin was bleeding from head to foot while I didn't have a scratch on me was immaterial. Multiple complaints had been made against him and he hadn't listened. He'd chased and harassed a member of staff and was currently screaming about biting my 'fucking nose off' in front of five security guards. He was definitely going down, no question about it. I was just worried that one day he'd get let out again and come looking for me then.

'Jerry is not your girlfriend,' I took the opportunity to point out, while pinned to the ground underneath a guard. 'You've never met her and you're never going to. You're a fucking nutter and that's all you are.'

'No I'm not, I love her and she'll love me. Why won't you just let me fucking talk to her?'

'No way, donut.'

'Okay, that's enough,' the security guard butted in. 'Save it for when the police get here.'

'Keep out of this, fatso. What's it got to do with you?' I asked.

'Yeah, this don't concern you, so fuck off!' Colin told him in no uncertain terms.

'Fucking right!' I agreed as the pair of us struggled

beneath £20 an hour's worth of security (that's four guards, to you and me).

And there it was, a single moment of solidarity between me and Colin; one last fittingly bizarre moment in a frighteningly bizarre relationship.

13: Fantasy, schmantasy!

Colin got eighteen months and was booked in for a thorough check-up from the neck-up, as Steve Wright used to say. It got him out of our hair for a little while, though I was dreading the day he was released. Insanely enough, he still wrote to Jerry after his sentence, professing his undying love and telling her what colour his piss was this week after being pumped up to the eyelids full of medication. We got three love letters in a month from him before they suddenly dried up and we never heard from him again. I have no idea what happened to him, maybe the authorities cottoned on and stopped him from writing to us, or maybe he suddenly sobered up one day and realised what a cunt he'd made of himself or, I don't know, maybe he just started fancying someone else. Probably the last one as it's easy to go off someone when you finally wake up to the reality that you have no chance whatsoever.

And talking of no chance whatsoever, that suddenly summed up my prospects of getting Wendy in the sack. I don't know what I'd done but the next time I saw her she was back to her frosty best with me.

'We still on for tonight then?' I asked when I passed her

in the morning, but all I got by way of a reply was a stern, steely glare that chilled me to my boots.

'What's up with her?' Stuart asked, seeing her reaction.

'I'm not sure,' I told him. 'Did Liverpool lose or something last night?'

Stuart thought about it for a moment then said he didn't know what that meant. This was one of the difficulties with working in the porn industry, there were so many phrases and euphemisms for everything that misunderstandings were commonplace. In fact, according to Paddy, it was more than possible for two people to have a completely different conversation with each other and not even realise it. This sounded like a load of old bollocks to me but I quite liked the idea.

I sat at my desk, lit a fag and told Stuart all about what had happened to me the night before, how I'd spent half the night down the cop shop giving the Old Bill a statement and numbers to check before they'd got hold of Peter and he'd told them to let me go.

I asked Stuart if I could go home early today but he wasn't having any of it. 'One of us has to stay here today, and I wouldn't put much money on it being me,' he said.

Stuart was out meeting freelancers this afternoon, which is what Editors do in all fairness, but that didn't alter the fact that I still wanted to go home – not because I was knackered or anything, I just wanted to go home and it seemed like too good an excuse not to use. But no, that was that. Stuart was out so I had to stay, meaning as soon as he went I could piss off over the pub all afternoon, so that was good enough for me.

Talking of freelancers, I had to deal with them too, sex copy writers mostly, who'd write our regular erotic fantasy sections. It was around this time, and in my regular monthly dealings with the freelancers, that I got involved with Sophie.

Now Sophie was completely the opposite end of the spectrum from Colin and it frustrated me no end.

She'd started writing sex stories for us a few months back and every few weeks she'd email her latest copy in, I'd read through it and have to have the same conversation with her; 'Keep it real.'

Now, I'm not saying this in a funky black Ali G way. What I mean is that the women in her stories were always far too keen and so willing to drop their drawers for no discernible reason that they bore no resemblance to real women – certainly not the real women I knew anyway. Therefore, the stories rang hollow and lost a lot of their appeal.

Like I've said before, most blokes don't get wanton gorgeous women running up and tearing into their boxers without so much as a 'Hello, how are you? Your shoes are nice. My name's Debbie,' unless they happen to be millionaires, though even with the most shameless of harlots, there's still a certain amount of pussyfooting around as they size up whether or not you seem like a good bet. Why do I say that? Why, because she knows, in fact, I'll just underline that, *she knows* that she can shag you. All blokes have a green light over their heads at all times and it takes an absolute minimum of skill on the part of a girl to get laid. You can brand me a sexist if you like but if you've got this far into this book I imagine you already have.

I've been down the pub before with girls when they're trying to get all sassy and impress me with their sexual prowess by telling me about their hyperactive sex lives and my answer's always been the same.

'Big fucking deal. If I had tits and a bush I'd be getting banged over this table right now.'

They go on to you about what nymphomaniacs they are and how many blokes they've had but the moment you try getting in their pants too, it's all, 'You wish,' 'In your dreams,' or 'Don't touch what you can't afford'.

Maybe it's me. Maybe I am an ugly cunt. Alright, okay, fair enough. But then I want to at least find some solace in porn and believe that the ugly cunt can get it too, so give me a decent reason as to why she's decided to shag this guy. Don't just tell me it's because she's horny and loves it, because I've met lots of horny birds who've claimed to love it and I've yet to make it into the pants of a single one of them.

So, this is my thinking and my rationale and I'd explain it to Sophie every month, and every month I'd get exactly the same story back.

'*Me and the girls got all dressed up in our sexiest clubbing gear and hit the Apollo. I was dressed in a little one-piece cocktail dress, with fishnet stockings and high heels and had no underwear on. I was getting loads of looks from all the blokes dancing around me and started feeling really horny. This guy came up to me and told me his name was Bruce. Bruce was a fireman and he had the body to match. Stripped to the waist, with a tanned six-pack and biceps I couldn't get both hands around, he pulled me close and I felt ten inches of solid meat against my leg. "Let's fuck," I said, dragging him off towards the toilets . . .* etc'

Now, this story isn't doing a great deal for me or my ego. For me to relate to this story it would need to read more like this:

'*Me and the girls got all dressed up in our sexiest clubbing gear and . . . yah-da yah-da yah-da . . . and I started feeling really horny. This skinny little bastard came up to me and told me his name was Bruce. Bruce worked in Pizza Hut and still had his coat on. He said he didn't like leaving it in the cloakroom in case they went through his pockets. We danced about to the music and he brushed against my leg every time he bent down to pick up his glasses. "Let's fuck," I said to him, dragging him off towards the toilets. "But I haven't got any Johnnies," he replied.'*

But then, this is stupid, because we all know for a fact that she wouldn't shag the Pizza Hut guy. I mean, why would she? And this is the secret to a good porn story. Come up with a believable reason for her to shag this fucking loser and you're half way home. Okay, the example's a slight exaggeration but tell me you understand what I'm banging on about, please?

Sophie could never grasp this. She'd send in story after story with absolutely no story to it and every month I'd have to email her and say, 'Look, I don't understand, why is she shagging her driving instructor?'

'Because she hasn't had it in ages and she's feeling horny,' she'd replied (via email).

So I'd say (again, via email. All this is via email), 'But she wouldn't. She might ask him for a drink or invite him round for dinner or something, if she fancied him, but she wouldn't just drive off up some country lane during her test and start sucking him off for no reason. Women don't do this sort of thing.' Then I'd go on and have to rewrite her story so that it was actually this girl's eighth test and she knew she'd failed it again, so she decided to use her powers of persuasion to get her licence. ('You can do anything to me, anything you want,' she said, baring her slender young arse as she bent over the bonnet . . . etc). I'm not claiming to be William Shakespeare here or nothing but a little twist like this makes it a bit more interesting than 'I was feeling really horny [for no apparent reason] and started grinding his cock like I'd been grinding the gears all fucking test'. It also makes me want to be a driving instructor.

But again, Sophie just wouldn't get it and next month I'd get a story about a hunky young shop assistant being dragged into the changing rooms by some old cockaholic housewife. It was very frustrating.

In the end, I tried to demonstrate my point to her by saying (at the end of my latest email to her), 'Look, let me put it this way. If I was to tell you to come down here and suck me off, you wouldn't, would you?' And she wouldn't. She was way up there in Birmingham, she had a husband and a couple of kids, she'd never met me and I had nothing to offer her. Of course she'd never do it.

Her email comes back. 'Who says I wouldn't? I've always fancied a trip to London. I'll be in touch. x.'

Well, I thought to myself, sew a button on that one.

The next day Sophie sent me a story in which I summoned her down to London, took her into my office (yes, in this story I had this lovely plush office with thick shagpile carpets and old 70s leather furniture) and made her do everything she'd ever written about with me to prove that she knew what she was doing. This story was the best thing she'd ever written and I couldn't help but print a copy off to take to the bog for a second read.

Boy, I needed that one.

At the bottom of the letter, just after she'd written 'Hope you like the story', she added 'Your turn. Tell me what you want to do to me.'

I got back to my desk, sat down and reread Sophie's covering email. I looked over my shoulder at Roger but he was redesigning his CV for the third time this week and paying no attention to me. Neither was anyone else for that matter. Everyone who was in today was in their corner of the office, either working or shirking, so I started quietly tapping my keyboard and didn't stop for another two hours. I attached my story to an email and sent it to Sophie, with the words 'Hope you don't mind but I got a bit carried away', then went and had another fifteen minute bog stop.

It was quite unnerving giving a complete stranger a glimpse into my darkest desires and I hoped I hadn't misread the situation. What if I had? What if I'd just emailed her a great long pornographic wish list of what I wanted to do to (and on) her when all she'd actually meant was 'Tell me what stories you want me to write for next month'?

I suddenly shat myself. I reread her email again and again, trying every which way to see how it could be interpreted, then sat there all afternoon panicking and working out plausible excuses as to why I'd done what I'd done if the jizz hit the fan.

Just as I was about to leave for the day I received Sophie's reply. This in itself was a small relief as I always hated those emails that disappeared into thin air. Like the email I'd sent Sophie, they almost always contained incredibly personal or highly incriminating stuff and I'd always panic that I'd somehow sent them to Stuart's computer or my Auntie Pat by mistake.

I stared at her name for a few tense moments, looked around the office to make sure no-one was paying me any mind, then clicked onto it.

'Oooh, Godfrey, aren't you a wicked boy? I don't think I've ever read anything so rude and filthy in all my life. It got me going like you wouldn't believe. I don't think I've wanked that much since I was a schoolgirl. Guess where my fingers are right now [I had a guess]. You made me cum, Godfrey. I just wish you could've been here to see it. And no, I don't mind at all the things you wrote. You can't say anything that'll shock me. The harder the better as far as I'm concerned. I want you to fuck my arse next time. Write to me again and let me know how you'd do it to me. Sophie xxx.'

This gave me a woody Pinocchio could've laid claim to.

That night I worked till eight o'clock bashing out another story for her and when I clicked SEND I almost popped in my pants.

I rushed into work the next day and logged onto my email and there was another reply from Sophie. This one said similar stuff to the first but she'd also attached another story in which I took her to a London hotel room and made her pose for the camera, then spanked her bum till it glowed like Rudolf's nose. Well, I didn't really get the spanking bit, especially when it was my turn and she used a big spiky hair-brush on my arse (yeah, try that with me in real life, love, and you'd get your lights punched out) but the rest of it seemed like something I'd definitely be interested in.

I wrote her back, asking her when she was coming down to London and she replied something along the lines of 'All good things to those who wait' or something like that. She thought we were being terribly naughty and it was turning her on no end just knowing that I was a short train ride away. 'Tell me what else you'd like to do to me. You can be as filthy and as dirty as you like. Go on, try and shock me,' she challenged, so I answered.

Over the course of the next week or so, her emails became the whole focus of my attention. I could barely concentrate on anything else as I fantasised about finally meeting up with her and nailing her into the wall. My wank-count went through the roof, so much so that Paddy asked me if I was eating okay.

More and more stories would arrive and more and more

replies would be sent. It got so that if I didn't get a reply from her that day, I'd stay late into the evening then go home all frustrated. I badly wanted to see her naked, and I didn't even know what she looked like. She'd described herself in one of her emails and she didn't sound half bad; early forties, big knockers, slim, brunette, big knockers, long legs, big knockers and big knockers. I could almost picture her . . . slamming up and down on top of me with her great big knockers in my face.

Oh man!

'How about this week? Can you get away for a night?' I'd email her.

'Aren't you the impatient little man? Are you hard thinking about me? What would you do if I came down tonight? Tell me what I can expect.'

I'd then run off 500 words of absolute depravity, send it to her, she'd read it and tell me how hot she was and how much she wanted me to do these things to her, but unfortunately she couldn't get away, so we'd just have to make do with our imaginations tonight.

'I'll fuck you in my head, my love,' she'd sign off and I had half a mind to reply, 'Well, you're certainly fucking me in mine.'

I spent the next week trying to pin her down as to when we could get together with similar success. Each time I'd suggest a day or a week, she'd side-step the question with some flirtatious reply and tell me what a bad boy I was being.

I told her if it was inconvenient for her to get away I could go up to Birmingham, check into a hotel room and she could come and see me one afternoon. Even if she could only manage an hour or so, at least we could finally get together and take out some of this pent-up frustration on each other.

If she needed it as badly as I did, even five minutes would've done. The next day I received a story in which she went along to some hotel room in Birmingham and fucked me silly for an hour during her lunchbreak.

And that was it – another story.

'When are we going to do this for real?' I asked.

'Very soon, I would imagine. How are you holding out? Did you like the hotel room story I sent you? Send me one about fucking me in the woods. Sophie x.'

I stared at those few words with confusion, frustration and mounting annoyance scrambling my brain, then went outside and smoked two fags in ten minutes.

What was this? Was she just stringing me along for laughs or something or did she actually want to meet up? Talking dirty to someone is a lot of fun, especially when you're swapping graphic descriptions of what you're going to do to each other, but it can only get you so far. Okay, you've hooked me, I'm ready, let's do it. Let's cut the chat and get to the real stuff, that was what I was interested in. I mean, didn't she think I read enough fucking porn stories all day long as it was? Just because these ones had my name in them, that didn't make them any different. It had, at first, but only because I'd thought they were a prelude to actual sex. On their own, they were nothing more than extra work.

When she went to a restaurant did she just read the menu for three hours?

I went back inside and replied to her.

'Dear Sophie, do you have any idea how much I want to have sex with you? I'm literally at bursting point and I want to meet up with you right now. My schedule is clear for the rest of my life. I can bunk any day, meet you anywhere and any time. All you have to do is say the word and I'll be there. We need to do some of this stuff for real. God' x.'

Her response came back within the hour.

'Dear God', what an absolutely wicked thought. I'm wet just thinking about it. Next time I'm in London I'll be sure to take you up on the offer. We could stay in one of those sleazy hotels where all the prostitutes go. I could dress as a hooker if you wanted and you could pick me off the street. Write me a story about that. Sophie x.'

This made me fucking furious.

'Fuck the stories, I don't want to read any more of your fucking stories. I want to fuck you for real, what is it you don't understand about this? Your stories are boring the fucking plums off me.'

I was so tempted to write this and send it back to her but I knew it wouldn't do any good. I suddenly realised that I'd been led up the garden path good and proper. She was never going to shag me any more than . . . well, any other bird I knew at that moment in time. All she wanted was a pen pal to have computer sex with. Devilishly naughty, if you're a bored old housewife, but ultimately very safe.

This wasn't what I was after.

I mean, Jesus Christ, I hadn't had it in so long, this was the last fucking thing I needed.

I took a few deep breaths (through a cigarette) and composed an email.

'Sophie, no more stories. I'm afraid they've lost any sort of appeal for me. I only started writing them because I thought they were going somewhere but now I realise they're not. I can't honestly see us ever getting together and this is just frustrating me. I'm sorry to be like this but I read porn stories all day. It's what I do for a living. And unless we actually get together, that's all they'll ever be. Just stories. I don't think this is going to happen so I'm going to stop torturing myself. All the best, God'.'

I clicked SEND then reluctantly got on with some work. Her reply came back later that day.

'Well, you certainly seem to know it all. How do you know we won't ever get together? Do you have a clairvoyant's ball? Who says I wasn't getting ready to come down for the weekend? I don't presume to read your mind, why do you presume to read mine? Sophie x.'

What was I, some sort of fucking mug or something?

'Dear Sophie, I'm not reading your mind. All I'm saying is that I don't think you're ever going to shag me. If I'm wrong, then that's great, but you're going to have to do it to prove it.'

'I don't have to prove anything to anyone. If you don't want me to fuck your brains out then that's your loss. Personally, I was rather looking forward to . . .' then she went into a 500 word description of what she reckoned she was going to do to me and ended it with, 'but I guess that doesn't appeal to you, does it? Sophie.'

'That does appeal to me, very much. But doing it, not reading about it. I mean, why not just send pictures of buns to Aid for Africa while you're at it? If you want to have sex with me then let's get together this week. I'll come up to Birmingham and you meet me at the hotel. Agreed?'

'I'm sorry, but if you're going to be like that, I don't think I want to meet up with you. Sophie.'

'See, that's what I'm talking about. This is never going to happen. Look, let's just drop the pretence and level with each other. I want to have sex with you, *for real*. Are you going to have sex with me, *for real*? It's as simple as that.'

'But it's not that simple. I want to have sex with you, I really do. Sometimes I get so horny just thinking about you but I'm married and I love my husband. It's not easy for me, you know. Please, try to understand that I was serious, I really do want to fuck you, I really *really* do, but it's just not possible. The intention was there, just not the timing. Where were you twenty years ago? Sophie x.'

And there it was, finally the truth.

I think this whole episode started when I tried to demonstrate a point to her, that her stories were a little threadbare as far as plots went and that women simply didn't behave the way she was writing about. Like I said in my first email, 'If I was to tell you to come down here and suck me off, you wouldn't, would you?'

She was the one that had responded, 'Who says I wouldn't?' starting this whole sorry saga.

Well, this finally proved my point. She wouldn't come down and suck me off because she couldn't and didn't, though I think this was still a little lost on her.

And who says you wouldn't, Sophie? I say you wouldn't and I should know. I'm not much at anything but I'll tell you this, I'm a fucking expert on the things women won't do.

14: Sexploitation

It was some seventy-two hours later and I was still pissed off about somehow drawing yet another blank. I was angry, frustrated, upset and disconsolate, so it was with rapidly evaporating patience that I found myself standing in a posh night club, listening to some boring rugby cock announcing to everyone within earshot that 'This bloke's got the best job in the world'.

I hadn't told him. I really wasn't in the mood. I'd come to the party with Paddy and Matt and word had just got out. I'd been cornered, bombarded with the same old questions and unable to escape. I'd only been here an hour and was ready to go home already.

Brian was his name and he just kept on saying, over and over again, 'Oh, I fucking tell you, man, what a laugh! What a fucking laugh!'

He was Australian to boot and therefore naturally given to over-enthusiasm for just about everything, so my job had him creaming in his pants. He'd bent my ear for more than half an hour before I'd been able to give him the slip, only for him to materialise next to me five minutes later.

'Oh, there you are,' Brian said. 'Here, this is my mate, also called Brian, no relation. Here, Godfrey, tell Brian what you was just telling me. Listen to this, mate, you're gonna love it.'

Oh, fuck me!

Fifteen minutes of minimalist recapping later, I had two new best mates called Brian, who I thought would never leave me again, but luckily some idiot off in the corner started singing Australian rugby songs and that was all it took. They announced to everyone that they had to have some of that, asked me if I wanted to join them ('Only if it's in a murder/suicide pact,' I think was my answer), then they bounded off with their tails wagging.

I thought I'd take the opportunity to slip away before they returned so I started filling my pockets with booze, fags, canapés and anything else free when this rather saucy little bird came over and said hello.

'Hello back.'

'Are you going?'

'Erm, I might do,' I told her, suddenly not so sure.

'What do you do for Philip Goss?' she asked, very deliberately. This was a Philip Goss shindig. He had tons of companies all over London, only one of them was porn. Most were respectable pin-stripe businesses – accountants, letting agencies, advertising and marketing firms, etc etc etc. The canapés I was slipping into my pocket were his property management company's by rights, but me, Paddy and Matt had been able to wangle ourselves a night of free booze by virtue of working under the same umbrella.

'Why?' I asked back.

'I want to know. What do you do?'

I gave her a good look over. She was a petite little brunette with cute freckles and a drunken slur. Lots of make-up around the eyes, short hair and an arse that looked like it had seen more than its fair share of action. I decided she'd do very nicely. Time to turn on the old charm.

'I work for one of his porno mags,' I told her.

This might seem like double standards, me volunteering this information to her, and that's because it is. I've never really minded talking about my job to women, because with women it serves as a useful device for cutting through all the usual old chit-chat and getting them onto the subject of sex without having to get to know them first.

'And why do you do that?' she asked.

'I don't know, beats working for a living, I suppose,' I said, giving her a cheeky little smile, which I didn't get back.

'So, you think it's okay to exploit women in this way, then?'

Oh dear, not this old chestnut, I thought, as the cheeky smile slipped from my face.

'How are we exploiting women?' I asked. 'What do you mean by "exploiting"?'

'I mean showing us to be pieces of meat rather than real people with thoughts and feelings. I just wanted to know if you think that's okay, and if not, how you can do what you do every day?'

'First off, we're not exploiting women, we never have done. This is some fucking buzz word that they teach you all at big fat feminist school that you love to throw about without really understanding what you're talking about. Exploiting women? How are we exploiting them? Okay, men like sex. Men have sex with women. Men enjoy looking at pictures of naked women because it reminds them of sex – and some of us need fucking reminding. Who have we exploited? Have we exploited you? No, because you weren't in the mag. Have we exploited the model? No, because she got paid for what she did and enjoyed the work. If anyone's exploited anything, it's the model who's exploited her own body and men's natural desires. Not us.'

'You use women.'

'Use them? What do you mean? Like banks use cashiers or restaurants use chefs. Then yeah, you're right, we do use women. We have to, most female glamour models happen to be women. It's a very hard racket for us blokes to break into. By that same token, I wouldn't rate your chances of getting into the Chippendales.'

'That's completely different.'

'I thought it would be.'

'The Chippendales are just a dance troupe, an evening's entertainment. It's choreography not pornography that draws women to go and see them.'

'Yes, and I can see how being ejected from the stage screaming, "I touched his willy! I touched his willy!" really helps you appreciate those moves.'

'I've never done anything like that.'

'No, you might not have but there are plenty of bir . . . er . . . women who have. I've never raped anyone, but that doesn't stop feminist writers like Paula Atkinson accusing all men of being "sleeping rapists" now, does it?'

'I've never even heard of her,' she told me, though that didn't surprise me, considering I'd just made her up. Still, sounded good, didn't it?

'We don't exploit women any more than calendars about polar bears exploits polar bears. Actually, we exploit women less because our women readily agree to be photographed. I don't suppose the old polar bears have that much of a say in the matter, do they? No, one minute they're having a shit behind a bush, the next they're up on the kitchen door of every conservationist in the country. How would you like that, hey? "Ahhh, look at her straining. Isn't she cute?"' I told her. 'Our girls get £50 extra if we want pictures of them having a shit. What do the polar bears get?' I added, just for a joke, but I don't think she realised it was one.

'It's humiliating for women. You humiliate women. You might think they're agreeing but you're actually taking advantage of their insecurities and doing their self-identification permanent long-term damage.'

'Have you ever even met a porn model?' I asked her.

'No, but that . . .'

'No, no, let me make my point,' I interrupted before she had a chance to get into her stride. 'I know plenty of porn models and it seems to me that you're making sweeping generalised remarks about a group of people you know nothing about.'

'They're women, and I think I know about women a bit more than you do, being that I am one.'

'No, they're not women, they're people. Personally I think that was a little sexist of you, but that's just me. I've met a lot of porn models and they come in all shapes and sizes; mentally, I'm talking about (most are almost identical physical clones of each other). They all have different reasons for doing what they do so I can't talk about them all, but I think I can safely say one thing – they'd all be pretty offended by some of the shit you've been coming out with.'

'Oh, shit, is it? Why is it then that hundreds of women are attacked every day by men who read porn?'

'Why? Because nearly every fucking bloke in the country reads fucking porn.'

'I rest my case.'

'Oh, you do, do you? Well, think about this; Holland has some of the most liberal laws in the whole of Europe as regards porn and prostitution, yet it also has some of the safest streets for women. Explain that one, Mzzzzzz Pankhurst.'

'The Dutch have always been more enlightened and more mature when it comes to sex.'

'Yes, they think porn and prostitution are fine. I agree with them. You don't. So who's being immature?'

'You think prostitution is the answer to solving hate crimes? You'd legalise the slavery of women, would you?'

'Legalise it? I'd make it compulsory, like National Service. Two years in a knocking shop for every bird over the age of eighteen. Actually, no, scrub that, just the good-looking ones, all the old boilers get three years in the ironing corps.' I don't know if she could tell, but my patience had finally expired and I was suddenly concentrating my efforts on mainly winding her up. I was doing a damn fine job of it too.

'Is your mother proud of you? Does she know what you do?'

'Are you joking? Of course she does. She was the first person I phoned when I got the job. "Hi, Mum, look at me. Look how low I've sunk." It was great.'

'How would you like it if she was in one of your sleazy magazines? That would be alright, would it?'

'I don't think we'd have her, if you know what I mean?' I said, pulling a face and whistling.

'You really are pathetic, you know that?' she said, turning on a heel.

'No, wait, wait, hold it. I'm only joking with you. This is a party after all, it's not *Newsnight*. What's your name?'

'I'm not telling you that.'

'Why not?' I asked.

'Why? Because you're a pornographer and I'm not giving my name to a pornographer.'

'Why? What am I going to do with it? This doesn't even make sense.'

'Listen, slimeball . . .'

'You can call me Godfrey if you like.'

'Listen, slimeball, you're not getting my name because you don't need to know it. You're never going to have call to use it five seconds from now.'

'Well, if we're never going to see each other again, another couple of minutes isn't going to hurt. No more joking, I'll be serious, I promise.'

The girl with no name dithered for a moment as she tried to make up her mind whether or not to give me a few more minutes of her life. Was it worth it? Was I going to listen to what she was saying or was I just going to use those minutes to make fun of her some more?

'Hey, you approached me. I think the least you can do is hear me out,' I told her.

'Hear you out? Hear out what, that I actually enjoy being looked at like a lump of meat?'

'Hey, maybe not you but you'd be surprised how many women do,' I told her. 'Actually, I'll take that back; you wouldn't be surprised, you'd be amazed at the amount of letters and phone calls we get every day from women who want to be in our mags. A lot of women get a thrill from it.'

'Oh, please. It's degrading,' she said scornfully.

If done right, I thought to myself, though I decided to keep my jokes to myself for now.

'You might find it degrading, but do you suppose every woman thinks the same as you? I've met a lot of women, not all models either, who get a real kick out of exhibitionism. One girl I knew never wanted to turn the lights off or close the curtains when we had sex, she wanted all the neighbours to watch.'

'Probably the only way she could get any excitement going with you,' she spat.

'Now who's being offensive? Though you're probably right. However, you do then acknowledge that there is a certain excitement angle to being watched? To having eyes roaming all over your body,' I said slowly, running mine up and down her in a way that made her shudder and tell me to stop. 'Here's a good example. A few months ago I was called into reception to see a girl who wanted to appear in *Bling* – that's the mag I work on. Anyway, she explained that she'd come in before but been told that, at only seventeen, she was too young to be photographed. Very sorry, come back next year if you're still interested. She tells me all this then shows me her birth certificate to prove she's now eighteen. It's only her birthday that day. "Can you photograph me now please?" she says. "It can be my birthday present to myself."'

'Poor girl,' my feminist friend said, shaking her head sadly.

'What? Where did you get that from?'

'Well, she was obviously deeply unhappy with herself.'

'Not necessarily. Some girls are just proud of their bodies and love showing them off. She certainly did and she's doing very nicely out of it these days.'

'These girls probably like showing off their bodies because they haven't had a proper education and they're trying to compensate for this with the only weapon they've got. How will this poor girl feel in twenty years' time when her looks desert her?'

'Oh, I wouldn't worry about that, she'll probably be long dead from all the crack we force-feed her.'

Femmy's jaw dropped in shock before she realised I was

joking again. Too good an opportunity to pass up. She didn't laugh.

'Look, you say it's down to a lack of education. Well, let me tell you this; half of our British models are university students and a hell of a lot more educated they are than I am. What does that do for your theory, hey?'

'Are they really? Is that true?' she asked suspiciously.

'Yes, straight down the line. I don't have to make this stuff up because it's all true.'

'Well then, it's obvious why they do it, they're doing it to supplement their student loans and pay their way through college . . .'

'And we're taking advantage,' I said, finishing her sentence for her.

'Yes, yes, you are. That's exactly it. And what happens when these girls finish their degrees and go looking for work? Who's going to take them seriously and look at them in any light other than brainless bimbos and whores after they've cheapened themselves in porn?'

'Well, no-one, if the world thinks like you.'

'Exactly, so you've ruined their lives.'

'We're just taking a few pictures of them, you're the ones waiting in the wings to tar and feather them. Why do you refuse to accept that some women might just genuinely enjoy porn as much as men?'

'There were a few black slaves in America 200 years ago who thought their lot in life was good. Some of them even pursued and caught other slaves that had run away out of misplaced loyalty to their owners. They even whipped their own brothers, and you know why?'

'For a laugh?'

'No, because they didn't know any better. Men have been oppressing women for centuries and pornography is just another tool of the oppressor,' she said, I suspect verbatim from some militant man-hating textbook.

'If you're going back a couple of hundred years, you know the Victorians used to cover up table legs because they thought they were obscene. This might sound daft to you and me in this day and age but the Victorians took it very seriously. Jesus Christ, it wasn't that long ago that *Lady Chatterley's Lover* was banned but who's going to crack one out to that these days? A hundred years from now I'm sure people won't be able to understand what all the fuss was about with our nudey pictures.'

'A hundred years from now, I hope to God people will be above this sort of thing and ban people like you altogether.'

'I doubt that. The way things are going the porn's just going to get harder and harder. It was only twenty years ago that people thought Benny Hill was a bit risqué and look at the shit that's on the box now.'

'If it hadn't've been for Benny Hill, perhaps there wouldn't be any of this crap today.'

'You could have a point there. Still, he was good, wasn't he?'

'He was a pig. And it's down to him and people like him that women have such a hard life today.'

'Not a fan then? Okay, but if you want to talk about hard lives, let's just get back to the old Victorians for a second. See, I seem to remember, from history and stuff, that in Victorian times ladies were required to be respectfully covered up at all times. If a Victorian could see what you're wearing today he'd probably take his belt to your backside and call you a harlot.'

'Yes, I'm sure *he* would.'

'But then aren't you contradicting yourself? It's our fault when you're all covered up. It's our fault when you've got your tits out. When exactly is it your turn to take responsibility for your own actions?'

'When we finally have control over them.'

'You do have control over them though, that's the point. Women can, and do, do whatever they like today. It's called equality. And if some of the women choose to take their clothes off and pose nude, hell, if some of them choose to suck six cocks on camera specifically for the titillation of men, then surely that's their choice. As long as they're not hurting anyone else, why shouldn't they be allowed to do these things?'

'Why? For exactly the reason you just said. They are hurting other people. They're hurting other women. They're betraying their sex and making life much harder and much more dangerous for all of us who don't choose to suck six cocks on camera,' she told me. It's funny, that was the first time I'd heard her talk sexy and it turned me on a bit. I wondered if I could get her to say it again.

'Dangerous? What do you mean dangerous? How is one girl sucking six cocks on camera dangerous for you?'

'Because men start to see us purely as objects of sex and that puts us all at risk of attack.'

'Not this one again? I'm telling you, porn doesn't make men attack women. Repression and censorship are probably more responsible for rape and sexual assault around the globe than anything else.'

'What utter nonsense.'

'Come on! Wanting sex is a perfectly natural urge and when you try and suppress it you're only asking for trouble. We've had it in this fucking country for years, all that "No sex please we're British" bollocks that's drummed into us from an early age. What's the upshot of it all? You said it yourself, one of the highest incidences of sex attacks and teenage pregnancies in Europe.'

'I notice you keep talking about men and what men want. You don't see women running around raping and killing men now, do you?'

'No you don't, because even the saddest, loneliest plain Jane can go out and get nailed from here till next week if she wants to. All she's got to do is ask enough blokes if they want a shag and she'll get one. The average equivalent bloke couldn't do that.'

'Rubbish. Men pick up women all the time.'

'Yes, but not all men are good at it. What I'm saying is all women can get a shag very easily without any effort, not all men can do the same. It's one of the last inequalities between the sexes and about the one card you lot have held throughout history. So look at us today, us men, we've chucked in all our cards but you still cling on to yours.'

'What are you talking about?'

'Look, put it this way, if blokes could pick up women as easily as women can pick up men, there would be no need for pornography and certainly no need to enslave you all as prostitutes. We would live in a truly enlightened age where men and women were equals and lived in perfect harmony with one another.'

Can you see where I'm going with this one?

'I really don't know what you're talking about. If men find picking up women is so hard, how come most women can't go out for an evening without being hit on all night?'

'Alright, put it this way; you and me, if you went up to ten blokes at this party tonight and asked them, straight out, "Do you fancy a shag?" how many of them do you think would say yes?'

'What has this got to do with anything?'

'Just answer the question. How many blokes would say yes if you asked them that question?'

'Well, I don't know, half of them I suppose.'

'Okay, now if I was to do the same, go up to ten girls and ask them the same question, exactly the same, how many of them would say yes?'

'With you? None,' she snorted.

'Exactly, so what do I do if I fancy sex tonight? Simple, I go home, get out my mag, lay it out on my favourite page and pound myself unconscious. You, if you want it though, well, you're alright, you've got fifty per cent of the field to choose from.'

'That's got nothing to do with me being a woman and you being a man, that's just you and the fact that you're a repulsive git.'

'What are you talking about? I'm alright! Not a bad looking bloke. I might not be Brad Pitt but I'm not Compo out of *Last of the Summer Wine* either. You want to take a look at yourself some time, you're hardly the Queen of fucking Sheba.'

'No. But I bet you'd still love to get me into bed, wouldn't you?'

'Yes, I would. Fancy a shag?'

This was the moment I'd been building up to. Now, readers of my magazine, I'm sure, would be expecting us to race off to the bog, lock ourselves in and fuck each other like rabid bunnies as we exorcised all this fiery pent-up passion for one another in an orgy of drunken sex. And indeed, this was what I'd been hoping for, but unfortunately this wasn't a story in *Bling*. Femmy looked at me with supreme smug satisfaction and savoured the moment as if it was the best three seconds of her life.

'Not if you were the last man on Earth,' she told me, with a big vindictive smile plastered right across her face.

I, at least, hoped the irony wasn't lost on her.

At this moment, one of the Brians reappeared, all sweaty and sung out. He'd hardly got his gabber hole open before she'd turned to him and asked him, straight out, 'Hi, do you fancy a shag?'

Brian's eyes lit up and he said, 'Strewth yeah,' or something like that, gave me the thumbs up and swept Femmy off to the cloakroom. Just as she was about to disappear from my line of sight, she turned back, gave me a little wave and started to laugh.

I won't even bother to describe to you how this made me feel, but you can probably guess. I grabbed an unopened bottle of Absolut from behind the bar when the staff weren't looking and headed off home.

I cracked open the vodka, got steaming drunk and half thought about sticking a porno on.

I didn't bother.

15: Tits? Out!

Another Monday. Another week.

People were always telling me how much they'd look forward to Mondays if they were in my shoes. Mondays meant the start of another working week for me and everyone knew the sort of crazy-ass job I had.

Boy, I tell you.

Girl copy, that was what I was writing. A few slutty dirty quotes to go next to the pictures in the magazine.

'*I want it hard and I want it now. Spunk on my tits and I'll lick it off. Wouldn't you like to see me do that?*' etc.

Stuart had given up any notion of journalistic accuracy so they were all down to my imagination.

'Just write whatever you think they'd be saying if you were there with them,' he told me.

So I did.

'*Urghhh!*'

'*Go away.*'

'*Not if you were the last man on Earth.*'

'*Please, try to understand, I really want to have sex with you, but I love my husband so I can't. Sorry.*'

They all got typed in and deleted over the next few hours as I struggled to come up with anything genuinely sexy. Not the sort of job you want when you haven't had it in ages and you're desperately trying not to think about sex. What misery!

In two hours, I think I got four sentences written before I gave myself the rest of the morning off and went to talk to Paddy and Matt.

'Hey, here he is. What happened to you the other night? Did you get hold of that bird I saw you chatting up?' Paddy asked.

'No. I didn't,' I replied.

'Oh, you should've man, she was cute.'

'Are you talking about Samantha? Short hair? Freckly bird?' Matt asked. 'She's meant to be a right dirty bitch.'

'How do you know that?' Paddy asked.

'My mate told me. Reckons she's a right shag monster. Loves it. Her bedpost is just a pile of sawdust these days. She was the one I was telling you about that sucked off her boss every night for a year and got a junior partnership out of it. She's a solicitor. Can't get enough of it, apparently.'

'Oh yeah, I remember. Oh, that was her, was it? Ohhh,' Paddy mused. 'Oh yeah, she's a bit of alright, she is. You should've steamed in there, God'.'

'I wasn't really interested,' I told them. 'And I was a bit tired too.'

And there had been me thinking I couldn't feel any worse about myself. Just goes to show, you should never underestimate the power of your mates to make you feel even shittier about yourself. What a day I was having.

'Anyway, besides,' I continued, 'she weren't exactly crazy about our chosen profession, was she? Got the old "exploiting women" bit chucked in my face.'

'Ohh,' Paddy nodded, understanding. 'I've had that before. You can never win those arguments so it's not even worth bothering. Just agree and walk away. I mean, boo-fucking-hoo, so what? If she don't like it, why don't she just go and live in fucking Russia,' he said, wringing mock tears from his eyes. 'What was it you said she did, Matt? A solicitor? They're the biggest fucking exploiters of the lot, so that just goes to show what she knows. No, she was probably just spoiling for a fight and you took the bait. In future, when some bird accuses you of exploiting women, just tell her to shut up and get her tits out.'

'That'll go down well.'

'It's not meant to go down well. It's meant to get her to either shut up or get her tits out,' he replied.

'I don't get it, how can she be a feminist and a shag monster?' I asked.

'Feminists like sex too,' Paddy said. 'Probably more than most, if you know what I mean, as long as they're the ones calling the shots. Probably.'

'I don't think we do exploit birds,' Matt ventured. 'All our models always look great, few old howlers but no-one can help that, not even them. They're always tarted up and made to look nice and shot just right so that they look on top of their game. Any bird would love to look like the sorts we publish. I reckon we do alright by them. Personally, I can't see how anyone can say what we do is exploitative in the slightest.'

'Naked tennis,' Stuart suggested.

Wimbledon was on the way and it was about this time of the year that every bongo mag in the country turned its thoughts towards getting an unconvincing Anna Kournikova porn-a-like to do herself with her racquet (under the obligatory unchanging headline 'New Balls Please').

'Didn't we have that last year with Tanya?' I asked.

'Ah, yeah, but that was in the studio. I'm talking about going down to an actual tennis court and doing an on-location two-girl shoot. It'll be a laugh. Get a few opening shots of them playing tennis first of all, then do all the usual close-up stuff with them sucking each other's tits through the nets and whacking each other's arses with their bats. What do you think?'

'Well, I don't know art, but I know what I like.'

'Good, because you're organising it. Get a couple of girls for Thursday, make sure they're stunners, not the usual old pigs you keep booking, and find us a tennis court we can use.'

'A tennis court?'

'Yeah, and it's got to be outdoor. I'll get the photographer, I've got someone in mind, a new bloke I wouldn't mind trying. You just find us a location. Right, let's get cracking.'

The girls were easy. Out of sheer laziness I just booked Tanya again. She was our regular girl after all, popular with the readers and always up for the work. I'd got to know her quite well from various shoots and from chatting to her on the phone, and she'd become my archetypal porn model. Stunningly attractive, fit as a ballerina, supple, flexible, with flawless skin and long slender dancer's legs, and about as interesting as a glass of water. I don't mean that in a cruel way, she was a lovely girl and all and I liked her a lot, it's just that she had only one topic of conversation – herself. In all the time I'd known her I don't think she'd ever asked me even one question (other than how much and when do I get the cheque?) yet she'd regaled me for hours on end about clubbing in the swankiest nightspots of Soho or Ibiza, dancing on music videos, flying out to the Middle East with eleven other girls to entertain (suck off and get bummed by) some Saudi billionaires and generally behaving outrageous, wacky and mad.

Okay, sure she had an interesting life compared to mine but telling me about it for six hours without pausing for breath and showing not even the slightest interest in me only rubbed my nose in it.

Still, she was a sight for sore knobs and I didn't half fancy her (with the sound turned down). She once told me that she'd do anything for money, absolutely anything, no inhibitions. I think she was just trying to impress me by being outrageous, wacky and mad, but if ever I win the lottery I'm going to make her eat her words . . . as well as the contents of my conkers.

The other girl I booked was Cindy, a stunning bubbly blonde with a thick West Country accent that always got me thinking about Dairylea and farmers' daughters. She was sweet as a button and incredibly cute, and I had several dozen JPEGS of her on my computer with her face covered in something that wasn't Dairylea.

Both girls were consummate pros and both were up for shooting outdoors in public if I could just find a court.

This proved to be the stumbling block. I tried a number of lawn tennis clubs but all of them balked at the thought of pornographers soiling their sacred turf. So I set my sights a little lower and tried a few athletics clubs, only to meet with similar objections. I tried colleges, local authorities and even a few hotels, anyone who might let us shoot on their court, all to no avail. No-one wanted anything to do with us.

I found this decidedly odd. If I had a tennis court and someone wanted to use it for a porn shoot, I couldn't see that I'd have a problem with it. Just as long as I could sit there quietly and watch, and maybe say hello to the girls at some point in a creepy weirdo way, then what was the problem?

No joy though. It got to Wednesday night and I still hadn't found anywhere. If I couldn't find somewhere before the next morning then the whole thing would have to be cancelled and I'd be the one to blame. This wasn't something I'd be allowed to forget so it was time to take desperate measures.

'Okay, you've got somewhere?' Stuart asked. 'Thank fuck for that. Where is it?'

'It's down in Tooting, on the Common. They're a long way from the road and it's a school day so there shouldn't be too many people about, but we might have to, you know, whip them off, snap snap snap, put them back on and be a bit careful.'

'You can see them from the Common?' Stuart asked.

'Yeah, well, there's a wire fence all around but yeah. Sorry, but it's the best I could do, I couldn't get anywhere else. What do you reckon?'

Stuart thought about it for a moment. We were sat around photographer John Cooper's studio while the girls went through make-up. Both had their hair up in curlers and fags dangling between their rich scarlet lips. Each wore a little white tennis outfit, bobbi-socks and pumps, but neither had knickers on. They really looked the business and were in playful high spirits. Tanya kept on flashing me her privates while Cindy repeatedly reached around and grabbed the front of my jeans every time I walked by to see if I had a hard-on.

'If the girls are happy to go for it, then we'll do it, but

you've got to take full responsibility, Godfrey. We keep the name of the mag out of it, don't mention it to anyone in case we get sued, and if anyone asks, you're in charge. Alright?'

I said it was, but what else was I going to do?

'Okay then, let's load up the car and get moving.'

The drive down to Tooting was unbearable. I'd sat in between the girls in the back, thinking it would be a nice place to spend a half-hour car journey, but they'd teased me so much that I was almost reduced to tears with frustration by the time we got to the Common. I've heard it said that girls can smell desperation. Well, I must've reeked of it because they didn't let up for a minute, flashing me their bits, asking me to touch their knockers, trying to undo my jeans and get at my old fella, everything. Seriously, I'm in the back and Tanya's holding my arms while Cindy's unbuttoning my flies and shoving her hand inside and all I can do is try and fight them off before they have my pants around my knees.

Stuart was in the front and none too happy about all this horseplay going on in the back but what could I do? Seriously, I spent most of the journey fighting them off, *à la* George Formby. It was something of a relief when we finally parked up and I could put some distance between the girls and my boxers.

'These them?' Stuart asked, staring across at a row of tennis courts.

'Yeah. Come on, we've got to go and see the man up in the hut before we start. Make sure everything's still kosher,' I told him, so we left John and the girls to bring up all the stuff. There wasn't much of it; a camera, a camera bag with rolls of film, a couple of tennis racquets and some strawberries and cream. Get the picture?

'I've booked all the courts for an hour, just for a little more privacy, but I also said we'd give this upstanding gentleman £50 for his trouble,' I explained, introducing Stuart to this mental stoner who took the money for the tennis courts.

'Yea', that's fiddy quid in cash, I don't take no cheques, ahhhight?' the gentleman added, wiping his hands down the front of his jumper. 'Come on, come on! Yeah, gi' dat to me, gi' dit ere, ahhhight.'

Stuart handed over the money, then gave us all a good laugh by asking for a receipt. The stoner looked at him for a minute, trying to work out whether he was serious or not, then just tore a page out of a blank notebook and wrote £150 on it.

'Dere, dat's fa you, I made it fa a ton more so's you's can gets more money, ahhhight? You wants annuver wun? I can rites you one fa a million quid if you likes. Makes you rich.' And he did just that. He ripped another sheet of paper out and scribbled on it '£100000 (a milloin pounds)' and stuffed it in Stuart's hand. 'If you get that, haff of it's mine, ahhhight?'

'Yes, well, okay. Come on, let's get cracking.'

John clipped together his camera and flash and shot off a few Polaroids, close-up and from afar, to gauge the lighting, but it was a beautifully clear and sunny morning so not much adjustment was needed.

'Alright, we've got an hour so let's get this done and get down the pub,' Stuart said, and we set to work putting the girls through their poses. All the horseplay went out the window now that we were doing it for real and under the clock, and we were able to snap off two rolls of intro and possible cover shots in no time at all.

'Okay, now both of you to the net and kissing. Yeah, that's it . . .' SNAP. 'Okay, Cindy, you lean right over the net so we can see your bum . . .' SNAP. 'Okay, John, get underneath them, that's it, down on the ground and you two stand over him so that he's shooting up your skirts . . .' SNAP. 'That's good, now let's do that one with pink . . .' SNAP SNAP SNAP.

The Common was pretty deserted so our little show went largely unnoticed. Two teenage truants who picked the day to end all days to bunk off school (but would never be believed by any of their friends in a million years), an old man and his Labrador, a couple of council labourers and a motorcycle courier were the extent of our audience. Them and, of course, our stoner attendant, who kept on trying to pass us a big fat joint every time we paused to change films. To anyone else who might've walked past, there was superficially nothing out of the ordinary. The girls still had their outfits on so the only obvious give-aways that something was amiss were the fact that a) they were absolute pin-up stunners; b) there was some bloke photographing their arseholes and; c) they were quite unbelievably shit at tennis.

'Here, mate, what are you doing this for?' one of the kids shouted over.

'Because we love tennis,' Stuart told him. 'Why aren't you at school?'

'Er, it's half-term,' he replied, standing there in school uniform with a satchel slung over his back. 'Are they going to get their tits out or what?' he asked.

'Yes, but you're only allowed to stay and watch if you've done your homework,' Stuart told them.

'We have,' they lied, making everyone except the old man and his dog laugh.

I was just starting to think we might even get away with it and do all we needed to do without attracting any unnecessary attention to ourselves, when all of a sudden, motorcycle couriers started pouring in from every conceivable angle. Word had got out; 'Forget your deliveries and get your arses down to Tooting Common quick, there's a porn shoot going on at the tennis courts.'

'We'd better get this done, and fast, before someone starts selling tickets,' Stuart said. 'Get the girls stripped off and do two rolls of fully naked shots and we can blow them up if need be, but I think we want to be on our way within twenty minutes.'

Before long there were a good three dozen assorted bikers and passers-by squashed against the fence watching us work, yet it didn't seem to bother the girls one bit. I asked them if they'd be willing to strip out of their dresses for the fully nude shots, expecting them to knock me back, but the girls didn't hesitate. A huge cheer went up as their dresses hit the deck and even the old man suddenly started cheering and clapping. The girls turned and posed for the audience, teasing them the same way they'd teased me in the car on the way down. They started kissing and stroking each other erotically, just yards from a swarming mass of excited testosterone.

'Get some of this,' I urged the photographer. 'Quick, take some pictures. Get the crowd in, this is fucking dynamite.'

The stoner behind Stuart started howling loudly as the girls got funky with each other. John knelt here, there and everywhere as he snapped off close-up shots of Tanya and Cindy doing the business. And it looked convincing to me,

I can tell you that. No more prompting was needed as suddenly I couldn't tell where simulation ended and real sex began. If anything, we had to calm them down to get shots we could use.

'Move your hand, pull your fingers out . . .' SNAP. 'Okay, lift your legs a little so you're not actually on her face' SNAP.

One of the bikers looked over at me, a tough, tattooed meat-head on a Yamaha, and said something I'd heard dozens of dozens of times before.

'Man, you've got the best job in the world!'

And you know what, at this precise moment in time, there was no arguing with him. It was a lovely sunny day and I was outdoors; I had two beautiful girls at my feet, screwing each other with everything they had, and I commanded total respect from every guy within a hundred yards of me. Days like these are few and far between. You need to fully appreciate them while you can.

'Hey, Godfrey, want to join us?' Cindy said, lifting her head out of Tanya's crotch and looking me right in the eye.

'Yeah, come on, Godfrey, get your cock inside me right now,' Tanya urged.

The rapidly swelling crowd (and by that I don't mean their numbers were increasing) cheered for all they were worth and suddenly started chanting my name. Stuart quick-stepped it over and told me to calm the girls down otherwise things were going to get really messy really quickly.

'How much more do we need?' I asked.

'Just a couple more shots. Give them their racquets and do one more roll, then we're out of here,' Stuart said, then looked at the crowd and added, 'if they let us.'

We urged John on and managed to temper the girls'

behaviour, though they were absolutely lapping up the adoration. My mind couldn't help but turn to my Femmy solicitor mate Samantha and wonder what she'd say if she could see me now. I didn't know, but I doubted her opinion of me would've improved.

With all the cheering and catcalls going on we didn't hear it at first. It was way off in the background, just one more noise in the traffic, something you hear every day in London and don't think twice about. The trouble was, it was growing louder and louder and it was coming our way.

'Shit! Police!' Stuart shouted and we all froze. The siren was turning into the Common and only a matter of yards away as we all suddenly ran around like headless chickens.

Stuart and John were at the top of their game though and were out of the courts and halfway to the car before I knew where my arse was.

'Holy shit! Quick, Cindy, Tanya, quick, come on!' I urged the girls, grabbing their dresses and bundling them butt-naked out of the courts and after the others. We sprinted across the grass and towards the car with one last cheer echoing in our ears before that was drowned out with a mechanical wail.

'Let's go, let's go,' I shouted as I ran between the girls. My mind was racing as fast as I was but oddly enough it wasn't with panic. Despite everything else that was going on around me, all I kept thinking, over and over again, was that I wished some of my mates could've seen me now. As it was, I was expecting to dine out on this anecdote for the rest of my life but an eyewitness or two would've been great.

'Stop, police!' someone shouted behind us, but we were way out in front and only fifty yards from the safety of the car. Ten more seconds and we'd be piling in the back and away. But suddenly we had even further to run as there were fifty-five yards between us and the car; then suddenly sixty; then seventy; then eighty; then ninety; then a hundred yards and then it was gone, disappeared off around a corner and gone.

They'd abandoned us. The utter utter bastards had abandoned us.

'What do we do now?' Cindy yelled, the confidence suddenly missing from her sweet West Country voice.

'Keep running or get nicked,' I shouted back and pointed towards the other side of the Common and a narrow alleyway leading to a housing estate. 'That way. If we can just find somewhere to hold up a minute, you can put your dresses back on and we can at least blend in a bit better.'

Yeah, two absolute stunners, wearing the skimpiest tennis dresses, walking down Tooting High Street. I was sure no-one was going to bat an eyelid at us.

I looked back around for the briefest of seconds and was lifted to see that one of the coppers had given up chasing us and was heading back to the car. We had a generous lead over the other one though and I reckoned we could lose her in the labyrinth of back streets and alleyways around the estate, long enough, at least, for the girls to get dressed again.

Dog walkers and joggers stopped in their tracks as the three of us ran past like an Electric Blue version of Benny Hill. As we approached the main road, I was half-hoping for one of those comedy pile-ups that you get in the movies, something to distract the attention of the police, but nothing like that happened – fucking careful drivers.

We charged across the road to a chorus of cheers and beeps and made it into the alleyway.

'Come on, this way,' I said, dragging the girls around a series of twists and turns, over a fence or two and into one of those electric generator areas. We ducked down behind the gate and tried to catch our breath.

The girls were sweaty, naked and excited and I was suddenly all alone with them. Tanya couldn't stop her giggling and I had to put my hand across her mouth to shut her up as the policewoman ran past outside. We waited a few heart-stopping minutes for the danger to pass and were relieved when it did.

'My heart is absolutely racing,' Cindy whispered, holding a hand to her heaving breasts.

'Mine too,' Tanya agreed. 'I haven't had this much fun in ages.'

The girls might've been loving the thrill of it all but I was more concerned with how we were going to get out of this mess.

'Here, here's your dresses, put them on,' I told them. 'We're not too far from Tooting Bec. There's a couple of pubs down there, we'll duck into the nearest one, have a quick drink and phone a cab. My place isn't too far from here and I can sort you both out with some clothes and cash to see you home. Agreed?'

'Ooh, Godfrey, you're our hero,' Tanya purred, both of them giggling in unison. 'Before we go anywhere, I think there's one very important thing we need to do first, right, Cin'?'

'Yeah. Let's do it,' Cindy grinned.

'What? What are you talking about?' I asked in confusion.

'A little unfinished business,' Cindy whispered in my ear as she unbuttoned my jeans and slipped her hand inside. This time, I didn't try and stop her.

'Oh, I see,' I said, my heart smashing violently inside my chest.

Tanya pulled my jeans and boxers down, then together, while hiding behind a fence and on the run from the police, two naked porn stunners gave me the best damn blow-job of my entire life.

Finally, I felt like a real pornographer.

16: Caught by the fuzz

Things went a bit downhill from there. When the girls went to put their dresses on, we found that we only had one of them. I must've dropped the other one during the chase and suddenly Tanya was naked for keeps.

'I don't think I can walk down the High Street like this,' Tanya said, holding her hands over her breasts.

'What are we going to do?' Cindy asked, pulling her dress on over her head.

'You'll have to leave me,' Tanya said. 'Go and get some clothes and bring them back for me. I'll stay here.'

Endorphins were swimming through my mind so I was pretty sanguine about just about everything. The Old Bill could peer over the fence and lock us all up as far as I was concerned, nothing was going to wipe the smile off my face. I think it was this attitude that helped me deal with the situation calmly and collectedly. What was it that Kipling said? 'If you can keep your head while all about you others are losing theirs, blahdy blahdy blah . . . etc'. I'll put money on it he'd just been gobbled off by a couple of right sorts just before he wrote that because I felt like a man . . . my son.

'No-one's leaving anyone anywhere. Here, take my t-shirt and put my boxers on,' I said, slipping out of my clothes and handing them to Tanya. 'I can go bare-chested, it won't matter too much. We might look odd but at least we're not breaking the law any more,' I told them as I pulled my jeans back on.

'Thank you Godfrey, you're a star,' Tanya said, covering herself up at last.

I peered over the gate, up and down the alleyway, but there was no sign of the police.

'We ready? Okay, let's go.'

We clambered back over the fence and dropped down into the alleyway. I knew I wouldn't be able to get in the pub now, not without a shirt, so we would have to walk back to mine. It was about a mile and a half but luckily I knew the back streets pretty well and already had a route in my head.

We quick-stepped it along the alleyway, then through a gap in a fence, along some waste ground and then through another alleyway.

People stared at us as we went by. Well, you would, wouldn't you? One bloke stripped to the waist, one girl in a skimpy junior tennis dress and one girl wearing boxer shorts and a t-shirt with Ron Jeremy doing it on the front. We were just walking along a side street towards the Broadway, when all of a sudden a police car crossed the road up ahead. The cop car didn't even pause for consideration when he saw us, he just stuck on his lights and started towards us.

'This way,' I yelled and we turned and started running in the opposite direction as fast as we could. If we could just get back to the gap in the fence and the alleyway and everything else, I was thinking, but it was hopeless, the Old Bill were nearly upon us. To make matters worse, Cindy stumbled on a loose paving slab and scuffed up her knee pretty bad. Blood started pouring down her leg and at that moment I saw that the game was up for her.

I had one last moment of clarity and handed Tanya a fiver and told her to make a break for it.

'Go on, go. The Tube Station's that way. Run. I'll take care of Cindy.'

Tanya was stuck in indecision so I shouted at her again and finally she sprinted off. Well, there was no point in all of us getting nicked, was there?

I bent down and put my arm around Cindy as the police car roared to a halt in front of us.

'Thank you, Godfrey,' Cindy said, her eyes full of gratitude. She leant towards me and tried to give me a kiss, but I pulled away at the last moment and kissed her on the forehead.

'Let's save it for another time, hey, shall we?' I said, sounding all heroic, though what I meant was, another time when you haven't just had my gunk in your gob.

'So, why don't you talk us through it again? What were you doing on Tooting Common this morning?' PC Butler asked me across the interview table. He and WPC Kensington remained completely expressionless, giving me a chronic case of the grins.

Talk your way out of this one, genius, someone was laughing way off in my brain.

Me and my Ron Jeremy t-shirt had been reunited, as unfortunately had Tanya and Cindy. All three of us knew not to implicate *Bling* or the company so it was agreed beforehand if it came to it that we'd have to take it on the chin (a bit like Cindy had earlier).

'Well, you're not going to believe this,' I started and PC Butler agreed, he wasn't. 'Tanya and Cindy are friends of mine. They're models. Anyway, we decided to meet up and have a game of tennis and we all just got a bit carried away.

We were having a game of dare-double-dare and, well, as you can see there's no calling their bluff.'

The two uniforms stared at me across the table, wearing uniform expressions.

'Whose idea was it for the girls to take their clothes off?' WPC Kensington asked.

'Er, I'm not sure. I think it was a joint decision all round, they suggested it and I said I thought it was a good idea, or I suggested and . . . er, vice versa,' I explained, tailing off at the end beneath their judgmental gazes.

'Why don't you tell us what you were really doing this morning?' PC Butler suggested.

'I have.'

'Well, I'm sorry, but I don't believe you.'

'Oh,' I said. 'What happens now?'

'Now you tell us the truth.'

'But I have,' I insisted.

'No you haven't, and you're just making things worse for yourself by lying to us,' PC Butler said.

'I can't help that,' I told them. 'I'm sorry that I'm making things worse for myself but this is the truth and I don't know what else you want me to say. Do you want me to make something up and tell you that? Wouldn't that get me into even more trouble?'

'You're in a whole lot of trouble already, you really don't want to get in any more,' WPC Kensington informed me.

'I know,' I replied.

'Okay then, now how about the truth? What were you doing on those tennis courts this morning?'

'Well, we were having a game of dare-double-dare, right, and I said . . .'

'Okay, let's stop right there, shall we?'

'What?'

'Mr Bishop, tell me something; what do you do for a living?'

'Er . . . oh . . . I'm a . . . I'm a journalist.'

'A journalist. And what newspaper do you work for?'

'Well, it's not really a newspaper, it's more of a magazine.'

'And what's the name of this magazine?'

'Um . . . *Bling*.'

'I see, and how would you describe the contents of *Bling*, the magazine that you work for?'

'Well, er, in a word – colourful.'

'Colourful? Can you be more specific?'

'Erm, not really, it's a very complicated question. I'm not really sure what you're getting at. I don't really do a lot on the design side.'

'Okay, let me put it like this, would it be fair to say that *Bling*, the magazine you work for, was full of pictures of women in the nude?'

'Hmm . . .' I mused, buying for time. 'It would be difficult to argue with that one,' I told him.

'Yes or no,' she insisted.

'Er . . . yes.'

'Let me ask you another question. I understand that magazines work two to three months ahead of publication. The edition that you're working on at the moment, when does it appear in the shops?'

'Ooh, well, now you've got me. I'm not really up with schedules.'

'June time?'

'Er . . . it could be, I don't really know.'

'What major sporting event takes place in June?'

'The Olympics?'

'Try Wimbledon.'

'Does it really? "Come on, Tim",' I said, raising a fist.

'So, you were shooting your Wimbledon edition of *Bling* on the tennis courts of Tooting Common, weren't you?'

'What? Absolutely not,' I gasped, outraged at the suggestion.

'Look, the sooner you admit it the sooner you can go home, so come on, that was what you were doing, wasn't it?'

'No.'

'Why was there a guy taking pictures then and why did he run off as soon as we turned up?'

'I didn't see any guy. He was probably just some old pervert with one of those long range lenses.'

PC Butler leaned back and snorted with frustration. I guess he thought they had me banged to rights and I'd cough it all just as soon as I was pinched. But what would be the point? I was caught, I knew that, and nobody could help me. Boo-hoo, where was the gain in grassing Stuart and John up? Okay, you could argue that I might get myself off the hook by claiming that I was just the monkey and that Stuart was the organ grinder, but if in order to unhook myself I had to stoop to the level of a snitch, well, let's just say I had a bit more self-respect than that. I mean, come on, I was a man, I knew what I was doing. I was a bit too old to go bawling my eyes out in front of the headmaster that it was actually a load of big boys who'd forced me to hold some first year's head down the bog and flush the chain as I heard the cane swishing behind me. And it didn't matter that Stuart and John had left us behind to get pinched because that was their level. This was mine.

'You know, they're really going to throw the book at you. You realise that, don't you?' PC Butler gloated. 'We have witnesses who claim that the girls were not only naked, but that you were instructing them to perform sex acts on each other in front of two fourteen-year-old boys. That will not be looked upon kindly by the magistrate. I'd be surprised if you weren't looking at prison time for that sort of thing and five years on the sex offenders' register. How would you like to have to disclose that every time you went for a new job or moved house?' he asked.

I merely stared at him, my cockiness suddenly gone.

'Is there anything you'd like to tell us now?' WPC Kensington asked when I failed to say anything.

I stayed silent a moment longer and thought about my options. That couldn't be true, could it? That I would be classed as a sex offender? Surely this was a bluff. But if it was, it was a very good bluff.

No, I couldn't believe that. People streaked at cricket matches all the time and only ever got a slap on the wrist. Mind you, streaking was one thing, wanking yourself off when you got to the stumps was another.

No, I couldn't believe it, it had to be a bluff.

Finally I answered.

'Only what I said before. It was a game of dare-double-dare that got out of hand.'

This time, though, I didn't smile when I said it.

WPC Kensington took me back to my cell and told me I'd have to stay in custody while they talked to the girls and decided what the charges would be.

She was just about to close the door when she looked up and down the corridor and spoke to me softly.

'Look, we all know what you were doing, between you and me, why don't you say something?'

'I can't and I won't. I'm sorry, but I'm just not a blabbermouth and I never have been.'

'Well, you're a fool to yourself,' she said.

'I know, maybe, but in my job you end up having to keep

a lot of things to yourself. Bit like your job, I would imagine.'

WPC Kensington laughed at that.

'Getting your kit off in public. That's hardly keeping things to yourself.'

'Well, yeah, fair point.'

'You know why we know that you were doing a Wimbledon photoshoot for your magazine?' she asked, but I stayed silent. 'Because another porno mag was arrested up in Walthamstow three days ago doing exactly the same thing. Every copper in the Met must've heard about it. We did. These things get around, you know. So, when we got wind that there was someone on our patch doing the same thing, we couldn't believe our luck. There must've been about six patrol cars all after you at one point this morning. Feel flattered?'

'Oh yeah, cushty.'

WPC Kensington smiled triumphantly.

'Let me ask you something, where do you find the girls to do that sort of thing? I mean, I wouldn't have the nerve. How do you find people to strip for you?'

I sensed she was trying to entrap me, but I couldn't quite see how. I answered her question very carefully, watching every word so as not to incriminate myself.

'Well, the girls volunteer for it. They read the magazine, then send in pictures of themselves and, if we like the look of them, we might invite them in to meet us.'

'And then you take pictures of them?'

'Yes,' I answered, unsure of where this was going. I didn't want to mention any photographers because I figured she was trying to drag John into this so I told her that I took the shots. Tell her this, I thought, and it might persuade her that this morning was no photoshoot because I wasn't found with a camera.

'And have you photographed many girls?' she asked.

'Oh yes, hundreds,' I told her. 'But I can't really go into it because, like I say, a lot of the girls don't want anyone knowing so I have to respect that,' I said, hoping that would throw her off the scent.

'Okay. Well, I've got to shut the door now but, look, don't mention this to anyone, and I mean anyone, but I wouldn't worry too much about that sex register stuff. I think that's very unlikely. Not for this. But, like I say, don't you tell a soul I told you. Okay?'

'Okay,' I agreed and breathed a huge sigh of relief as she shut the door.

But then, why would she tell me that? What was her game? God, women were such conniving bastards, weren't they? I decided I had to be even more on my toes around WPC Kensington than her mate PC Butler.

He might've been a cunt, but at least I knew where I stood with him.

17: Buck rogered

It was another five hours before we were eventually released. PC Butler and WPC Kensington had one more crack at me but I stuck to my story and refused to budge an inch. The girls must've done the same because at about six o'clock all three of us were charged and bailed to appear before the beak two weeks to the day.

The charges: Public Indecency and Breach of the Peace.

That didn't sound too bad to me, a fine at worst, I figured, so the three of us left to go home. Tanya and Cindy were provided with clothes, which put the mockers on me getting them both back to my place, and I had to make do with a kiss goodbye from each of them at the Tube Station.

What a day!

I had a dozen messages from Stuart waiting for me on my answerphone when I got home that evening but I couldn't be bothered to respond to any of them.

The next morning I'd barely got my arse into my seat when Stuart called me into his office and drilled me about what had happened.

I told him all about it (leaving out the blow-job) and asked him why they'd just shot off and abandoned us. Stuart said that that was John. It was, after all, John's car and John had been the one behind the wheel but Stuart could've made him stop.

'I tried, I even threatened him but he refused,' Stuart insisted.

'Well, the girls were fucking furious with you,' I told him.

'Never mind all that, what did you tell the Old Bill? You didn't mention *Bling*, did you?'

'No, I didn't,' I replied and gave him the whole story of what I'd said and what I'd been charged with. When I was finished Stuart went off to see Peter and I was left to my own devices.

'What was all that about?' Paddy wanted to know, so I went through the whole thing again, although this time I replaced the martyrdom and resentment with exaggeration and high comedy.

'You fucking silly cunt,' Hasseem laughed as the story poured out.

As I was talking, Roger answered my phone and called over to me that Peter wanted to see me in his office. He wanted to see me in his office, right now.

What now?

'Maybe he wants to talk to you about your pay rise,' Matt suggested.

I knocked on Peter's door and found Stuart in there already. I took a seat and tried to look as innocent and as non-threatening as possible.

'Okay, Godfrey. Why don't you tell me about yesterday?'

So, I told the story again, this time adding the words, 'So Stuart said . . .' or 'Then Stuart told me to . . .' or 'I wasn't sure but Stuart reckoned . . .' etc, at the start and end of every sentence.

When I was finished, I was dismissed for the time being and heard nothing more that day.

In fact, I didn't even see Stuart again. He and Peter went out somewhere and didn't come back.

So, I did what I always did on such days and went to the pub for the afternoon.

First thing Monday morning, I'm talking eleven o'clock here, I was called in to see Peter again.

In his office was himself, Stuart and Peter's solicitor. I thought I'd been called in to be given legal advice for my upcoming court appearance.

In fact, I'd been called in to be fired.

'What?'

'I'm sorry, but the company cannot leave itself open to litigation,' Peter told me. 'The police have been in contact with us, as well as the parents of two teenage boys. If we don't act we are, by definition, admitting responsibility.'

'Yes, those kids' parents could take us to the cleaners,' Peter's solicitor explained. 'Disciplinary action must be taken against you, and all links between you and the company must be severed.'

'But this was your idea,' I said, pointing accusingly at Stuart.

'My idea was the shoot, my idea wasn't to do it in public where the whole world could see it happen. You should've booked a private court. I told you that this was your responsibility and you agreed to it.'

'Yeah, but I didn't think I'd be fucking nicked and sacked for it.'

'That's what responsibility's about, I'm afraid, holding your hands up and accepting the consequences,' Stuart said without even the slightest trace of irony.

'You fucking cunts . . .'

'Now hold your horses,' Peter said, stopping me before I

could get into my stride. 'I think you should listen to our proposal before you say anything else. Nigel?'

All eyes turned to the plank in the pin-stripes. He paused for effect, like he was Rumpole of the Windmill or something, then turned to me. Or should that be, looked down at me? Even though we were both sat at roughly the same height, some people have an unerring ability to make it seem as though they have to look down at you in order to establish eye contact. This was how Nigel talked to me and I yearned to see him trapped in a burning bus.

'Naturally, the company regrets the events of the past few days and, short of admitting any sort of liability, we would be prepared to offer you terms.'

'Buy me off, you mean?'

'No, that's not it at all, we're . . .'

'Look, it's okay, let's not beat about the bush here, I am for sale. What are we talking about here?'

Nigel looked at Peter, who nodded at him to continue.

'Well, taking into account your salary and today's current job climate, together with age and . . .' Nigel cut the spiel when he saw me doing the universal spin-on gesture. 'Six grand.'

I thought about that for a second, then suggested, 'Twenty.'

Everyone laughed, then Peter's face turned serious again and he just said, 'No.'

'Ten then.'

'Six.'

'Come on, meet me half-way here, eight grand?'

'Six.'

'Come on, another grand for goodwill. It's not going to fucking bankrupt you, for fuck's sake.'

Peter thought it over.

'Six grand,' he said. 'Take it or leave it, we don't have to give you anything if we don't want to.'

'Alright, six grand,' I agreed, caving in. 'But I want that tax-free.'

Peter and Nigel swapped loving looks and finally conceded some ground.

'Now let's turn to the matter of your court appearance,' Nigel said. 'Do you have a solicitor?' he asked.

'No, I was going to defend myself.'

Again, laughter all round.

'Sorry about that,' Peter said, wiping a tear from his eye. 'Oh dear, right, well, we're prepared to appoint a solicitor for you and meet all the costs. They'll be someone not directly associated with the company, but they'll be a very good solicitor nevertheless. Are you happy with that?'

'Er . . . yeah, okay. And the girls too? You'll get one for Tanya and Cindy too?'

'They'll act for all three of you,' Nigel assured me. 'Furthermore, the company is prepared to pay any fine you receive as a result of this case on the condition that you sign a document admitting sole responsibility.'

'What if I don't get a fine? What if I get Community Service or something?'

'We've thought of that; again we're prepared to pay you compensation of £10 an hour for every hour of Community Service you're sentenced to. Same with prison time, although this is highly unlikely. We'll pay you £50 for every day you spend in prison. Again, we don't have to do any of this, but the company wants to look after you,' Nigel assured me, and for a moment I thought he was going to give me a big hug. 'That is the offer, I think you'll find it's fair. Take it or leave it.'

'And the girls too, you'll pay their fines?'

'You should just worry about yourself,' Peter suggested.

'No, bollocks. I'm not signing anything unless you agree to pick up the girls' fines too,' I told them in no uncertain terms. Now, you might think that this was uncharacteristically noble of me, and you'd be right. But you know, everyone should try being a hero once in their lives, just to see how it fits. Besides, I knew it was probably the last opportunity I'd ever get in my life to ingratiate myself with two fucktastically foxy porno models and that sort of realisation concentrates the mind.

Peter and Nigel asked me to step outside for a moment and when I stepped back in they agreed.

I could see Stuart's cogs whirling over and knew I had to make phonecalls to Tanya and Cindy before he did, otherwise he'd try and nab all the credit.

'Okay, that's all agreed. You'll be paid up to the end of the month and receive a copy of the amended agreement along with a cheque. If you'll just sign here in three places then we won't keep you any longer. You can clear your stuff and go,' Peter told me.

'And you'll definitely pay our fines, no matter how big they may be?'

'It's in the agreement, the confidential agreement, I should add. Yes, we'll definitely pay your fines,' he assured me.

'Okay then, where do I sign?' I asked, really looking forward to punching the magistrate in the throat.

18: Hello hello hello

In my limited experience, I've come to the conclusion that things usually happen to you when you're least expecting them. Some days you can get all threaded-up and go down Fanny Fandango's Discotheque brimming with confidence, dentist-white teeth and immaculately gelled hair, yet go home at the end of the evening with nothing more than two pieces of chicken and chips. Other days you can go down the supermarket in a six-day-old t-shirt and slippers and end up meeting the woman you'll spend the rest of your life with. You never can tell. I think it's God's way of keeping us on our toes.

Or women's.

After I left Peter's office, I spent the next three days drunk. I would've spent the Thursday drunk too but the police phoned me in the morning (just before the pubs opened) and asked if I'd be home that evening. What was I going to say, no? So, I sat around watching telly and working out convincing answers to every possible question. I half-thought about phoning my newly appointed solicitor to have him present, but I couldn't be bothered and figured I'd handle the situation myself. Well, I'd done alright so far.

I just wouldn't say anything. I'd appear to co-operate but I wouldn't add anything to what I'd said already.

Just after seven there was a knock at the door and I went down and found WPC Kensington staring back at me.

'What's this, CID or something? Where's your uniform?' I asked.

'Oh, I got off duty an hour ago. This is nothing official, I just wanted to ask your advice about something. May I come in?' she said.

'Yeah, sure. Come on up.'

WPC Kensington came in and followed me up the communal stairs to my first-floor room. She shut the door behind her once inside and came and sat on the sofa next to me.

'Did you pay a lot for this room?' she asked.

'Only in terms of social standing,' I replied, a well-worn joke of mine that has yet to win a single laugh. 'You wanted to ask my advice about something?' I asked suspiciously.

'Yes, but this is strictly confidential, you understand. You have to give me your word you'll never tell a soul about this without my permission, my job depends on it,' she told me. 'Do I have your word?'

'Of course, anything you say will be strictly between the two of us.'

I wondered what the hell she was going to say and sensed a little tension in her voice. She'd come across at the station as a stern sort of fish but now here she was apparently nervous.

Hang on a minute. She wasn't thinking about . . .

No. That couldn't be it.

Could it?

'Well, basically, I'm kind of interested in how you . . . how I . . . might go about appearing in one of your magazines.

Like I said, you can't tell anyone because I could lose my job over this, so I just wanted to sound you out first, find out about the procedure. Would I be able to do it anonymously? Not show my face or have to use my real name?' she asked. It took me a moment or two to gather, first, my thoughts, and then my socks, as they'd blown right across the room.

'Erm, well, yes, it's possible. Hardly any of the girls use their real names anyway and as for covering your face up, yes, some women do that. Though I should say not in the mags like *Bling* that use professional models. You'd be better off sending in your pictures to someone like *Froth*, who deal with the er . . . (how shall I put this?) amateur enthusiasts. With *Froth* you can just send in Polaroids or normal 35mm snaps that you take at home and get those printed. You would have to send in ID and a model release too though, not for publication or anything, just for our records. That would probably be your best bet,' I told her. I'd have to make sure I got hold of a copy of that issue of *Froth*, that was for sure.

WPC Kensington gave this some thought and said she liked the sound of it.

'How do I go about getting my pictures taken?' she then asked.

'Well, you just, I don't know . . . do you have a husband or a boyfriend or someone who could take them for you?'

'Yes, but I really don't want anyone I know to know about this. I'm just doing this for myself, no-one else,' she explained.

'Well, you could set the camera up on a self-timer.'

'That's a possibility, I suppose. Or you could take them for me,' she then suggested, and I had to go over and collect my socks again. 'I know it's a bit of a cheek, me asking you this, but as far as I'm concerned the fewer the people who know about it the better, and you are a professional. Could you do this for me?' she pouted. 'I've got money, I can pay you for your time.'

How does that expression go? Fuck me!

I couldn't believe my ears, here was WPC Kensington, who only last week had me in cuffs, offering to give me money to take pictures of her rhubarb. Naturally, this didn't need even a second's hesitation, though I tried not to act too keen in case I gave her the creeps.

'Of course I'll take them for you, and look, don't worry about the money. It would be my pleasure,' I told her, and she could be sure about that.

WPC Kensington broke out into a big nervous smile and thanked me.

'Do you want to do them here, tonight?' she asked.

'Yes, but I'll just have to nip out across the road and get some film for my camera. I won't be five minutes, it's literally just across the road. You will wait, won't you?'

She merely nodded her head by way of reply and gave me a little smile.

I pretended to check my pockets for my keys while adjusting the lie of my jeans, then jumped up out of the sofa and headed for the door.

'Just five minutes, that's all I'm going to be. Don't go anywhere,' I almost pleaded with her.

I threw myself down the stairs and out of the front door as if the hounds of hell were after my ass. The late night shop, which was usually a leisurely ten-minute stroll away, suddenly seemed like the other side of Middle Earth. I sprinted as fast as my legs could carry me, terrified that WPC Kensington would get cold tits and do a runner while I was away. I kept pleading to whoever was listening, 'Please, please, please, let this happen,' almost sobbing at the prospect of returning home and finding her gone. I didn't think I could take the disappointment if that were to happen.

But then, what was I getting so worked up about? I was, after all, only going to take pictures. She hadn't promised to shag me or anything. In fact, the possibility of sex seemed distinctly unlikely, seeing as she had a 'husband or boyfriend or someone' and had approached me because I was 'a professional'.

Oh, bollocks.

Should I try it on? Should I try it on like that other photographer did and suggest some pictures of her sucking someone off (and leave it up to her to work out who I was talking about)? Oh yes, very smart move. She'd see right through me and have her clothes back on and me in cuffs for the second time this week before I could say 'Jack Toff'. Of all the people to try it on with, a policewoman was perhaps not the smartest.

In fact, what if this thing was a ruse, a honey trap to get me to incriminate myself even further and I was walking right into it?

That thought stopped me in my tracks.

Of course that was what this was. How was I being so blind? My little head was doing all the talking and my big head was listening but it would be both of us, together with our attractive virgin backside, that would end up in the slammer.

No, wait, that couldn't be it. That would be entrapment. She'd asked me to take the pictures, there was nothing illegal about that. As long as that was all I did, take a few pictures of her, there was nothing they could get me on. It would be a completely wasted operation. In fact, it might even be a good way of getting the other charges against me dropped, by showing persecution. Okay, so that's all I'd do, just take a few pictures.

I wondered how far WPC Kensington was prepared to go with the ruse.

Would she actually do as she'd said and take her clothes off for the camera, or would she bottle out at the last moment when she realised I wasn't taking the bait?

I returned with two rolls of film after fifteen minutes and found her still sitting on the sofa.

'I hope you don't mind, but I helped myself to a scotch just to calm my nerves,' she said, and I told her that was quite alright. She could have as much as she needed.

I loaded up my camera, a simple 35mm Canon, and asked her if she was ready.

'Shall we move you over onto the bed then?' I suggested, and she downed the last of her glass.

'Okay, let's do it.'

I put on some music to relax us both and positioned her on the bed. She had a knee-length skirt on and dark stockings and when I told her to open her legs, I saw that she had on matching pants and suspenders. I snapped away as she lay there spread-eagled in front of me and my woody soon lost all reservations and returned with interest.

'Undo a few of your buttons on your blouse,' I told her and she complied. If this was a sting, I had to admire her dedication. Time to get her to do something dirty.

'Okay, rub the front of your panties with one hand and pull down your bra with the other,' I half-said, half-choked. Again she complied without hesitation and when her nipples popped into view I felt a head rush I'd not felt since watching Zoe strip all that time ago.

'That's good, that's really good. Now lose the blouse completely. Take it off and sling it to one side . . .' SNAP

SNAP SNAP . . . 'Now the bra, lose the bra . . .' SNAP SNAP. 'Okay, cup your tits and lick one of your nipples . . .' SNAP SNAP BLIMEY.

At least I knew she wasn't wearing a wire. There was now no hiding the bulge in my trousers and I even pointed it out to WPC Kensington to diffuse any potential awkwardness.

'It doesn't matter how many of these I do, I just can't help getting a hard-on.'

'That's good,' she smiled, eyeing my packet. 'I'd be upset if you didn't have one.'

'Take your skirt off,' I told her (SNAP).

WPC Kensington lay just in front of me in her undies and high heels, rubbing herself all over, panting hard and looking me straight in the eye.

Okay, I thought to myself. Let's see if you're really ready to go through with this.

'Lose the pants.'

She didn't even flinch. She lifted her bum and slipped them off, then opened her legs, showing me everything.

SNAP SNAP SNAP SNAP SNAP SNAP SNAP SNAP SNAP SNAP SNAP SNAP SNAP SNAP SNAPPIDY SNAP . . .

'Damn it, hold on, I've got to change the film already,' I told her. I knew I should've got 36 exposures. Unlike most models I knew, WPC Kensington didn't attempt to cover herself up while my shaky hands attempted this fiddly operation. She just lay there, stroking herself all over and staring at the ceiling.

God, I wanted to shag her so badly. She might not have been as stunning as Tanya or as cute as Cindy, and she'd need a little airbrushing around the tits before she could be printed, but she was still a looker, no question about it.

I had the film back in and was standing over her again, this time considerably closer.

'Tell me what you want me to do and I'll do it,' she said. 'Make me do things.'

'Pleasure yourself in front of me and I'll take some pictures.'

WPC Kensington went straight into it. She whacked herself off more frantically than . . . well, I knew I would whenever I remembered this rainy Thursday in Tooting.

SNAP SNAP SNAP.

She was moaning like a banshee now and I was right there with her. I knew it was the wrong thing to do and that I was meant to be a professional but this was absolutely killing me. Okay, sure, yeah, it was probably a trap, but even if it was I couldn't help but walk right into it.

'Okay, right, listen,' I grimaced, unbuttoning my flies, my heart absolutely smashing against my ribcage. 'I just want to get some pictures of you with this in your mouth.'

WPC Kensington leant up and looked at my meat, then seized it like a girl possessed and stuffed it into her mouth. I'd never known such a wanton blow-job in all my life. So much so in fact that it made me wonder if this was what it would be like to be sucked off by a Velociraptor.

'Oh God, yes!' I called to the heavens as she worked me like a suction pump. SNAP SNAP SNAP.

WPC Kensington was so short of breath that it took her three attempts to tell me to take some pictures of me fucking her. I pushed her back on the bed as she ripped the shirt off my back and yanked my trousers and pants down, painfully twanging the old fella. As I climbed aboard I felt an overwhelming sense of relief that I was finally going to get to experience sex, rather than disappointment.

However, I should just say that the mind can play funny

tricks on you. I know it sounds stupid, but even at this point, with me rogering her bandy, I still wasn't one hundred per cent convinced that I was actually going to get to shag her properly. I'd gone through such a cruel drought (Tanya and Cindy aside) and known so many last-minute knockbacks that my mind refused to take for granted the fact that we were now having sex. I continued to SNAP away just for show and it was only when I told WPC Kensington that I was having difficulty taking pictures with her moving about so much and she replied, 'Well, put the fucking camera down then,' that I finally accepted the facts.

'Oh yeah, give it to me! Give it to me hard!' she was yelping, slamming me in and out of her for all she was worth. 'Now from behind.' 'Now with me on top.' 'Now up against the wall.' 'Now me doing you with this.'

'What?'

I'd never known anything like it. Yes, it had been a long and arduous drought and yes, I'd pined for sex more times than I cared to remember, but fuck me, it caught up with me with a vengeance.

She was insatiable. That was the only word for her, absolutely insatiable.

I had gouges out of my back, bite marks on my nipples, cuts and bruises all over and a black eye before the night was out. We must've done it every which way but loose, and then done it loose, for there was nothing left taut on either of us by eleven, and I put in the performance of a lifetime.

I don't know what her home life was like but she was the dirtiest girl I've ever known. She told me that she just couldn't bring herself to do these things with her boyfriend because she'd be too embarrassed all the rest of the time, but with me, a low-life scumbag pornographer, she could do or say anything because I didn't matter to her one little bit. I was just a fuck.

Then she asked if I wanted her to piss on my face.

'Not especially, but thanks for the offer.'

'You want to piss on mine then?'

'Er . . . not really,' I told her. 'Besides, I can never go when someone's watching me.'

'Let me know if you change your mind,' she said as she attempted to coax one last fight out of my battle-weary cock.

And she got it too, though it weren't much to write about, so I won't bother.

Just before midnight she showered, gargled and thanked me for a spectacular evening (her words, not mine), then asked me what I was going to do with the pictures. I told her to photocopy her birth certificate and passport and send me a copy along with a letter confirming her address and telephone number so she could be contacted by Jackie or Mary for verbal confirmation.

'We have to go through all that?' she asked, reluctantly.

'I'm afraid so,' I told her.

'I'm not sure I want to give out my details and I certainly don't want anyone ringing me at home. Can't you just slip a couple in somewhere discreetly?'

It would be difficult now that I'd lost my job (though I didn't tell her this), but possible if a few of the boys were willing to do me a favour or two.

'I'll see what I can do. Now you take care.'

Well, it might be breaking the rules but how could I refuse a woman who'd only minutes earlier had my spuds in her mouth.

19: Court rogering

You know, I always wondered if there was a God upstairs who looked down over all of us. Well, now I know for a fact there is – and he has a really creative sense of humour.

'Okay, I've spoken to the clerk and told him that you're all here so we just have to wait for our case to be called. Don't go wandering too far away, because if we miss our turn we'll get bumped right to the end of the day's business,' Samantha told me, Tanya and Cindy.

You may remember that I'd met Samantha before. She was my femmy solicitor friend from the Philip Goss party and I was the evil skin trader. Well, here she was now representing me and two of the women I exploited. She didn't choose to take us on, moreover, she was 'asked' by her boss as she was the firm's only woman and it was felt that female representation might look better from the bench. I know this because she told me three days earlier when we all went to see her. But hey, you know, what could she do? I suppose she could've claimed a conflict of interests and explained to the senior partner that representing such a person went against her high moral principles but, considering she'd sucked her boss off more times than he'd had hot and salty dinners just to get her arse in the chair in the first place, I don't suppose that would've cut much mayonnaise with him. Besides, solicitors don't have to like their clients and I doubt there are too many that do.

'Isn't she that bird you were chatting up at that party?' Paddy asked as Samantha walked away. Paddy, Matt, Hasseem and even Hazel had all come along for support. Also, Paddy had a little camera with him and he figured he'd try and get a few shots of Tanya and Cindy quickly whipping their bits out when no-one was looking and get a spread out of it for the mag. Unbelievably, Tanya and Cindy agreed (for a fee) and had already slipped out of their panties and done a couple of shots on the steps outside.

'Yeah, that's her,' I replied.

'Nice arse,' he commented. 'You reckon I can get a couple of shots of her with the girls?'

'What, for *Ace*? Yeah, she'd love that.'

'You never know,' he said.

'Ask her anyway. It'll be a laugh whatever.'

'Alright, hang on here, I'll go and have a word,' he said and I watched him jump up out of his seat and go after her. I was looking forward to seeing her reaction but at that moment I was distracted by someone walking past who I knew would be well up for anything I could think of.

'Hello, WPC Kensington, isn't it?' I said, stretching out my hand. WPC Kensington shook it and gave me a polite smile.

'Hello, Godfrey, how are you?'

'Oh, fine. And you? I haven't seen you since the day you arrested me,' I told everyone within earshot.

'Yes, that's right, you haven't,' she confirmed, unbelievably stilted. We looked round and saw Matt staring at the both of us suspiciously. A lengthy awkward silence followed before WPC Kensington explained that she had to get on, but she'd see me in court later, so I said 'cheerio' and wondered if this was a good time to ask her if she still wanted me to piss all over her face.

'Well, I'll be off then,' she said, then added quietly, 'I'll give you a call next week' and wandered away.

'What's going on there?' Matt asked when I sat back down.

'I'll explain later,' I told him, and I'd need to as I had a couple of photos for him, but I didn't really want to get them out here.

The day dragged on, as days sat around waiting usually do. The morning turned into lunchtime, lunchtime turned into pub-time and pub-time unfortunately turned into afternoon, so it was all back to the magistrates' court to sit around and wait some more. Happily, though, we all had a healthy glow about us now and those few beers (or in the case of Tanya and Cindy, four G&Ts each) made a boring few hours a little more bearable.

I was up and wandering around, just to stretch my legs, when I walked past the toilets and Tanya emerged from the ladies.

'Hey, Godfrey, have you got the camera?' she asked, looking from side to side.

'No, Paddy's got it.'

'Go and get it. I'll wait here.'

I thought what she wanted was to do a couple of shots by the bog door but when I returned she bundled me into the ladies and then into one of the cubicles.

'It's alright, they're all empty. Let's do a few rude shots,' she said, hitching up her skirt and spreading her legs. I know, I should've refused and told her she was going to get us both nicked again, but then sometimes you just have to do these things, don't you? Besides, I was bored out of my mind so taking pictures of Tanya's smoo was a nice distraction.

She stood on the seat and squatted down as I dropped between her legs and started SNAPPING away.

'Do pink,' I told her and she spread herself with one hand while balancing against the cubicle wall with the other. 'Nice,' I whispered as I took more shots.

'You like?' she said, slipping a finger inside herself then wiping it over my face.

We both giggled and tried to be quiet but neither of us could help ourselves as she clattered and slid all over the plastic seat. The situation was so fucking preposterous, here we were in the court bogs, doing exactly the thing that had got us to court in the first place. Jesus, if we got nicked for this they really would throw the book at us, but fuck it all, this was something I was going tell my grandchildren about.

I don't know which of us instigated it or how it came about, but before I'd shot more than half a dozen pictures, I had my pants around my ankles and was doing Tanya hard up against the door.

'Yeah, yeah. Fuck me, yeah,' she panted, and I was half-tempted to answer, 'I am'. Suddenly, I didn't care if anyone heard us or not, I was fucking an absolutely stunning porn model and everyone else could go to hell. I knew for a fact – for a fact – that I'd never have anyone this gorgeous again so I wasn't stopping for anyone until the deed was well and truly done. Life was all downhill from this moment on anyway.

They could bang me up for five years after this, I wouldn't care.

Tanya's breath smelt sweet on my face and she smiled mischievously as I piled in up her for all I was worth. Her body was firm and light and she complied to my every touch like a pro. Wow, this was great! This was fucking great, I kept thinking to myself. First Tanya and Cindy noshing me off, then WPC Kensington, and now this. I think it is safe to say I was experiencing something of a purple patch and loving every second of it. Thank you, God. Thank you, thank you, thank you.

'Oohh, you're pretty good, you know, Godfrey.' I can't remember if she actually said this or not but I thought I'd chuck it in anyway.

Tanya ruffled up my hair with her fingers as we kissed and at one point I couldn't tell which was my tongue and which was hers.

This was great! This was fucking great!

Tanya transferred her attention to my earhole and the pair of us almost went crashing to the ground.

The sudden unexpectedness of the whole situation combined with the thrill of doing something really wrong (and really fucking stupid) had the two of us overdosing on adrenaline. I'd heard the expression 'drunk with lust' before but I'd never really known what it had meant until this moment.

It's something I can wholeheartedly recommend.

'You're so big, Godfrey,' Tanya probably said.

Reality came crashing back to the pair of us with a knock on the cubicle door. Tanya and I froze in mid-thrust and we barely dared to breathe. After a moment or two, Tanya shouted out, 'Won't be a minute, just going to the toilet,' then she looked into my eyes and did something that I'll take to the grave with me. It might not sound much to you, considering what else we'd been doing, but it's the thing I think about most whenever I revisit that afternoon in my mind – there we were, against the cubicle door, our bodies entwined and breathless with passion, and she leaned forward and planted the tiniest, most gentle little kiss on my lips.

It was a moment of genuine true affection and I loved her deeply at that moment.

'Tanya?' a voice asked from the other side of the door.

'Yes?' Tanya replied, her eyes fixed to mine.

'Who have you got in there with you? Is Godfrey in there with you?' she asked and I recognised it as Samantha's voice.

'No,' Tanya told her and gave me another little kiss.

Samantha went into the next cubicle, climbed up on the bog seat, as was the vogue of the day, and peered over the wall at us.

'What the bloody hell are you two doing?' she demanded.

'Making babies,' I told her, and me and Tanya laughed.

'Get the fuck out of there right now, if anyone catches you you'll be strung up.'

I considered this, not for very long admittedly, then told her, 'I haven't finished yet.'

Tanya smiled at that and slowly we started grinding again.

'I don't give a shit, get out of there.'

'Not a chance,' Tanya replied, responding to my every touch.

'I'll get the Clerk of Courts if you don't stop that right now,' Samantha threatened, so I told her she could go and get Lawrence of Arabia if she wanted, I wasn't stopping for anything.

'Look, you're our representation,' Tanya said, looking up at her. 'So go and represent us by keeping a look-out.'

'This is madness, you can't do this,' she said.

'Watch us,' I told her, mildly exciting myself at the thought.

'Christ al-bloody-mighty . . .' Samantha ranted to herself, clambering off the toilet seat and out of the cubicle. 'Are you coming out or what?'

'Not just yet,' I said, driving in and out of Tanya with mounting urgency.

'I mean it, I'll go and get the Clerk.'

'No you won't.'

That seemed to take the wind out of Samantha's sails because she dithered about for a few moments longer, then said, 'Well, just bloody hurry up then.'

'Will do, keep an eye out for us, will you, we won't be long.'

'No, I don't think we will,' Tanya gasped by way of a reply. 'Oh yes!' she moaned. 'Oh yes, that's it. Oh God.'

It's funny, she hadn't been that vocal before Samantha had appeared but all of a sudden she couldn't keep her trap shut.

'Oh yeah. Oh no. Don't stop. That's fantastic,' Tanya told me and Samantha. 'Oh yeah! Oh yeah! Oh yeah! Oh God. No. No. No. Yes. No. Oh fuck!'

I didn't have a clue what she was banging on about, all I knew was that I was getting rave reviews and you can't argue with that.

'Oh God. Oh God. Oh God,' she kept on crying. 'Yes yes yes. Oh God, yes, that's it, I'm going to come. Oh yes, don't stop that. Harder. Harder. Ooooohhhhhh!' she howled in my ear, tensing up and crashing against the door, then going all limp on me.

Suddenly there was no stopping me, I was like a jack-rabbit on Viagra and I slammed her against the door again and again and again. Tanya could only hold on for the ride as I galloped up the last straight and headed for the finishing line. She bit my ears, kissed my neck and made short work of my carefully gelled hair until eventually, with one final deep thrust, I exploded inside her.

'Oh YES!' one of us called out, though to this day I've no idea who.

We stayed in that position for a few brief heavenly seconds as the endorphins washed over us, and kissed one more time before reluctantly disengaging.

Jesus, I was absolutely done in as I tried to straighten myself up. I don't know quite how to describe it. I guess the only way would be like this; you know how when you go swimming and you're not very fit? You do ten lengths of the pool and just about manage it, but when you go to get out of the water you can barely stand? Well, that was me opening the cubicle door, all slack-jawed and wobbly kneed. Tanya looked fit to drop herself and when we emerged, the gobsmacked look on Samantha's face was worth all the curry in India.

I staggered past her without stopping, but gave her a little wink as I exited the bog. Behind me, just as the door was swinging shut, I heard Tanya tell Samantha, 'Now that boy knows what he's doing.'

And this time, she really did say it.

About ten minutes later, out in the waiting hall, Samantha asked me if she could have a quiet word. I prepared myself for a long stern lecture, or guessed she was planning on telling me that she was ditching the case, but instead she just handed me a plain envelope and told me I'd dropped it in the ladies.

'I didn't know whose it was so I had to look inside. Isn't that that policewoman?' she asked, as I checked all the photos were there.

'Oh, yes. Thank you. Don't say anything to anyone, okay? You could get her into a lot of trouble.'

Samantha racked her brain for the right words, though in the end all she could manage was, 'I don't get it. I just don't get it. How do you do it?'

Most of my life I've been a plank, but there are some moments, just very occasionally, when I surprise even myself at just how cool I can be. I know it was corny and a cliché but I took the envelope, tucked it into my pocket and replied, 'Why don't I tell you over dinner, once we get all this nonsense out of the way?'

Samantha stared at me, absolutely lost for words. I have no idea what she was thinking because at that moment our case was called and we had other things to concentrate our minds on.

All I know is that she didn't say no.

Paddy, Matt, Hasseem and Hazel wished us all luck and went and found seats at the back of the court, and WPC Kensington gave me a smile of encouragement as we took our places for kick-off. Samantha saw this and again looked at me in complete confusion.

'All rise,' some bloke said, so we all did.

Mine was the first name he read out and I was asked to confirm my name and address. He then asked me my occupation and I was about to say 'unemployed' when I remembered that Moonlight were picking up the tab so I could be as cocky as I liked.

He asked me again when he didn't get an answer

straightaway and a broad smile broke out across my face. I looked back at Paddy and the lads and suddenly I knew the answer I had to give. All eyes in the court stared at me as they waited for me to reply and when I did a cheer went up behind me.

'Pornographer,' I told them.

Epilogue: Seriously, are the letters really real?

Dear Bling,
I'm not sure if you can help me but I was thinking about selling my body to females for sex and I'm not sure how to go about it. How do I set myself up as a prostitute and what should I charge. I would like to do this but I don't know how viable this idea is as I will be sixty years old this year and I think perhaps, if girls are having to pay for it, they might want someone with a younger body. Your advice would be much valued.
John, Birmingham

Dear Tanya,
Please could you answer the following questions and return this form in the envelope provided? Just cross out the answer you don't want.

1. Would you like to play with my cock? YES — NO
2. Would you like children? YES — NO
3. How many? 1? 2? 3? 4? 5? More?
4. Can I be there at the birth? YES — NO
5. Would you shave my cock for me? YES — NO
6. Can I shave yours? YES — NO
7. Can I spank you? YES — NO

8. Will you spank me? YES — NO
9. When would you like me to come to London? ______
10. Can you help me? YES — NO
11. Can I suck your toes? YES — NO
12. Will you push your tongue in my ass? YES — NO
13. Can I do it to you? YES — NO
14. Will you finger my ass, then fist it? YES — NO
15. Can I do it to you? YES — NO
16. Can I fuck you in the pussy over and over again? YES — NO
17. How about your ass? YES — NO
18. Can I drink your pee? YES — NO
19. Will you drink mine? YES — NO
20. Will you marry me? YES — NO
21. How soon? ______

I look forward to reading your responses, Tanya. Take care, my darling. I'll be thinking of you (while I'm wanking).
Hugh, Manchester

Dear Gemma,
I saw you for the first time this week and think you're fab. I would like to eat and drink out of you. I would also like to give you an enema and put a see-through pair of knickers on you and watch you go to the toilet. I don't get enough sex off my wife and use brothels but I still can't get someone to do this for me. I am forty-six years old (though I only look thirty) and I am a long-distance lorry driver who owns my own wagon. If you are interested in doing this for me I will make it worth your while. If not, could you arrange it?
Glen, Stoke

Dear Bling,
I like your sexy letters in *Bling* and would like to add one of my own.

I'm a young white male aged twenty-five. Last year I lost my virginity with a twenty-year-old girl who I was fucking for the first time, but to tell the truth it was pretty shit. For starters (1) she did not scream out when I spunked and (2) she did not get pregnant. (3) I asked her for a blow-job and she said no because I didn't have any condoms and she would not swallow my spunk. All I got was a kiss on the cock and that was just boring so I didn't bother licking her back. We just had sex and I sucked on her tits and chewed on her nipples but no milk came out of them. She is only twenty years old but weighs twenty stone already. True story. Her name is XXXXX and she lives at XXXXX. Next time I want to fuck one of your models like Claire. Please send me her address so I can fuck her.
Baz, Sheffield

Dear Tanya,
Fucking hell!!! How are you? I hope you are in good health and happy. My name is David ——. I am twenty-six, single and my hobbies are smoking spliffs, drinking Hungarian red country wine and watching TV (soaps, boxing, football, porno). What are your hobbies Tanya? I like to buy *Bling* and look at your lovely body. You are so perfect and lovely and I only ever wank over your pictures Tanya. What is your favourite colour? My favourite colour is black & white. What films do you like? I like *Slut Woman* and *Cum Shot Starlets* and *Saving Private Ryan*. That's all the news for now. Bye my love. Write back soon.
David, Devon

Dear Bling,
Please can you get more photos of naked newsreaders? Me and the lads in my regiment have just returned from the Gulf where we saw stacks of top quality female reporters and some of them looked well up for it (a bit boring though). Fiona Bruce on the news and Sophie Raworth are particularly edible, is there any chance of seeing them bent over the news desk with their arses stuffed full of cock? Tell them it's for the lads in —— if that'll help. They're always talking about us all the time so perhaps it's now time for them to shut up and give something back. Carol Vorderman is another popular celeb with the lads. I'd like to see her with my cock in her gob while my mate Taffy fucked her in the arse. See how she likes those numbers. Or perhaps getting fucked by a load of lads against the *Countdown* clock as it ticks down. When it gets to the bottom, everyone hoses her down with her mouth open. Another of my mates, Brian, reckons he's still got a thing about ABBA. He says he'd like to see those two sorts getting fucked by the rest of the band like in a porno movie, though he doesn't want them to play any of their records. Not sure if this one is possible and besides, they're probably knocking on a bit these days so who wants to see that (other than Brian). Keep up the good work from all the boys. Looking forward to your next issue already but for now, just have to go and clean a few goat herders out of the tank tracks.
Mullet, BFPO

Dear Jerry,
I am your biggest fan and would really like to do a photoshoot with you. Please reply to me and we can arrange this for real. I have spoken to Don at *Bling* and he says it is fine and we can do a photoshoot with each other and so I am

now just waiting for you to call. I have a very big dick and I am really great at sex. Please please please reply to me now and this can actually happen. I have enclosed a picture of myself wanking myself off all over you in the magazine so you can see I am serious about this (just imagine how fantastic that would be for real????). I also enclose a SAE so that you don't have to buy a stamp and also a phone card if you want to call me on the phone instead. I very much look forward to hearing from you soon. Your biggest fan.
Colin, London

Dear Traci,
You look like a right dirty sort. Don't worry, I mean this as a compliment. At the moment I am stopping on at one of Her Majesty's hotels as I used to be a bit like Batman, as in I couldn't go out without robbin'. Fingers crossed though, I'll be out this time next year. We should get together when I get out, I don't mind travelling. It would make a nice change in fact. Please send me a picture for my wall? Can you sign it and write something on it like, 'To Bex, the best bloke in all the world, nobody does it better'? Look forward to seeing my release on you. Ta.
Bex, HMP Erlestoke

Why not get a laugh out of Danny King's other Diaries, published by Serpent's Tail?

The Burglar Diaries

'One of the few writers to make me laugh out loud. Danny King's brilliant at making you love characters who essentially are quite bad people' David Baddiel

'This is the sweet-as-a-nut, hilariously un-PC account of the jobs [Bex] has known and loved — the line-ups, the lock-ups and the cock-ups. If ever there was an antidote to *Bridget Jones's Diary* this is it. *The Burglar Diaries* is the first in a series. Long may it run' *Mirror*

Meet Bex — he works funny hours. He's your average small time housebreaker, working the streets of suburbia, stealing what he knows (and he doesn't know that much).

Bex and his long-time partner in crime Ollie are not the sharpest tools in the box, so they get into more than their fair share of scrapes. But they stick together, have a laugh, and make enough cash to stay in the pub all weekend. A confident and lippy raconteur, Bex frequently shares his thoughts on life that are as dodgy as he is and offer an hilarious insight into the mind of the petty criminal.

Burglars, fences, petty villains, dope heads, bent coppers, angry homeowners and one long-suffering girlfriend; you'll meet them all in *The Burglar Diaries* and like every one of them. Just watch your bag, that's all . . .

The Bank Robber Diaries

'It's low on morals but big on laughs, so if you can thieve one, by all means go for it!' *BBM*

'Danny looks set for a long and healthy career going straight . . . to the top of the best-sellers list' *Penthouse*

'*The Bank Robber Diaries* is the best (and funniest) British Crime novel since *The Burglar Diaries*, which was also written by Danny King' *Ice*

'The characterisation is — well, superb. . . . Extraordinarily well conceived and compellingly written . . . if you liked *The Sweeney* and *Two Smoking Barrels*, you'll like this' *Shots*

'I'd like to make a withdrawal' . . . Chris Benson idolises his older brother Gavin. In fact, everyone looks up to him. But then they have little choice when they are lying on their stomachs in the middle of the Halifax with a gun shoved in their face . . .

When Gavin gets sent down for a fifteen-year stretch the somewhat unprofessional trio of Chris, Sid and Vince are left without their ringleader. As if Chris hasn't enough to deal with already with his adulterous partner Debbie spending money faster than he can nick it, his lovelorn, sexually frustrated sister-in-law to 'console', and the Neighbourhood Watch scheme to look after . . .

The Hitman Diaries

'Once again the comic genius and hilarious one-liners have you warming to the anti-social protagonists of Chris, Sid and Vince; more cock-ups than hold ups . . . a thoroughly un-pc but rewarding novel' *BBM*

'The action flows as thick as the blood and the jet-black humour will leave you wondering whether to laugh, cry or vomit' *Jack*

'An action-packed tale of murder, mayhem and dating . . . it'll have you hooked' *Mayfair*

For Ian, being a hitman is just a job. Good money, security and a never-ending supply of contracts. It sometimes causes problems with his lady friends but, by and large, they are understanding and accept his frequent absences. Ian faces a moral conflict when given a contract to get rid of Janet, the love of his life, the only woman to really understand him. And moral conflicts are not something that Ian can cope with.

The Hitman's Diaries continue Danny King's unique take on what makes low-life characters tick.